NEVER DEAD

NEVER DEAD

Wonny Lea

Never Dead

Copyright © Wonny Lea 2015

Published by Accent Press 2015

ISBN 9781783752607

The Author asserts the moral right to be identified as the author of this work.

Chapter One

Ellie was grateful that her mother was staying with a friend, and so she hadn't needed to explain why a police car brought her back yesterday. She'd forced herself to concentrate on getting ready, but the thought of breakfast was so nauseating that she simply poured herself another cup of coffee.

Just as it had been doing all night, her mind went back over yesterday's events – a day that had started the same way as this one, with Ellie getting herself ready for work and catching her usual train to Cardiff Central. Her boss hadn't been too pleased when she rang to tell him what had happened on the train, and he was less than enthusiastic about her having to go back to the police station again this morning. He could understand why, as the person who had discovered the body, she would need to be interviewed – but surely that should be a five-minute formality and not require a return visit?

Ellie had tossed and turned all night. There was something she hadn't told her boss about. She was positive that she didn't know the elderly man who had died on the train yesterday morning. So how was it possible that the police had found *that* photograph in his pocket? She had recognised it instantly – a photograph of a young woman and a baby. A photograph identical to the one she had discovered inside her favourite book.

The book had belonged to the man that Ellie had always known as her father. Gwyn Bevan had died when Ellie was just ten years old, but the news that she was not her parents' biological daughter had only come during one of the increasingly frequent teenage rows with her mother, Joanne.

1

The photograph too had only been revealed through chance. After her father's death, Ellie had asked if she could keep his most treasured book, a copy of *Animal Farm* from his schooldays. Although Ellie had kept her dad's book safely in her bedside drawer ever since, she had only discovered the photograph during an uncharacteristic burst of anger a couple of weeks earlier. It had been her father's birthday, a day she always celebrated, but Joanne hadn't even remembered. Upset, Ellie had sworn at her, storming off and slamming her door. She had thrown herself onto her bed in her temper, knocking the book to the floor and dislodging the small paper pocket that was glued to the inside of the front cover. She'd always known it was there, but as far as she was aware it only contained the prize-giving card, etched in beautiful copperplate, from when her dad's teacher had presented it to him.

Picking it up to stick it back in place, Ellie noticed that there was something else beneath the card, folded and wedged snugly in place. The photograph. She didn't recognise the baby or the woman pictured there, but her heart had turned somersaults when she read the single word printed on the back – *Harriet*. Instantly her mind had gone back to the time of her father's death, eleven years earlier.

Ellie and her father had been putting the finishing touches to her bedroom makeover on a Saturday morning, ready for her tenth birthday. At the time Ellie had loved *Teenage Mutant Ninja Turtles* and in spite of her mother's insistence that a Barbie bedroom was more suitable for a ten-year-old girl, Ellie had prevailed. She remembered her father stepping off the last rung of the ladder and standing back to admire his handiwork. That was when her whole world had turned upside down.

She'd been unable to do anything other than watch as her father's face distorted and, in obvious agony, he clutched his chest and fell to the floor. Even after all these years the memory brought fresh tears to her eyes and it was only recently that she'd been able to make any sense of what he'd said before he died. Ellie remembered how she'd held his hand and begged

2

him to get better. She had become even more upset by the fact that he didn't seem to know who she was in those final moments. Her dad kept looking at her but calling her Harriet.

Ellie, frightened and confused at the time, couldn't really remember what had happened next, but according to her mother she'd screamed for someone to help her father. The little girl had never seen anyone dead, but even before the ambulance arrived she knew that her father was gone forever. She'd refused to go back into her bedroom after his body had been removed and slept in the spare room until the day of her father's funeral. It was arranged that Ellie would stay with a neighbour, but when the woman called to collect her Ellie was nowhere to be found. Gwyn's sister Julie, who had travelled from Swindon for the funeral, eventually opened the door of Ellie's room and found a bewildered little girl sitting cross-legged on the floor, sobbing pitifully, and almost completely covered in shredded Ninja Turtles wallpaper.

Ellie remained eternally grateful that it was her Aunt Julie who had found her. Instead of screaming at her, as her mother most certainly would have done, Julie had called down the stairs to inform the departing mourners that she would not be coming. Joanne, tearful and drunk, and some of her friends returned to the house four hours later to find Ellie and Julie sitting at the kitchen table eating toast and drinking hot chocolate. Joanne was usually no more than a social drinker, having a routine few drinks at the working men's club every Saturday, and so Ellie had never seen her mother under the influence of alcohol until that day.

Despite revealing her daughter's true parentage in a fit of anger, Joanne had never gone into the reasons for why she and her husband had adopted Ellie. Joanne had always disliked anything changing her routine and that had included becoming pregnant. Watching her friends grow fat on the fruits of love made her determined not to follow suit. Gwyn had assumed that having a family would be the natural outcome of their married life together, but after the wedding Joanne had made it very clear that she was never going to allow her body to be distorted by some 'little parasite', as she mentally pictured a baby growing inside her, though she was careful to present quite a different picture to her new husband. She told Gwyn that she was terrified at the thought of giving birth and related graphic descriptions of nightmares she pretended to have had. Her performance succeeded in persuading her young husband that if she became pregnant it would end in disaster, and he looked on sadly every time he watched his wife swallow her contraceptive pill.

Outwardly, though, the early years of their marriage would have seemed perfect. Gwyn was a hard-working and doting husband, and they always had a nice home and surplus cash. He was proud to be able to indulge his wife, but struggled to come to terms with the fact that he would never have a child, especially with his parents constantly reminding him how much they looked forward to becoming grandparents. Worried that she was in danger of losing her husband, Joanne suggested that they consider adoption, and before she could change her mind Gwyn put the wheels in motion.

Although they were questioned as to why they were not starting a family naturally, Joanne managed to convince the psychiatrist who assessed her during the adoption process that her fear of childbirth was real and deep-seated, and he sympathetically signed the couple's papers. After that there were nine months of waiting, and though Gwyn pleaded with the social worker she reminded him that it was no longer than the time it would have taken if Joanne had conceived and carried a child naturally.

Joanne and Gwyn had asked the adoption services many questions about the baby they had taken into their lives, but for the most part they would have to take her on trust. They were not entitled to know specific details regarding her genetic family and were simply told that their new daughter's mother had been very young and the family had decided that placing the baby for adoption was in everyone's best interest.

Joanne accepted this information at face value, but there

4

were many times when Gwyn stared intently at the little girl he soon came to love so deeply and wondered how anyone could give up such a precious gift. He knew that his wife would never really love Ellie, would just use her to prove to the world that she had the perfect family. As Ellie learned to talk and walk, and was later recognised by her teachers as gifted, it was Gwyn who hugged her and shared in her delights.

Even Detective Inspector Pryor had been sceptical about the photograph being an exact copy of the one Ellie kept in her dressing-table drawer. He'd suggested that it wasn't difficult to mistake one baby for another, especially as the photograph was old and had been folded.

After some initial questions DI Pryor and DC Cook-Watts had driven Ellie home from Cardiff, but Pryor had been obliged to swallow his words when Ellie had shown him her photograph. Beyond all shadow of a doubt the two were identical. Yet even with some gentle prodding Ellie had been unable to throw any light on the mystery of how the photograph had been found in a dead man's possession for, other than on the train in the last week, she had never seen the man before.

Ellie looked at her reflection in the long mirror, attached to the end wall of the small hallway, in what she always referred to as her mother's house. She had wondered many times why she didn't call the house her home. Ellie had been twelve weeks old when a social worker had taken her to the Bevans' freshly painted house in Ton Pentre, and since then apart from the occasional sleepover at a friend's and a few short holidays she had spent every night of her life there. Her friends and colleagues always talked about 'going home' but when asked about her plans for the evening, if Ellie didn't have a date, she would simply say she was going to her mother's house. Perhaps it just didn't feel like a home to her since her dad died. She tried to remember what she would have said when he was alive, but his death, the most tragic day of her life, had been just before her tenth birthday. She was going to be twenty-one next week.

Ellie felt unable, or possibly unwilling, to ask her mother

about the photograph and since she had discovered it she had pondered every possibility regarding the identity of Harriet. Common sense told her that it was a picture of her and her mother, but where had it come from? Was she Harriet or was that her mother's name?

And just who had that poor old man with the sad eyes been?

Chapter Two

'I really wasn't expecting that!'

Helen Cook-Watts fastened her seatbelt and turned to look back at the house she and her colleague had just visited.

'Me neither! I thought Ellie must have made a mistake about that photo.'

Matt Pryor slammed on his brakes as a handful of children suddenly poured out of a lane, seemingly hell-bent on hitching a ride on his bonnet. Both detectives shook their heads in unison. Today's kids seemed to be scared of nothing, and even the sight of a marked squad car didn't stop them randomly hopping on and off the kerb.

'Times have certainly changed,' Matt said dryly. 'When I was a kid we'd have run off with our tails between our legs at the mere sight of a police car. Now anyone official seems to be fair game, and it's a case of "take us on if you dare".'

Helen nodded. 'I only came back last Monday from that two-week training course, and one of the best lectures was from our very own Sergeant Evans. One of his stories was about the sessions he's done over the years with local primary schools. Back as a young constable he'd have to persuade the kids that he wasn't there to lock them up because they'd been naughty. On his last visit, a six-year-old boy announced to the class that they shouldn't listen to the police, because his dad said they were all a bunch of liars and should be locked up in their own jails.'

'Bloody hell. What chance have we got if kids are fed that sort of stuff? I wouldn't be a teacher these days for all the tea in China – I probably *would* end up locked in one of our jails, because there'd only be a certain amount of cheek I could tolerate before strangling the little blighters.'

Helen laughed at what she knew was a suggestion alien to Matt's nature. She was new to CID, but had known Matt since she was in uniform, and like the rest of the staff had been treated to his anecdotes regarding his twelve nieces. It was obvious to everyone that he was a doting uncle, though lately Helen had heard a hard edge to his voice that was uncharacteristic. She knew he was only joking about strangling cheeky kids but over the last couple of weeks she'd noticed something different about him.

Matt looked tired. The decision to promote him to detective inspector had recently been announced, along with a number of other substantial changes to the setup in Goleudy, and Helen knew Matt was more than pleased with the outcome of the recent 'root and branch' organisational review. Not only had he got the rank he'd been hoping for, but the new setup meant that he would still be working with DCI Phelps, albeit in a slightly different capacity.

Helen also knew, via station gossip, that Matt had recently become involved with a nurse, rumour having it that he was quite smitten. Maybe things weren't working out between them? Helen felt for him, but she didn't feel able to broach the subject: the man was still her boss, and despite her concern it was none of her business.

'How come Ellie got to see the photograph that was in the dead man's pocket?' she asked, changing the subject.

Matt was driving faster now as they'd left the twists and turns of the small Valleys roads behind. 'Of course! I'd forgotten you didn't actually see the scene on the train. We're not sure, as yet, when the man died, but as the train pulled into Central Station it lurched slightly, and the deceased, who'd been propped upright in his seat, fell sideways, virtually into the lap of an elderly woman. Ellie rushed forward to help as apparently she knows the woman and she'd seen the man on the train before.'

'But she didn't actually know him?'

8

Matt turned onto the road leading to Cardiff Bay. 'No, the older lady, a Mrs Wiseman, gets the train every Monday and Thursday, when she's met in Cardiff by her daughter. Ellie usually sits next to her, and she said she's got to know quite a bit about Mrs Wiseman and her family – but she only saw the dead man for the first time last week. He was already on the train every day when she got on, all week.

'Apparently, as soon as it became clear to the other passengers that the man was dead the carriage emptied quicker than rats leaving a sinking ship. Only Ellie and the elderly lady stayed and so they were the ones interviewed.'

Matt parked the car and carried on speaking as they walked up the back steps towards the office that for the moment he still shared with two detective sergeants. 'It was PCs Davies and Mullen who were first on the scene, and in an attempt to discover the identity of the dead man they looked through his pockets – that was when the photograph was discovered. According to Davies he was more surprised by Ellie Bevan's reaction to the photograph than to finding the dead man on the train.'

'He's getting a reputation for finding dead bodies,' laughed Helen. 'We were first on the scene when that body in Coopers Field was discovered. But this sounds more like the man had a heart attack or something. Was there anything else in his pockets to tell us who he is?'

'No, that's the weird thing. Apart from the photograph all he had on him was his train ticket, a set of car keys, some notes and loose change, a folded handkerchief, and a half-eaten packet of wine gums. No bank card, driving license, nothing. I spoke to Professor Moore and he's agreed to do the post-mortem this afternoon. I'm to take the lead on the investigation. We have to treat it as a suspicious death due to the circumstances, but I guess you'll be proved right.

'Give me a few minutes,' Matt said as they reached the door of his office, 'and *then* ask Davies, Mullen, and DS Matthews to join us in Incident Room Three. As it looks likely that it'll be you, me, and Matthews working together when the new structure is fully implemented, we may as well cut our teeth on something simple. At the moment we have an unexplained death in a public place, and it's likely to be due to natural causes. The photo link will probably turn out to be a thing for the family to sort out, and nothing to do with us.'

'OK, guv,' Helen said, heading off to round up the others.

Matt allowed himself a brief grin as he noted it was the first time he'd been called 'guv'. As a DI heading up his own team it was a title he'd be happy to get used to. The problem was that he felt anything but happy. Despite the good news at work, the rest of his life seemed to be falling to pieces.

He was grateful to find the office empty and sat at his desk. Ignoring the usual pile of paperwork in his in-tray he leaned back in his chair and closed his eyes. His mind ran briefly over the scenario at the train station. Although there were one or two points that needed addressing, he couldn't see that CID would have much input. The death would of course be referred to the coroner, and he would be called to give evidence, but it wasn't as if he had a major crime to solve and so it wasn't enough to distract him from thoughts of more personal problems.

He had last weekend, for the first time in his life, got seriously drunk for a reason other than social pleasure, and a nagging thought was telling him that the oblivion it had brought was something worth repeating. It didn't seem all that long since he was happy, playing the field both on the rugby pitch and with a succession of girlfriends. An injury sustained in capturing a criminal had put paid to the rugby, at least for a while, but the women – or woman – was another matter.

Since Matt had met Sarah he had thought for the first time about settling down and having a family of his own, but now, with the thought barely ignited, it was being extinguished.

What was it about life? He had to admit that, in spite of what could be considered a traumatic childhood, he'd done well at school and university and his chosen career was proving to be everything he'd hoped for. It would be the icing on the cake if he and Sarah could join his sisters and play happy families but on more than one front that dream was fading fast. He knew that the thought of losing Sarah was the main reason for him feeling at the lowest ebb he could ever remember, but the potential breakup of not one, but two, of his sisters' relationships was also keeping him awake at night.

Matt thought back to his own childhood. His parents had separated when he was seven, and as far as he knew his father had returned to his hometown of Tropea in Italy. For years Matt had avoided asking questions about his father, as they inevitably resulted in his mother crying and his older sisters shouting at him. It had been his sisters who brought him up after their mother died. He couldn't remember a time when his mother hadn't been ill, although there was no specific problem that he could recall other than chronic anaemia, which he now knew had been the result of years of almost constant pregnancy and numerous miscarriages. Their mother's last wish had been that her children revert to her maiden name, and so at the age of thirteen Matthew Fattore had become Matthew Pryor.

Although he hated himself for having the thought, he had to admit that in many ways things were easier after his mother died. His sisters were old enough to take over the running of the house and although Carlo Fattore had abandoned his Welsh family there was, up until Matt's twenty-first birthday, a generous monthly cheque.

As, one by one, his sisters flew the nest, Matt ended up alone in the family home in Pontprennau. He had since become the favourite uncle to twelve nieces, and his eldest sister Cara had been known to joke that there was more Italian than Welsh in all of them than they would care to admit, as on one occasion all three sisters were pregnant at the same time. Matt got on well with his sisters' partners and was included in all aspects of their family lives, so it was a terrible shame that things were going wrong for two of them.

The sound of his phone ringing caused him to jump out of his skin, and feeling a bit unsure of what he was now supposed to call himself he stuck with what he knew.

'DS Pryor.'

'Good afternoon *DI* Pryor, and congratulations on your

11

promotion – you're going to have to get used to your new title! This is Mrs Williams, Professor Moore's assistant. The Prof has asked if it's possible for you to look at something he came across during his post-mortem examination of the gentleman found dead on the train this morning.'

'Thanks, Mrs Williams, I'll be with you in a few minutes.'

Matt replaced the receiver and dragged his mind back to what he remembered about the body. The man looked like he'd simply fallen asleep, and there had been nothing obvious to suggest anything other than death by natural causes. However, it was *extremely* unlikely that the Prof call him in to look at the damage caused by a massive coronary thrombosis, or a cerebral haemorrhage, or any other naturally occurring fatal phenomena.

As he walked up towards the domain of Professor Moore on the fourth floor of Goleudy, Matt wondered what exactly was going on. He'd been hoping for a meatier case, but now he was wondering if he should have been more careful about what he wished for.

The familiar smell of the hypochlorites and alcohols used for general laboratory disinfectant reached Matt's nose as he got nearer to his destination and as always it made him feel slightly queasy. He could see Mrs Williams hovering at the doorway of the changing rooms and made his way towards her.

'We're in his usual room,' she said. 'The Prof's suggested you look at the trousers that were taken off the dead man, and I'm to tell you that the stain on the upper right leg is new and is blood. I've put a set of lab clothes and overshoes out for you, and the trousers I mentioned are on the table just as you go in, along with the rest of the gentleman's clothes and belongings.'

She left him there. Her ear was tuned to the man she had worked alongside for many years, and although Matt heard nothing, she had obviously picked up a sound that indicated that the Prof required her immediate help. As the Prof got older he seemed, to everyone except Mrs Williams, to be getting more and more cantankerous. His brilliance, as both a forensic scientist and a lecturer, was being increasingly recognised, and offers of lucrative lecture tours were pouring in from all over the world. Fortunately he was something of a home bird and so Cardiff was privileged to retain his services. According to DCI Phelps, that was mainly based on the fact that the Prof would have no desire to demonstrate his skills without Mrs Williams at his side – and she was no globetrotter.

Matt pushed open the door of the changing room and walked over to the table where the dead man's clothes were laid out and labelled. There was a dark blue, lightweight raincoat, a cream cotton shirt, and a very traditional set of white pants and vest. The first thing that struck Matt was that all the clothes were in excellent condition and looked more likely to have been bought in John Lewis than Peacocks. The shoes certainly looked expensive: soft black leather and, like the rest of the clothes, giving the impression of money and good taste.

As far as Matt could see there were just a few belongings, but they would possibly help with identification. There was what looked like a solid gold watch, a thick, plain, gold ring, and the contents of the dead man's pockets he'd already seen. He turned his attention towards the trousers and immediately noticed the stain Mrs Williams had mentioned. Although it appeared as if the Prof was absorbed in the post-mortem examination, he must have had one eye on Matt and told him to come nearer if he wanted to see the reason for the blood.

Grateful that he hadn't been around when the first incision had been made Matt moved to the foot of the examination table. He didn't mind watching these sessions but he couldn't get over the nauseating feeling he got when witnessing the Prof's scalpel first cut into the cold flesh. That moment was well passed and all eyes were now on the right leg of the deceased man and more specifically on a small area of skin that had been damaged.

The Prof seemed to grow a few inches in stature as he proceeded to give Matt a bit of a lesson in human biology and ran his hands over the leg.

'This group of muscles is known as the quadriceps, and the individual muscle that has been pierced is the rectus femoris. I missed this puncture wound initially, but when I'd finished the post-mortem and couldn't come up with a cause of death, we retraced our steps from head to toe and we found this little bleeder – didn't we, Mrs Williams?

'We then did a bit of detective work of our own and found the bloodstain on the trousers. Your SOC people will want to have a better look at those, and I will be pushing for early toxicology results as I am certain they will tell us the cause of death.'

'Are you saying this man was injected with something that proved to be fatal?'

In his usual dismissive fashion Professor Moore looked over the top of his half-rimmed glasses and raised his eyebrows.

'You're the detective, my friend! All I will be able to tell you is what caused this man to keel over on the train. It will be for you to discover if he gave himself a fatal injection, or if someone else decided he should be dispatched from this world. I understand you're leading this case in the absence of DCI Phelps, and it looks to me as if you *may* have been handed your first solo murder.'

Matt could barely remember changing, scrubbing his hands, and walking back to his office. His mind had suddenly become completely focused and, although one part of him wished that Martin Phelps was on hand, he was feeling a big rush of adrenaline at the opportunity of going it alone. He mustn't blow it.

Matt reminded himself of the techniques he had learned during his time as Martin's DS. Martin was famous as a stickler to his methods, but Matt would have to find his own way of doing things now, and quickly if this really was going to be his first lead on a murder investigation.

He walked along a short corridor towards Incident Room Three and pushed open the door to find the small team he had requested already waiting for him. PC Mullen was handing out mugs of coffee and moved one to the edge of the tray.

'I'm told yours is strong with just a dash of milk and a spoonful of sugar. I hope that's right.'

'Perfect,' replied Matt. 'I try to cut out the sugar sometimes but I don't last long. How DCI Phelps drinks his coffee strong and with no milk or sugar is beyond me – it tastes like poison.

'Talking about poison brings me to a bit of news that will surprise you all as it did me. I've just left the Prof, who has completed the autopsy on our mystery man. I was expecting him to tell me that the deceased had suffered a heart attack or something along those lines, but far from it – unless the gentleman gave himself a lethal injection it looks as if we have a murder on our hands.'

Matt went on to tell the team about how the lack of any obvious cause of death as a result of internal examination had led to an almost microscopic examination of the surface of the body.

'The man has quite hairy legs, especially for someone of his age, and what looks like nothing more than a pinprick is, on closer examination, something more significant. There is a small amount of dried blood surrounding it and whatever caused the injury was delivered through his clothes. There is a recent blood stain on the upper right leg of his trousers and before I left the fourth floor I asked Mrs Williams to get all his belongings sent to Alex Griffiths for the SOC team to look at them.

'Although he wouldn't commit himself without toxicology results, I am sure the Prof is expecting to hear that the man was killed by an injection of a fatal substance. If he'd injected himself we'd have found a discarded needle and syringe near the body, but there was nothing. What we need to find out is who injected him and why but I guess the first thing we need to know is who he is.'

Matt stopped for breath and took stock of the effect his news was having on the team.

Helen Cook-Watts was the first to speak. 'I didn't see the man whilst he was on the train; in fact I haven't actually seen him at all, but from what I was told I just expected a simple "death from natural causes" verdict with us just needing to discover his identity.'

'Well, I did see him slumped in his seat because I got there just before DI Pryor and I spoke to the woman who was sitting next to him.' DS Matthews paused and looked deep in thought as his mind ran back over what he had been called to witness. 'When the train lurched as it stopped that apparently caused the man's body to fall forward and the woman, Mrs Wiseman, cry out as a dead man fell into her lap! The station staff did say the carriage would be taken out of service, but at the time we weren't even considering it as a potential murder scene so we didn't seal it off or anything. Shall I ask Alex Griffiths' SOC to go over the carriage with a fine toothcomb?'

Matt nodded. 'Yes, and we need to interview other the people who were on that train and that's not going to be easy, although I suspect many of them will be regular commuters, catching the same train every morning.'

PC Mullen voiced her concerns. 'Yes but one of them, according to the Prof, is a murderer, and a pretty cool customer to kill someone in a public place like that. I guess if it was death by lethal injection, the act could have been done by a man or a woman. It doesn't require brute strength to jab a needle in someone, does it?

'The only two people left when we arrived at the scene were Ellie Bevan and Mrs Wiseman, Hilda. The older lady was naturally in a state of shock, but calmed down when her daughter was escorted to the train by one of the porters. Apparently the daughter had been waiting in the foyer for her mother and had heard the buzz of conversation regarding a death on the train, and so she was half-expecting to find her mother had passed away.

'After taking her contact details we were more than happy for Mrs Wiseman to be taken to her daughter's house. Maybe if we'd suspected foul play at the time we would have detained her. After all, she was best placed to do the deed and it would have been easy for her to hide a syringe in that rather large handbag she carries.'

Matt shook his head. 'Nothing is beyond the realms of possibility, but an elderly lady killing some random man by injecting him with a syringe full of poison that she keeps in her handbag is stretching the boundaries of madness. What possible reason would she have had?

'Now, we still have to wait for the blood analysis to be one hundred per cent sure that we *are* talking about murder, but we can go public on a suspicious death and ask for anyone on the train to come forward and help with our enquiries. I'm not expecting the killer to oblige us, so it will be the usual slog of examining all the CCTV footage from the platform and station exits. I suggest we look at a timeslot of five minutes from the time the train arrived at the station. If I had just committed a murder I don't think I would have hung around for longer than that.'

Now it was Helen's turn to shake her head. 'I use the train quite regularly and one thing's always the same: everyone rushes about! If we're looking for someone in a hurry to get out, that will be the majority of the passengers and probably most of the staff.'

'OK, fair point,' Matt said. 'For the moment let's just secure all the tapes that are relevant to the timeslot and concentrate on a public appeal for witnesses and getting a thorough examination of the carriage. I'm going to have to re-interview Ellie Bevan and consider the possibility that she murdered the man or at the very least explore the connection between them.'

Matt reconsidered his words. 'I can't see her being the killer, as the last thing she would have done would be to draw our attention to that photograph. She told us she was adopted but has never been in touch with her real mother or the family, and knows nothing about them. This man could be one of her biological family, so what do you think the relationship would be?'

'I was going to say not her father, because of the age gap, but I remember reading about Charlie Chaplin being seventy-odd when he fathered his last child,' said Helen. 'We need to find out who he is – what about dental records?'

Matt nodded dubiously as he knew that would take some time. 'I'm more inclined to try matching his car keys with a vehicle that could have been left at one of the stations. The train starts at Treherbert but I don't know how many stops there are between there and where Ellie got on.' Helen volunteered to check it out.

Matt made his first stab at creating some form of methodology. He didn't draw columns on the whiteboard, as Martin would have done, but rather a series of bullet points to list the actions that were needed. When he had exhausted the list he gave each task a number and his small team were allocated specific jobs. He was happy with the way he had brought everything together, but as this was now likely to be a full-scale murder investigation he would need more help.

He headed towards the stairs and tried to remember some of the tricks Martin had taught him about negotiating with the powers-that-be for additional resources. At least he was now fully occupied and could put his personal problems on the backburner by replacing them with his first murder …

Chapter Three

'But that was eleven years ago and to be honest I don't even remember much about the case – I think it was before I came back to Cardiff from Swansea. I've been through all the paperwork, as you suggested, and although my approach would have been very different it's unlikely that I would have found anything else and –'

DCI Phelps was interrupted by Chief Superintendent Colin Atkinson. 'We both know that the odds are you would have found more leads – that's what you do and that's what I want you to do now. It's likely that you will reach the very top of our profession, Martin, but for the time being I'm greatly relieved to have someone with your ability staying at DCI level, albeit in a different role, and with your salary enhanced to the limit of what is within my power to give.'

Martin grinned. 'Yes, thanks for that, sir, and it's possible, in the not-too-distant future, that I will want to move onwards and upwards, but for now any sort of desk job is just not for me. What I do need is some more information regarding my new role. Things like who'll decide on what old cases I look at, and who I'll be reporting to.'

'That will be me on both counts, and I must tell you at the outset that the arrangements have not gone down well with one or two officers who probably see themselves as sitting between you and me in the chain of command. Their egos have taken a bit of a knock because they weren't asked to head up my new section, but I think I've managed to massage their self-esteem by suggesting they are invaluable to me in their current positions. Anyway, let's get some coffee and make ourselves comfortable, because explaining what I have in mind is not going to be a five-minute job.'

The two men had been sitting on opposite sides of the large desk that took up one corner of the chief superintendent's office on the top floor of Goleudy. As they moved towards the small table and two easy chairs at the other end of the room, the door opened and two mugs of coffee on a tray seemed almost to float towards them.

Martin laughed. 'Now that's what I call power! I have to ask for coffee, or get my own, but you only have to think about it and it appears.'

The young woman who was responsible for the arrival of the coffee smiled at Martin. 'No power or magic involved on this one, just the fact that it's eleven o'clock and the superintendent is a creature of habit. Your take it black and strong with no milk or sugar – is that right?'

'Brilliant, thanks.'

Martin took both mugs of coffee and even before he had placed them on the table he heard the door close behind her and he and the super sat down. Colin Atkinson had a smug grin on his face and Martin raised an enquiring eyebrow in his direction.

'We need more women at the senior level of this organisation. They already head up some of our key departments, and of course we have our chief constable, but I'd like to see more at DI and DCI level. I'm just thinking of all the brilliant women who work here. There's Jackie my PA, who you just met, Iris who manages the staff dining room and mothers everybody, including me, and there's Mrs Williams who manages Professor Moore. I'm thinking of applying to the Royal Mint to get a medal struck for her.

'Speaking of brilliant women staff, how is Mrs Griffiths coping with her pregnancy? I spent a few hours with her during my induction week when I first arrived in Cardiff and it's the measure of the woman that although I got to learn a lot about her family, I was never subjected to any negativity regarding her need to be in a wheelchair.'

20

Martin nodded. 'Charlie is one of the most upbeat people I have ever met, The only time I've ever heard her raise any question about her health was in the early stages of her pregnancy when she self-diagnosed narcolepsy. That was until she discovered that falling asleep at any time of the day is pretty common in the first trimester, and then she enjoyed swapping amusing stories in the antenatal clinic. She's a real tonic, and to answer your question, mother-and-baby-to-be are apparently coping very well.'

The chief superintendent sat back and took on a more businesslike demeanour. 'And now it's my turn to answer some of your questions about the role I have in mind for you. I understand and appreciate your desire to remain at the sharp end of the business, and it's because of your success in closing cases that I want you to head up a new venture. I'm not going to call it a department or section because I don't anticipate it being a permanent feature. As you know, we already have a department that constantly reviews unsolved crimes and cold cases, but one of the reasons I got my current job was because I suggested a different approach. Not to do away with what that team are doing, but to implement ad-hoc intervention on a grand scale.

'You're right in your assessment of the level of politics involved in the higher ranks of the force – it's a constant factor, and fuelled by the almost daily reporting of the police failing to bring to justice the perpetrators of murders and other serious and violent crimes. Our figures here in Cardiff are no worse than other forces', but they are increasing steadily and I'm on a mission to change that.

'The new structure I've proposed will see fairly traditional teams of DIs, DSs, and DCs, and I've done a lot of work with John Evans regarding the deployment of named uniformed officers to each of the teams. It won't always be possible because of shift patterns but there seems to be evidence that the results are better when the team members aren't just thrown together, as they sometimes can be.'

Martin nodded. 'Although my experience wouldn't stand up

to scientific scrutiny, I'd definitely support that theory. If I'm heading up an investigation into a serious crime, it's always a relief to see uniformed officers whose personalities and skills I know, and they prefer to feel like part of the team and not optional extras.'

'I will be taking a direct role in the assignment of particularly difficult or sensitive cases,' Atkinson continued. 'Where it's appropriate I will allocate a DCI to the team, but generally they'll work as movers and shakers when investigations aren't progressing. I want us to be more focused, and I will juggle resources so that every effort is put into solving every crime and my objective is to ensure that no more cases are added to the files of UCOS.'

'I'm with you on everything so far,' said Martin. 'What I'm still unclear about is my role.'

'Walk with me, Martin,' suggested the chief superintendent with something of a twinkle in his eye.

Somewhat puzzled Martin followed Atkinson out of his office and along the corridor that led to the opposite end of the top floor. Unusually, the door to this section of the building was locked but the chief superintendent, this time with a broad grin, opened it and stepped aside to allow Martin through.

'Wow!' exclaimed Martin. 'We all knew something special was going on up here, but the biggest bets were on it being some sort of swanky facility for visiting dignitaries.'

He wandered around the state-of-the-art amenities, pressing buttons and examining some of the equipment. There were side rooms as well as the main room, and although Martin was loath to admit it he welcomed seeing a very large whiteboard alongside the latest in electronic presentation aids.

'This area will be your baby, Martin,' explained the chief superintendent. 'Goleudy is already one of the most up-to-date facilities in the country but new criminal detection aids are constantly being trialled and I put us forward to be a national test centre. You can access all departments in Goleudy from this unit, but I'm the last person you'd want to demonstrate how everything works, and I think I can hear the arrival of someone who's much more familiar with all the ins and outs of the technology.'

With that the main doors opened, but it wasn't the low hum of the motor or the entrance of the wheelchair it powered that caught Martin's attention – it was the beaming smile on the face of the occupant.

'Like it?' asked Charlie. 'I've been spending so much time up here, even sneaking up after my normal working hours, Alex thinks I'm up to no good! If it wasn't for my increasingly obvious pregnant state I think I would have been accused of having an affair.' She laughed and looked down at her rounded abdomen. 'Even Alex would find it difficult to believe anyone would fall for what will soon be a pumpkin on wheels, but as I was sworn to secrecy about this project I haven't been to tell him anything.'

Chief Superintendent Atkinson walked towards the door. 'I'll leave you to it! Martin, I don't want to set up regular progress meetings, but keep me up to speed and schedule a session when you think it'll be useful – good luck!'

Charlie was already demonstrating how different bits of technology linked together but as the chief super left she looked up and they exchanged knowing smiles.

'I really like that guy,' she told Martin when she was sure Atkinson was out of earshot. 'He's no computer expert, and a lot like you in that he doesn't understand the technology but he does know what he wants from it. I've been reined in several times when my suggestions for this place have been more like a personal wish-list and have included pieces of kit more fitting for the NASA space-station than Goleudy – but then you know me, I'm just a techy addict.'

Martin grinned and although he had the benefit of being able to walk on two legs he still had difficulty keeping up with Charlie as she whizzed around the room, randomly demonstrating how everything worked.

'You'll love this,' she announced as with the press of a button a very large screen was revealed and Martin could see some sort of camera alongside it pointing towards him.

He looked puzzled. 'What's it do exactly? I don't want to appear unimpressed, Charlie, but it just looks like a super-sized flat screen TV – is that what it is?'

'No,' teased Charlie. 'Think of it more as a porthole, but before I can demonstrate how it's going to be of use to you I need to make a phone call.'

She took the opportunity of giving Martin a quick introduction to the links attached to the phone system before pressing number four on the standalone keypad and getting straight through to Mrs Williams.

Although Martin could only hear Charlie's side of the conversation, it was obvious that the call had been expected and that both women knew what was going to happen next. If Mrs Williams was in on the operation then it was a pound to a penny that Professor Dafydd Moore was lurking somewhere in the background.

'Watch,' suggested Charlie as she directed a remote control towards the screen and brought it to life. Occupying most of the screen, and with scalpel in hand, the Prof looked up and Martin could not only see him but could hear him too.

'The age of Big Brother has well and truly arrived, DCI Phelps. Now not even the sanctity of my own PM rooms is sacred, and you'll be able to watch any post-mortems of interest to you without suffering the smell or the inconvenience of walking to the fourth floor. However, as you have just witnessed, it does need a phone call to Mrs Williams in order for the facility to be activated from our end – so we can just shut you off ...'

In order to prove his point the Prof did just that and Charlie laughed.

'He's been brilliant regarding the installation of this technology and, well, you know what an old show-off he is, so not surprisingly he's looking forward to doing a full show for you and whatever team is up here with you. Mrs Williams is a little more self-conscious but she'll get used to it.

Martin nodded. 'I take it the cameras and speakers mean that it's a two-way arrangement and if necessary I can speak to him and ask questions about his findings? If he hadn't been so quick to turn us off I'd have liked to ask about the post-mortem he is doing right now – I hadn't heard of any new cases, but then I had a day's leave yesterday and I've been on the fifth floor ever since I got here this morning.'

'It's probably Matt's man who died on the train,' suggested Charlie. 'Rumour has it that what looked like a sad but natural death may be something more sinister, and our Matt is in charge of the investigation. Alex and I were talking about Matt last night actually. We thought he would be over the moon with his new promotion, but he's not, is he? He seems a bit withdrawn and generally not happy with life. I know he's still seeing Sarah so I think things are OK on that front, but he's definitely not the Matt we know and love at the moment. I think I'd better cook him a supper and see what I can find out. It's not that I'm nosy or anything – I just hate to see him unhappy.'

Martin raised an eyebrow at the very idea that Charlie could be considered nosy and thought that if Matt was having personal problems then they couldn't be in better hands. He still had lots to ask about the new technology, but there was a more pressing task at hand.

'Forget the speculative tour and instructions and give me a for-real example of how all this technology will help me solve an actual crime. The boxes of paperwork on the table there relate to a murder in Roath eleven years ago, and I've been asked to take a fresh look at it. I've had an initial trawl through the case notes and they are poorly presented. There's not half the information I'd expect to see, and what's there is all over the place.'

'Easy-peasy,' interrupted Charlie. 'We've got a state-of-the-art scanner that, if I link it to a particular programme on the computer, will put all that stuff into date order – if that's what you want. I tend to use dates whenever I'm trying to sort police files because it's the one thing you can rely on. It must be drilled into every new constable, and it works, because I've never picked up a piece of paper in this place without the first piece of information being the date!'

Martin laughed as he recalled that even when he was just making rough notes the first thing he did was to put the date in the top right-hand corner. 'Yes, that would be a good start, and it'd help me work through the case as if I'd been involved with the original investigation.'

It only took Charlie a couple of minutes to get a substantial batch of material scanned, and working from a twinned computer screen Martin was able to start transferring the data into a format he favoured. He had drawn three columns on the white board and was quickly filling the first column headed 'Actual Facts'.

'I wasn't around when this murder was investigated, but I remember the publicity that surrounded it. The body was discovered by a couple of kids on their way to school, dumped on a piece of waste ground near Roath Park. The kids were a boy and a girl and at the time they discovered the body they were both ten years of age, so that would put them in their early twenties now. I wonder if they ever think about it?'

Martin suddenly realised that he was talking to himself as Charlie was totally engrossed and had only stopped sorting and scanning briefly to take a call from her husband. After checking with Martin she told Alex where to find her and assured him that he would be welcome to join her on the fifth floor, provided he brought a cappuccino and a cup of black, no sugar, for her companion.

'So Martin's with you, is he? What are you two up to?' had been Alex's reply.

'Less of the questions and more of the coffee,' was the last Martin heard before Charlie ended the call and returned to the job in hand.

It was a good ten minutes before they both looked up as the door opened and another tray of coffee sailed through the air, this time ably supported by Alex Griffiths, head of the SOC section.

'Bloody Nora! What's all this?' Without pausing for breath or waiting for a reply he put down the tray and took in every aspect of the facilities with an eye trained to scrutinise crime

26

scenes.

'Should have known it would be technology and not another man that was stealing you away from me. There's certainly enough here to keep even your techy brain amused. But what's it all for?'

Alex's last question was directed at Martin who went on to explain the operation that Chief Superintendent Atkinson had set up. Nodding his approval, Alex enthusiastically offered his support in relation to any re-investigations. His interest sharpened as he read the details that Martin had written in his first column.

'I remember this one! It was the very week I joined the SOC team and although as a rookie I was basically just carting the equipment about, I was keen to learn. I was really disappointed when the case was technically closed with just about every question left unanswered. We never discovered the identity of the victim and I don't remember a single clue in relation to the killer. It was the first time I had ever seen a victim at the scene of a crime, and if I close my eyes I can still see him – still see his mottled, naked body and what looked like a dark red, almost black necklace around his throat. Of course it wasn't a piece of jewellery, it was where some kind of wire had been used to cut deep into his throat. He had in effect been garrotted, although as I recollect it the cause of death was asphyxia. He had drowned by inhaling his own blood.

'When we arrived at the scene the body was partly covered with two coats and a couple of kids were being comforted by Sergeant Evans and a PC whose name I can't recall. The boy and girl were wrapped in blankets, it was their coats giving the victim some dignity. Of course the kids were scared out of their wits but we were all impressed by their actions. Apparently the route they were taking to school didn't attract many walkers, there was no real path and quite a lot of uneven ground to contend with.'

Alex looked further down Martin's list and some of the detail refreshed his memory. 'Yes, it was early on a Monday morning when the body was reported and the call was made from the small convenience shop nearby. Apparently Owen, the boy, agreed to wait with the body, while the girl, Erica, ran to the shop for help. What amazed us all was that it was a freezing cold morning but that hadn't stopped the children giving up their coats to cover the neck and the genitals of the dead man. We were all really impressed, and there was a whip-round in the staff canteen to raise the money to buy them some new coats and give them a bit of extra pocket money.

'There were a few purists who moaned about how the kids had possibly contaminated a crime scene, but that was rubbish because their actions could easily be factored out of any SOC investigation.'

Martin listened with interest because this was an insight into the crime that he had never anticipated and one that could be more valuable than sifting through the paperwork, even with the help of Charlie's technological miracles.

'I don't suppose you remember who did the post-mortem, do you? The style doesn't fit Professor Moore's, and there's no way I could see Mrs Williams allowing such a flimsy report to leave her office.'

Alex shook his head. 'I didn't know any of the main players really well at that time, but Sergeant Evans should be able to help you out.'

'There is a name, but it's handwritten and I can't make it out – and like you I wouldn't recognise names from eleven years ago. Yes, I'll speak to John, and he may be able to fill in some background details too.'

Charlie had finished what she was doing and beckoned Alex over for a guided tour of some of the less obvious features of the new setup.

The arrangements with Professor Moore's department brought a smile to Alex's face. 'Matt would have liked a detached visit to the Prof's domain rather than the stomach-churning session he had earlier. Thanks to the Prof's meticulous examination he has a murder to investigate, and I've just come back from scrutinising a railway carriage where it seems that a man was killed with a lethal injection of something as yet unknown. I hope our efforts will produce more clues to today's murder than they came up with in Roath eleven years ago.'

'Well, I don't know about clues,' replied Martin 'but I can already think of a dozen or more questions that weren't asked back then, and I'm getting the feeling that for some reason this case was prematurely closed. I'm going to find John Evans and see if that old copper's nose of his can help me find out why I think something doesn't smell right.

'When you report back to Matt tell him I wish him well with his first lead case, and that it looks like we both have our work cut out. I know he'll be as excited as I was – but I actually think I'm even more elated by the possibility of solving a murder somebody wanted to bury all those years ago.'

Chapter Four

'I don't know where the hell he is so there's no point in you questioning me. He's been getting up at the crack of dawn and going somewhere every day for the past week, but he's back by late afternoon most days. I didn't hear him leave yesterday morning, but he must have done and I've not seen him since.'

Lizzie had confronted her mother regarding her father's whereabouts, but even as she did, she knew she was wasting her time. Catherine Ferguson was already putting on her cream leather gloves and heading for the door.

'Get a grip, Lizzie! Your father is big enough and ugly enough to take care of himself. It can't come as any surprise to you that we've been husband and wife in name only for more years than I care to remember ...'

Catherine turned back towards her daughter and for a moment looked as if she was going to bare her soul, but with a shrug of her shoulders she thought better of it. At the best of times she was a cold fish, and the smiling images of her fronting her latest charity campaign belied the real Catherine Ferguson. She adored being in the limelight, was the ultimate social animal and an excellent fundraiser, but ultimately everything she did was in her own best interests.

After marrying Edward she'd moved into the Ferguson family home on the outskirts of Malmesbury, and since the death of Edward's parents the mansion had been theirs. Being the lady of the manor fitted Catherine even better than her tailor-made gloves, and it was the reason she hadn't sought a divorce although their marriage was a farce.

'But aren't you even a bit worried about him?' persisted

Lizzie. 'I've never known him go off anywhere without letting me know …'

'Yes, but he didn't know you were going to be here, so he wouldn't be expecting you fussing around like a mother hen. There's nothing whatsoever unusual about the lack of communication between your father and I – we live our own lives and that's the way we like it. Why are you here anyway? I thought you had some new protégée you were coaching to do what you never managed to achieve. What is it they say – he who can, does, he who cannot, teaches!'

'Why do you constantly find the need to remind me of how, in your opinion, I failed? Most mothers would be proud that their daughter got to number three in the world, and everyone says if it hadn't been for my shoulder injury I would have made it to number one.'

'Change the record, Lizzie, that's all your father ever goes on about – but we'll never know, will we? When he does turn up, tell him the BBC want to film here next week when I launch the latest appeal. They like that someone from such an affluent background as this is highlighting the plight of a particular group of Somalis. I'm happy to do the PR from this end, though I draw the line at handing out food parcels with the minions.'

Lizzie watched through the window as her mother walked towards her car and remotely zapped the driver's door open. Catherine Ferguson had turned sixty last year but women half her age would give the world for her looks and figure. She had been the perfect blue-eyed blonde, and although the years had taken some of the colour from her hair it had been skilfully replaced by her expensive hairdressers. Her skin miraculously showed none of the effects of several decades of heavy smoking, but then it had been seriously helped by everything short of the surgeon's knife. Not that Catherine hadn't considered cosmetic surgery, it was just that even temporary post-operative disfigurement was too much to contemplate.

Lizzie couldn't remember the last time she had been hugged by her mother. As far back as she could recall, the nearest they came to any contact was the affected air-kissing ritual Catherine had perfected, and used whenever the two women met in public. The routine was not reserved for her daughter – it was for anyone of a certain social status, and recipients were left with the intensely flowery fragrance of her Jean Patou perfume. For Lizzie the ultra-expensive scent of 'Joy' could never mask the fact that her mother chain-smoked, and the lingering combination of perfume and cigarettes made her feel quite sick.

Lizzie watched the black Land Rover crunch over the gravel surrounding the house. It always surprised her that her mother didn't drive a flash sports car. The sturdy vehicle easily negotiated the uneven quarter of a mile stretch to the rear entrance of the property, where the metal gates could be operated from the convenience of the dashboard.

In spite of what she'd just told her daughter Catherine knew exactly where her husband had been going. In recent years he'd barely left Woodcanton Hall, so when he'd returned after his second successive morning outing she'd known he was up to something. Rummaging through his pockets when he was asleep, she found railway tickets from South Wales, and she guessed he was organising something he'd hankered after for years. She had to find out what exactly he was doing, and so calling on the help of some unsavoury friends she'd had him followed.

Initial reports suggested he was stalking a young woman. He'd apparently watched her from the corner of her street and then at the railway station. Then for two days in a row he'd caught the train that she normally used, but at a point further up the line. He just seemed content to have her in his sights. The reports suggested that he was behaving like an old man besotted with a young girl. Catherine demanded a photograph of her, and the image left her in no doubt that this was Lizzie's daughter. The old fool was looking to reconcile with his granddaughter.

Catherine had always belittled Edward for his measured ways but now she was grateful for them. It wouldn't have been in his nature just to turn up on his granddaughter's doorstep and introduce himself. He would need to convince himself that a meeting would be in her best interests. Catherine couldn't see that as the act of a kind and caring man; it just reinforced her opinion of him as weak. It also gave her the opportunity of stopping that meeting from ever happening …

Lizzie would have been amazed had she been able to access her mother's thoughts as she watched the Land Rover drive off. She thought about where her dad could be, but even before Catherine's rear numberplate disappeared from view she was distracted by the persistent buzzing from the intercom in the hall.

'We're here, Lizzie – wow, what a place! Let us in, we can't wait to get a better view.'

Lizzie pressed the release button for the gates at the main entrance and opened the front door ready to greet her visitors. Della was driving and Basil had his head, shoulders, and most of his body through the window, waving his arms as if to demonstrate the sheer size and splendour of the surroundings.

Della caught sight of Lizzie's car and pulled in alongside it.

'So this is where you were brought up – you lucky sod! How could you bear to leave? Will you inherit this lot? Where are the tennis courts?'

'Take a breath, why don't you! Follow me and we'll grab something to eat, and then I'll show you around before we work out some sort of training plan. I take it you still have the next few days free so we should get through quite a bit in that time.'

Della Pugh was the protégée to whom Catherine Ferguson had been referring. Their arrangement was barely five months old, but Lizzie was convinced that with her as the coach and Basil Copeland as the fitness instructor, Della would make it all the way to the top of the tennis tree. Just seventeen, she already had a number of junior titles under her belt. Their plan was to follow the tournaments in warmer climes during the winter and break into the European scene in the spring.

Normally their training sessions were held at the Waverley Tennis Club, but they were starting to attract too much attention and so Lizzie had suggested using the facilities at her parents' home. She knew that the danger of introducing her partners to what was on offer was that they would always want to come to the Hall, and it wasn't somewhere she wanted to spend too much time.

As a child she had adored the house and the gardens, but during school holidays it had been a lonely existence. She had an older brother, but he was the apple of her mother's eye and had spent his school holidays being introduced to the great and the good of London society. It was obvious from a tender age that he was heading for a career in politics and that their mother was going to help him get to the top.

Due to difficulties with the family business, Lizzie's dad, Edward, hadn't been around much when his children were growing up. Lizzie remembered that it was after the guests had left her fourteenth birthday party when he made an announcement. It seemed that he had brought the business back from the brink of financial ruin and secured a number of unbelievably lucrative contracts that meant his company was solid and he could hand over its management to a board of trustees.

Catherine made it perfectly clear that he was too late to be influencing his son's future in the direction of the family business. Instead of feeling the disappointment he might have expected, Edward felt relief. His son was so much like his mother it was uncanny. They both fed off a mutual admiration, embracing people they deemed to be important and leaving no space for others – not even members of the family.

For the next year, at every opportunity, Edward had spent time with his daughter, often playing tennis. It didn't take him long to realise that she had a real talent for the game and he hired a personal coach. If her mother had been around more and had been a little less besotted with her son, she would probably have noticed that the coach was more interested in what her fifteen-year-old daughter had to offer off the court than rather than on it.

The revelation that Lizzie was not just pregnant but also beyond the point of a legal termination split the family even further. Charles Ferguson was convinced that a front-page story, of his underage sister being raped by a celebrated tennis coach, would ruin the promising political career that was opening up to him. His mother wholeheartedly agreed, and Lizzie's pregnancy, delivery, and the adoption of her child were all taken care of like a covert military operation.

Until recently Lizzie believed she'd been able to put that episode of her life behind her. With the help of her father and a new tennis coach, she had gone on to make a name for herself – one that even her mother and brother approved of. She became the darling of the British nation, not just because she was the ladies' tennis star they had been dreaming of, but also because she was a charismatic and attractive young woman. It wasn't difficult, with all the resulting attention, for Lizzie to bury a section of her life that, when she did bring it to mind, caused her to feel dead inside. Yet lately she was finding it more difficult to put a lid on the past, and frequently found herself wondering what had happened to her baby. She was already in her mid-thirties, her biological clock in full swing, and she was discovering strong maternal feelings that had been well-hidden until now.

'We won't get anything done if you don't stop daydreaming!' Della interrupted Lizzie's thoughts. 'Basil's already found the tennis courts. I can't believe how lucky I am! Are you sure your family won't mind if we use them? Shouldn't you ask someone if it's OK for us to just park ourselves here? I keep getting the feeling that someone will turn up with a shotgun and order us off the premises.'

Lizzie laughed. 'My father's been nagging me for years to make use of the things he set up for me. A while ago he went to the length of looking at developing a live-in training hostel for underprivileged children with a passion for tennis.'

'I love the sound of your father! What stopped him going ahead with his plans? Is he around – I'd love to meet him.'

'I'm hoping he will turn up or at least give me a call sometime today. I didn't tell him I was coming here – I know he'll be absolutely made up with our plans and I wanted to surprise him. To be honest I can't think where he's gone, he doesn't use his car that much and when I think about it, I can't remember him having a night away from here, not in years.'

'Can't you call him?

'He's practically allergic to mobile phones! I've bought him two over the years but I suspect they're still in their boxes, unopened –'

Basil had returned from investigating what was on offer to him as a trainer and interrupted. 'What car does your father drive?'

'He's had the same make of car for donkey's years – or is it donkey's ears, I can never remember. Anyway, his latest Jaguar's about five years old and the same colour as all the others and that's about all I know. Why do you ask?'

Instead of answering the question Basil asked another. 'Is it a deep burgundy colour?'

'Yes, but how the hell do you know that?'

'There are only two things parked in that row of garages and outhouses near the tennis courts, one is a huge motorised lawnmower and the other is a fantastic Jag. I wouldn't have a clue about what model it is but we seem to agree on the colour.'

'Parked in that row of garages,' echoed Lizzie. 'But that's impossible! None of us ever uses those garages, they're going to be converted into living accommodation if my father's tennis school ever comes to fruition. We all park outside the house, just like you did earlier. I need to check this out.'

A few minutes later Lizzie was standing with her arms folded looking accusingly at the bonnet of her father's car.

'There is no way on earth my father would have left his prize possession here – and look at the state of it! He'd never have parked it with mud on the hubcaps and bits of leaves and stuff caught up in the windscreen wipers. No, this isn't right. I wish to God I could have persuaded him to carry a mobile phone.'

Lizzie peered through the passenger window because she could see her father's coat draped over the seat.

'What's that underneath his coat?' She moved aside so that Basil could get a better look.

'I think it's a wallet but I can't see it properly.' He bent down to view the interior of the car from a different angle. 'No. It's a small brown leather case with a zip and some sort of pattern like Chinese writing on the top.'

'It's not Chinese writing – it's my father's initials laid one on top of the other. His full name is Edward Philip Ferguson, and as a child I made him what I called his personal logo. Starting with the E, the P a bit bigger and to the left, and finally the F, slightly to the right and biggest of all. He loved the design and started putting it on lots of his personal stuff.'

As she spoke Lizzie was attempting to open the car doors and the boot and it was clear that she was getting more anxious.

'Don't mess around with the doors anymore,' urged Basil. 'I'm surprised you haven't already set off the alarm. Is there a spare set of keys anywhere? Surely there must be some way of you contacting your father – what about your mother, would she know how to get hold of him?'

Lizzie shook her head. 'If you knew my parents you wouldn't ask that question. I can't see me thinking about tennis strategies for the moment. Why don't you two settle into the rooms I pointed out to you earlier, grab something from the kitchen, and make yourselves at home. Use all the facilities you want, and just take a look at the programme I've drawn up – it's designed to get Della match-perfect in time for the Australian Open. I'll catch up with you as soon as I've sorted out what's going on with my father.'

Lizzie crossed the strip of grass and made her way towards the house. She looked back towards the garages and remembered that the last time she was at Woodcanton Hall there had been two cars parked in those garages. Her father had told her that they belonged to some friends of her mother, but when she'd asked her mother about them Catherine told her to mind her own business.

Her father had been a bit more forthcoming, explaining that he had overheard Catherine talking to two of the men about some sort of lecture tour to raise money for the Somali charity. Lizzie had seen three men leave in one of the cars later that afternoon and she'd reproached herself for being judgemental.

38

She'd thought that all three looked like thugs – but her mother was clearly at ease in their company.

She remembered them now and the memory seemed to be encroaching on her worries about her father, even though although the connection didn't make any sense to her.

As she reached the front door the sound of the telephone ringing interrupted her thoughts and she subconsciously realised that it had been ringing for some time. So much so that by the time she picked up the receiver the line had gone dead. Worried that she had missed a call from her father, Lizzie dialled 1471 but only to hear that the caller's number was withheld.

She made her way to her father's room with the intention of looking for an address book, or something that may have contact numbers for some of his friends. Even before she had reached his room, on the second floor, the telephone rang again and she rushed ahead to pick up the extension at his bedside. She paused after the caller spoke, before saying, 'Yes, this is the home of Edward Ferguson, but I'm afraid he's not here at the moment. I'm his daughter. Who did you say you are?'

There was a moment of hesitation on the line as Matt fought hard to find the right words.

'My name is Detective Inspector Matthew Pryor and I'm investigating the death of a gentleman who was found on a train in Cardiff yesterday morning. He had no means of identification on him, but we have traced his journey back to a car that was left in the parking area of Treorchy station and the car, a burgundy Jaguar, is registered to a Mr Edward Philip Ferguson.'

Before Matt could say any more Lizzie interrupted. 'Look, Inspector, what you say doesn't make any sense. It's true my father has the type of car you describe but it's not been left at any train station – it's here, in one of our garages, I saw it less than ten minutes ago!'

'Are you sure?'

'Absolutely, and there are another two people here who can confirm the fact.'

'I'm not disputing what you say, but I can't make sense of it because we know for certain that the Jaguar parked in Treorchy is registered to your father. When you say he's not there at the moment what exactly do you mean? Do you know where he is?'

Lizzie was starting to feel more anxious and vented her feelings on Matt.

'No, I don't know exactly where he is. My mother told me earlier that she thinks he was here yesterday morning but I don't live here so I don't know.'

'Look, I'm really sorry to push you on this, but if you could describe your father it could help.'

'He's tall, six feet or just about, and is slightly built with grey hair and dark blue eyes.'

'Does he own a gold and steel Cartier Santos watch?' asked Matt.

There was no reply.

'We do believe that the gentleman I told you about could be your father. Is someone there with you? I don't like the thought of putting you through this on your own. Is your mother around?'

'I'm not on my own, Inspector. I'm a big girl and haven't needed my mother for years, but, anyway, you've definitely got your wires crossed. There is no reason on earth why my father would end up on a train in Cardiff Central station – either dead or alive.'

Hearing movement in the kitchen below, Lizzie put her hand over the receiver and called down to Della and Basil.

'Come up here, will you? I may need you to confirm that my father's car is in the garage.'

Returning to the phone, she gave Matt some more details about her father.

'Once again, I can't tell you how sorry I am. But neither can I ignore the fact that your description absolutely fits ours. If you add that to the fact that your father has not been seen since yesterday –'

'I'm coming to Cardiff to see for myself,' Lizzie interrupted. 'I'm sure you're wrong, Inspector, but I'm not comfortable with the feeling I've had ever since my mother told me she hadn't seen my father since yesterday. Just tell me where to come and I'll be there as soon as I can.'

Matt gave Lizzie the details but warned her about driving in her obvious state of anxiety.

'Don't worry, Inspector, I have someone who will drive me. And please don't stop trying to identify the body, because in a couple of hours I'm going to prove you wrong – it's not my father.'

Chapter Five

'Don't you bloody well tell me what I can and cannot do! You well and truly owed me that one, and it's not as if it was the first time you've sorted out a problem. I know the identity of *at least* two more British citizens who are no longer of any concern to those who paid you to get rid of them. *And* there are the numerous nameless, faceless wretches that didn't quite make it to the wondrous new life we enticed them with …'

What Catherine Ferguson lacked in physical size, she more than made up for in volume. She cared little for the fact that the three men in the hotel room with her were all of substantial build and, as in the view of her daughter, 'looked like thugs'. She was acutely aware that the men she addressed would have no qualms about putting a bullet in her and so she constantly told them about her insurance policy.

'Let me remind you, once again, that should anything happen to me, the relevant authorities would immediately be made aware of the truth behind this particular charity – the truth behind your precious Somali SOS. I have made a detailed account of everything I know and it's in a very safe place. Naturally, I wouldn't want it discovered while I'm alive, as it doesn't only implicate you – it certainly strips me of all the glory the British people have been stupid enough to shower me with.'

She laughed. 'My one regret is that, all being well, I will never see the looks on the faces of some of the people we've conned. Some very senior politicians have publicly spoken up in favour of my work and there are well-known businessmen who have poured thousands and thousands of pounds into helping our poor refugees. It's been a pleasure to take their money! And if some dear old pensioners really want to give some of their paltry income to add to our national appeals, who am I to deprive them of that warm glow?'

Two of the men in the room were seen by the British establishment as caring businessmen who were pulling out all the stops to help the people of Somalia, their homeland, cope with natural and man-made disasters. They had been entertained by the great and the good in business and in politics, and Catherine was one of just a handful of people who knew about the dark side of their operation.

Although most of the people, both at grass roots level and higher up the chain, were dedicated to Somali SOS and did good work in Somalia, there were a hundred different ways to make dirty money from the charity – and Samatar Rahim and Omar Hanad knew them all. It never failed to amaze Catherine that so little was done to follow up the money that was donated. She had been part of the setup for nearly fourteen years and her role had been mainly a public relations one. As well as the charity's work in Somalia, some refugees were helped in their quests to obtain residency or reunite with family members in the UK, and they were often the ones that were used to promote Somali SOS.

They could be relied upon to smile sweetly at the camera and, with their limited English language skills, express their gratitude at the charity's assistance in freeing them from oppression, poverty, or torture. The words were supplied for them and the public never knew the price they had paid for their 'freedom'. There was a heavy financial cost in being chosen, despite there being a specific large fund just for that purpose. Often families sold everything so a relative could have the opportunity of a better life. These were the publicised success stories, but the real money was in the illegal transport of people.

If there was nobody in the UK waiting for a person, false papers would be provided – at an additional huge cost. The sums were crippling, but some people were desperate enough to give everything they had.

44

Catherine also knew that the number of people who paid for passage from Somalia was always greater than the number who arrived in Britain, but she never wanted to know what had happened on the journey. If some of the people didn't make it to Britain, well, then profits for her and her associates were maximised. She was happy to remain ignorant of just how those people went 'missing' along the way; it was a way of salving her conscience.

The third man skulked in the background and barely heard the argument. The things he'd witnessed since he was a small child had made him immune to evil. He was now prepared to do anything in order to keep the lifestyle he had become accustomed to – and his associates knew that Ahmed Hassan provided them with the perfect way of keeping their hands clean, whilst getting unsavoury jobs done.

Ahmed was available to anyone who would pay him for murder – he had been conditioned to consider human life expendable, even more so if linked to a cause he could be persuaded to support. He did not consider the evil of his actions. Morals had not been a part of his life since, still a boy, he had watched his mother and father shot, his nine-year-old sister repeatedly raped before being left to bleed to death …

Ahmed believed that the two men he worked for respected him for the services he provided, but he was fooling himself. His own lifespan would be measured by how useful he was and at any moment he too would become expendable.

The voices of the other three were suddenly louder, and his attention was caught by something he didn't hear very often – at least not from them. An element of fear in their voices.

'How do you know the case has been reopened?' demanded Catherine.

'I make it my business to know these things,' retorted Samatar. 'It's not only been reopened but it's been given a high profile, and from what I have heard, unlimited resources. There is an expectation that someone called Detective Chief Inspector Phelps will be able to find things that were invisible to the first investigation team.'

'Shit! I cannot *believe* I'm hearing this ... it's been, what, ten, eleven years? Why now?'

Samatar scowled. 'I guess we all considered the episode to be well and truly buried, but clearly it's not.'

He looked at Omar, and then caught the eye of Ahmed. 'We three have suddenly found that the US of A is in need of our business expertise, and so we fly out of Heathrow later today. I doubt whether the so-called unlimited resources Phelps has at his disposal will stretch to him chasing us to New York for questioning.'

'You *bastards*! So you're just going to piss off and let me face his questions? What am I supposed to say? I can't remember exactly what I told the police at the time. They'll undoubtedly have records of their investigation – what if I say something different? I can't even remember who it was or how he died.'

Samatar walked to a table, poured a large glass of whisky, and handed it to Catherine.

'Drink this and get a grip. The only reason you and I were interviewed by the police at the time was because the post-mortem examination revealed the likelihood that dead man was Somali. It was during one of our big, nationwide campaigns to raise awareness and so they were interested in some of our projects.'

'Yes, I know that, but there were a few hairy moments when the numbers didn't tally with official records. I still don't know how we got away with that.'

'In the same way we usually get away with the mismatch of documentation. There is always a corrupt official willing to doctor official lists if the price is right. 'A greedy Home Office official was more than happy to massage the figures back then. It was good for us, but although he got a nice little back-hander it wasn't one of his best decisions because we now have a tight hold over him, and in his now considerably elevated position he is of great benefit to us. The bloody idiot is caught like a rat in a trap, and scared senseless that someday he will be called to account for perverting the course of justice.'

'Stone? Will he fall apart if he's questioned?' Catherine took huge gulps of the whisky and re-filled her glass.

'He's got too much to lose. As he climbs the slippery pole of success he becomes ever more dependent upon hiding the sins of his past. Paradoxically, Patrick Stone is one of the best civil servants around, and from what I can gather there are no other blots on his copybook. I can just imagine his face when he gets to know this case is to be reopened – his job, his pension, and his reputation will all be screaming at him.'

Samatar Rahim looked as if he was deriving considerable satisfaction from the potential misery of another human being. *Samatar* when translated means 'someone who does good', and *Rahim*, 'mercy'. Maybe his parents had some sort of vision about what sort of man their son would grow into. If so, they had got it drastically wrong.

'You really are a bunch of bastards. Why didn't you arrange for me to travel to the States with you? We've done it before – we've campaigned in America. It wouldn't have been seen as strange. It's typical of your lot to leave a woman to face the music.' Catherine was flushed and the whisky was having the opposite effect to the anticipated calming one.

'I think you are forgetting something,' Omar taunted.

'Like what?'

'Like your need to play the grieving widow,' he smirked.

There followed a few moments of silence and then Catherine poured herself yet another whisky and sat on a high-back chair.

'Christ, I'd almost forgotten about that! His body *must* have been identified by now. I expected to hear from the police yesterday, and I was amazed to get away this morning without at least a phone call. My daughter turned up unexpectedly, so she's bound to be the one to receive the news when it does come. At least *her* grief will be genuine.'

Samatar gathered together some papers and picking up a small case indicated that the other two men should follow his example.

'Catherine, I am relying on you to keep a cool head. If you have to get in touch with me use the business phone and make

47

the call professional. If during the conversation you tell me that you are devastated by the death of your husband, I will take it as a signal that you need to talk, and we will resume contact on our untraceable phones.'

Before Catherine could reply, she was faced with an empty room, as Ahmed slammed the door behind him.

She'd been assured that the police would put her husband's death down to natural causes, and nobody would have expected her to go looking for him, but what had seemed like a perfect plan suddenly seemed to be full of holes.

Hopefully the holes were only in her imagination. There was only one way to stop those thoughts. Looking at what remained of the amber liquid, Catherine figured that the almost half-full bottle would be more than enough to send her into the oblivion she craved.

She knew that her anxiety had nothing to do with her husband and everything to do with the reopening of the old murder case. There was nothing that would connect her to her husband's death – and there'd be absolutely no reason for them to think outside the box of natural causes. However, if the police discovered the perpetrator of an eleven-year-old crime then there certainly would be a trail back to her.

Catherine suddenly felt very sick and contemplated ringing Wincanton Hall and finding out if there had been any police calls. She was trying to remember if Lizzie had said how long she was staying and had a vague idea that tennis coaching had been mentioned. If she did ring and if Lizzie was already distressed by the news of her father what then? She had no idea how long it normally took the police to inform relatives of a death.

She briefly considered ringing her son. He would put on a convincing public display of grieving for his father but Catherine knew that there was no love lost between the two of them. He was his mother's son and had inherited her hard-nosed view of life, and both were used to pandering to Joe Public while hiding a personal agenda. If his political career to date was anything to go by, it was serving him well.

The difference between Catherine and her son was an uncontrollable violent temper – his. Even as a child he would suddenly lash out when things weren't going his way but his most horrific explosion was when he had heard about his sister's pregnancy. Suffice it to say that the tennis coach responsible for her condition had not set foot on a tennis court from that day to this.

In spite of his injuries, the coach decided to play a dangerous game, reasoning that the potential financial rewards of blackmail were worth his own possible exposure as a rapist. Money changed hands, though Lizzie Ferguson herself never knew, any more than she knew that the father of her child was rendered a cripple by her brother. She also had no idea that her tennis coach, after his third attempt to secure more money for his silence, was himself silenced, permanently. He was one of the other two British men that Catherine had spoken about earlier.

Although there were parts of Catherine's life that beggared belief they were extremely well hidden, and that's how she wanted them to stay. She supposed she would have to tell her son about this bloody case being reopened and just hope that, as before, he would not be linked to any part of the investigation.

Thinking was becoming difficult. Although it was still the middle of the day, with the last of the whisky drained Catherine drifted into a confused mix of sleep and unconsciousness.

Chapter Six

'Why have we chosen a cold, wet, and windy Saturday in November to wander aimlessly around Roath Park? Sorry, scratch that. Why have *you*? I love the fresh air, Martin, but there's a cosy cottage with a warm log fire beckoning and I know where I'd rather be.'

The strong gusts of wind made it impossible to use an umbrella and so Shelley Edwards snuggled up to Martin and hid her face from the elements.

'OK, let's just go to the end of this stretch and then we'll turn back.' Martin stopped and squinted a few times to get a better look at the lake and the paths and surrounding gardens. It suddenly became obvious to Shelley that he wasn't just attempting to admire the view and she punched him, not too lightly, in the stomach.

'It's work, isn't it? This outing has nothing to do with "making the most of our few hours of winter daylight" and everything to do with police business. I'm right, aren't I?'

Martin grabbed her and kissed her. 'You're getting to know me far too well.'

Shelley shook her head and her hood fell off, just as the heavens really opened and the drizzle turned into a deluge.

'Run,' shouted Martin. He grabbed her hand and made for a small path, but it didn't lead to the main road as he thought it would. They took shelter under some trees and then, just as suddenly as it had started, the rain stopped, and a watery sun appeared.

'Say what you will about our weather, but boring it never is – look, there's a rainbow. OK, Mr Detective, I've rumbled you, but as we're here now and the clouds appear to have done their bit for today, we may as well take a proper look around. In fact, I could give you a guided tour because my friend Alice lives in that house there.'

Shelley pointed to one of the large detached houses overlooking Roath Park lake and asked Martin if there was a particular spot he needed to see. He started to tell her about the case he was looking into when she interjected.

'Oh, I remember when that happened, and I could take you to the exact spot where the body was found.'

Martin grinned. 'I never had you down as a ghoul! We often have to beat the murder-watchers off with a stick at our crime scenes, but I wouldn't have put you alongside them.'

'I'm not, you cheeky blighter – I'll leave all that ghoulish stuff to you. The reason I know is because of what I told you just now. Alice lives in that house and along with everyone else in the neighbourhood she was interviewed by the police. On top of that, her younger brother went to school with one of the kids who found the body. It was the boy – he was called Owen and I remember his name because he became something of a local celebrity. Heaven knows what he's doing now.'

'In what way was he a local celebrity?' asked Martin. 'According to what I read, the two children who found the body were both given some sort of award for their exemplary behaviour. I don't know what the thinking was back then but I do know that now, if some kids witnessed something as upsetting as a naked dead body, they'd be offered counselling.'

'The girl may well have been in need of some sort of therapy but the boy certainly cashed in on his experience.' Shelley smiled and shook her head. 'He was taking groups of children from his school on guided tours of the area and charging them for the privilege. Alice was in her final year at Swansea Uni at the time, but she had younger sisters at the same school as the boy and so heard how it all ended in tears for him.

'Lots of parents complained that their children were being forced to pay young Owen for giving them nightmares! I can't really remember the outcome but there was something awful to do with the boy's family. It may have been a suicide – Alice would remember. Do you want to see if she's at home?'

'You can't just drop in on someone you haven't seen in ages with a man she's never met who wants to ask her about an eleven-year-old murder! Can we?'

Shelley nodded and dragged Martin in the direction of her friend's house. 'I haven't seen Alice since her birthday last January, but we do keep in touch and she does know about you. She's got two young sons, and she and her husband moved to Bath about eight years ago but the marriage didn't work out and now she's back here living with her mother – her dad died a couple of years ago.'

Martin had reservations about just turning up unexpectedly but he could see that Shelley had the bit between her teeth and anyway there was always the chance that the meeting would be useful to him.

He needn't have worried, as even before they had reached the front door, it was flung open and a short plump woman was dragging Shelley into the house.

'Shelley Edwards, what a lovely surprise – and you must be Martin. What took you so long to make a move on Shelley?' she asked him accusingly. 'The poor girl was smitten for months before you finally got round to asking her out!'

Shelley blushed and glared at her friend but Martin laughed and shook his head.

'I've asked myself that question many times and I still don't know the answer.'

'Don't just stand there dripping, take your coats off and come into the kitchen.' Alice collected the wet clothes and spread them out over the backs of some chairs. 'Go through there, Shelley knows the way.'

Although Shelley hadn't been in the house for many years she did know how to get to the kitchen, and as on previous visits had the feeling of going back in time. The house was semi-detached Victorian. The lounge at the front of the house overlooked Roath Park lake, but the kitchen was at the rear of the property and quite dark.

Martin remembered when he and Matt had interviewed a couple in one of the other houses on Lake Road West, regarding a hit and run incident. That couple's modern kitchen had been like something out of a glossy magazine. The kitchen he was standing in now had moved on from the Victorian era, but was nowhere near the twenty-first century.

There were two boys sitting at the super-sized wooden table were much more up to date, and even though a total stranger had walked into the kitchen, they didn't look up from the iPad they were sharing.

'That electronic device has turned my kids into zombies,' complained Alice, but the boys had undoubtedly heard this allegation before and their eyes remained glued to the screen.

Alice tried another tactic and threw a tea-towel over the screen. Bingo!

'Mum, don't be mean – we were just having a …'

It was then that the oldest boy, Evan, realised that they had company and his embarrassment registered on his face. Martin felt an immediate sympathy and although his own early teens were a distant memory, he could still remember when his face would turn crimson at the most inappropriate moment. He removed the tea-towel and an image of a skeleton brandishing a hangman's noose filled the screen, obviously stemming from a recent Halloween party.

'The quality of the pictures on these things is amazing. Is that you looking for a neck to fit your rope?'

With something else to focus on, Evan's hormones relented and his confidence returned. He stretched the screen so that the face of the skeleton was enlarged and easily recognised as his own.

'Yeah, that's me, and the green gremlin sitting next to me is Alyn.' He nodded in the direction of his brother.

Martin hadn't even noticed the gremlin and watched as Evan enlarged other parts of the photograph and his actions brought to light another three Halloween monsters.

The two women were catching up on gossip and rustling up some coffee, and Shelley was amused to see how easily Martin crossed the generation gap and made friends with the two boys.

'So you took all these photographs yourself? I can see you've had a great time with the special effects. We used to say the camera never lies, but I would never recognise you in some of these pictures.'

Evan grinned and had great pleasure in demonstrating to Martin that costumes could also be transformed, and turned his brother from a gremlin into a fairy!

Alice placed a tray on the table and suggested that her sons had things like homework they should be doing. A few mandatory objections were voiced but Alice had heard them all before and ushered the boys out of the kitchen.

'Shelley tells me you take your coffee strong and black, which is just as well as those two reprobates have drunk all the milk. Not only finished off the milk but on every other front eaten me out of house and home – so I've got nothing to offer you. I swear those sons of mine have hollow legs'

'If the coffee tastes as good as it smells I'll be more than happy, but what about you two?'

'There's no need for milk – not in a large glass of pinot noir! I've persuaded Shelley to join me in a decadent pre-lunch tipple.'

'I didn't need much persuading,' said Shelley. 'I've been telling Alice what brought us here this morning and she certainly remembers the upheaval when the body was discovered. I told her the police are re-opening the case and that you've –'

Alice interrupted. 'I was in university halls during the week, but the body was found on a Friday and I came home for the weekend later that day. Quite a few of the houses around here have been bought and renovated by well-off professionals but the majority are still owned by families like mine who've been here for ever. The whole area was in shock.'

'From what I've read so far, no one was able to identify the body,' said Martin.

'We were all shown a photograph, but I didn't come across anyone who had even seen the man, let alone anyone who knew him. He looked like an emaciated version of a boy doing the same course as me, but he was Kenyan, not Somali. It's strange, but even as a child I never really gave much thought to people's ethnic backgrounds – I suppose it's because Cardiff has been a great big melting pot for a very long time.'

Alice perched herself on a stool. 'Do you really think there's any hope of you getting to the bottom of that death – after all this time? What I most remember is the chain reaction. The two kids that found the body were hailed as heroes at first. The local press made a big thing of the exemplary way in which the youngsters had behaved – but the story closed down pretty quickly, I guess when it was discovered that the boy, Owen, was making money out of the situation.

'His family were accused of elaborating their son's story. I don't know if that's true but they certainly sold it to the press.

Apparently his mother committed suicide not long after, but I don't know if that had anything to do with what had happened. Last I heard was that Owen and his dad had moved to Southampton.'

'Where were they living at the time?' asked Martin.

'Not really sure, but judging from the direction the kids were walking to school I would say on the east side of the lakes. Sorry I can't be more helpful.'

Martin smiled. 'Well the answer to your question is yes, it happens time and time again. A case of what is likely to be unlawful killing reaches, pardon the pun, a dead end. It isn't worked on for years but during that time technology moves on and a fresh look throws up new possibilities, which are what I'll be trying to find.'

The kitchen door burst open and Evan and Alyn returned to make it clear to their mother that they were starving. Alice shrugged her shoulders and looked apologetically towards her friend.

Shelley gave her a hug. 'It's OK, Alice, we only intended this to be a flying visit, so we'll make a move.'

Minutes later they all left the house together, with Alice and her sons heading for the shops and Shelley leading Martin to the scene of the crime.

She took him back through Roath Park and to an exit furthest away from where they had been.

'The schoolchildren who found the body would probably have come from this area but it could be much further back. The catchment area for the school they went to could go back for miles – I don't know. Anyway, this is the road that would take them to school from anywhere around here, but a bit further down is the shortcut that some of the kids use.'

As predicted, just a few steps ahead, was a patch of rough ground and a faintly trodden path leading off the main road. Martin looked around and took in the position of a couple of shops at the end of a terrace of houses. He remembered that the boy had retraced his steps to a nearby shop, possibly one of those.

They went over the path and could see why it wasn't well used. True, it cut off a corner of the route but it was uneven and with the recent rain it was wet and slippery.

'Remind me to bring my wellies next time you invite me out,' teased Shelley. 'Seriously though, Martin, it looks as if we won't get much more than ten minutes before another batch of rain and it's going to take five of those minutes to get back to the car.'

Martin looked at the threatening dark clouds and caught Shelley's hand. They hurried on and were almost back on the main road when Shelley stopped.

'This is it. This is the place. It was just before this path came back onto the road.'

Martin looked around. There were houses in the area but nothing overlooked that particular spot and it seemed as if all the windows had deliberately turned away from the scene. At the edge of the rear wall of one of the houses was a group of smooth stones that were shiny and were out of place on the rough ground.

'Some sort of shrine,' suggested Shelley in response to Martin's unspoken question.

They both bent down to get a closer look at the oval-shaped

stones that were arranged like the petals of a flower.

'It's quite beautiful and strangely moving but what amazes me is that it's not been vandalised. I think the stones have been polished too. Someone is obviously tending this simple memorial. Do you think it's something to do with the body that was found here?'

'Don't know,' replied Martin. 'I've read all the paperwork and the area is just as described, but there's no mention of these stones being there then. It's not uncommon for people to set up shrines at the site of a road traffic death, or even a murder.'

Martin used his phone to take some photographs and it was clear to Shelley that the cogs of his brain were working flat out.

'Park those thoughts, Martin Phelps, and concentrate your attention on a living body – mine! I'm wet and starving and in need of some TLC, and I'm claiming back the rest of this weekend.'

It only took Martin a few seconds to catch up with Shelley as she headed back towards the car.

Chapter Seven

Less than twenty minutes after putting the phone down, Lizzie's red Volvo was on the M4, heading for Cardiff. She had sort of promised the detective who had phoned that she would get someone to drive her, but one look at Della's car had changed her mind. It didn't look as if it would make it to the end of the drive and Della admitted that the fuel gauge had been in the red zone for the last twenty minutes of their journey to Woodcanton Hall.

Basil had offered to drive the Volvo, but he was a notoriously bad driver and Lizzie wasn't going to take a chance at the moment. She had initially suggested that Della and Basil stay and make a start on the training programme she had prepared, but they were determined to support Lizzie and go with her to Cardiff.

During the first five minutes of the journey Basil had repeatedly asked Lizzie if she was OK to drive. He stopped asking when it was made clear to him that she was using the familiar process of driving to keep her mind from wandering too far into fantasy.

'I don't know what to make of that phone call with Inspector Pryor, there are things that make no sense whatsoever. They got my father's name by checking out the number plate of a car, left at some station in Wales – I can't remember the name of the station … yes I can! It was Treorchy, like the Treorchy Male Voice Choir, they gave a concert in aid of one of my mother's charity campaigns.'

Lizzie kept her own thoughts as she remembered that the concert was at a point in her career when she was wowing the tennis world. Her mother had, at that time, been only too willing to wheel her daughter into the public spotlight, because of the additional publicity it gave to her cause.

'What I don't get is how my father's car can be in two places at the same time! We all know it's parked at the Hall, albeit not where I would have expected it to be, and not in its usual pristine condition.'

Basil interrupted. 'When you were upstairs getting your phone and handbag I nipped to the garages and took some pictures of the car with my phone, so we can show the police where it actually is.'

'Thanks, Basil ...' Lizzie's mind was now running away with random thoughts and coming up with some impossible questions. 'What if the body they've found *is* my father? It wouldn't be impossible for him to have gone to Cardiff – we do know people living there ... but he would have driven straight to their homes. He would have no reason for being on a train.'

Lizzie slowed the car down to a crawl and threw the loose change she'd collected from Basil and Della into the coin bin as she steered her way through the Severn Bridge toll barrier.

'Was the body the detective told you about found on an intercity train or a local one?' asked Della.

'He didn't actually say, but if the car they believe belongs to my father was found in Treorchy, then I suspect it was a local train. What am I saying? I don't know! The only reason I didn't tell Inspector Pryor that he was off his trolley is because I don't know where my father is.' Lizzie's eyes filled with tears.

'Hang on, Lizzie, we'll be there soon and, fingers crossed, it will all have been just a big mix-up – it wouldn't be the first time the police have got things wrong,' said Basil. 'Pull over onto the hard shoulder if you want me to drive.'

'No, I'm OK. I'm worried, of course, but I'm trying to keep the lid on it until we really know if my dad's just staying with one of his pals or ...'

Knowing that Lizzie Ferguson was on her way to Goleudy prompted Helen Cook-Watts to get the body moved from the post-mortem room to the viewing room. She remembered the first time she had taken someone to view a body, the distraught adoptive parents of a man who had been brutally murdered. This time, the elderly gentleman looked as if he was merely asleep, and she hoped that whoever identified him would take comfort from his peaceful demeanour.

She joined DI Pryor and was pleased to see that the team, previously just Davies, Mullen, and Matthews, had been substantially enhanced. The case, now a full-blown murder investigation, had been moved to Incident Room Two and Helen could see Alex Griffiths talking to her boss and a woman she recognised, but didn't really know.

Matt Pryor called her over and made the formal introductions.

'Helen, this is Detective Sergeant Shaw, and Margaret, this is Detective Constable Cook-Watts. DS Shaw is on a three-month secondment from the Wiltshire force. I jumped at the opportunity of getting her help with this case, given that our victim may well turn out to be from that part of the country.'

The two women exchanged smiles and DS Shaw's smile turned into a spontaneous laugh as she told Matt that the only person who ever called her Margaret was her mother – and only then when they were having a disagreement.

'I'm Maggie to everyone, but of course I'm DS Shaw to the public and most people outside the team. Does that fit in with your normal way of working here?'

'OK, Maggie it is,' smiled Matt. 'People use whatever they feel most comfortable with, and we don't stand on ceremony amongst ourselves, though outside this building we generally stick to formal titles.'

'It's great to be able to get stuck into what promises to be an interesting case – I only hope I can be of some use to you.'

'Let's get this show on the road.' Matt looked around and suggested that they take things in the order they had happened and invited PC Davies and PC Mullen to start the ball rolling.

Davies stood up and referred to his notebook.

'The initial call came through to Goleudy at 08.34 as a result

61

of a diverted 999 call from a Mr Eric Lloyd, one of the managers at Cardiff Central. He'd summoned the police and ambulance services, but it didn't take the paramedics long to realise that their presence was surplus to requirements. We arrived on the scene at 08.55. By that time the platform was virtually empty and Mr Lloyd took us to the carriage where the dead man had been found.

'The paramedics were still there but had focused their attention on an old lady, a Mrs Hilda Wiseman, who was distraught because the man had died close by her. Her daughter had arrived a few minutes before us and we all thought we were about to have a second body on our hands.'

PC Mullen spoke from her seat. 'Fortunately, the other woman who stayed when the train stopped, Ellie Bevan, was brilliant in pacifying the old lady.'

'As I understand it Mrs Wiseman wasn't interviewed and left the scene fairly quickly, to be taken to her daughter's home in Canton,' Matt said. 'I'd like DC Cook-Watts to visit her there as soon as we've finished this session.'

Helen nodded and Davies continued. 'At the time everyone, including the paramedics, was under the impression that the man had had a heart attack or a stroke – no one suspected murder. We've obviously heard since that this is a murder investigation but I for one have no idea how he was killed. There was no sign of a struggle – no blood – nothing to make us suspect foul play.'

'I'll come on to that in a moment,' said Matt. 'Would you just describe the situation that arose when you tried to discover the identity of the dead man?'

'Sure. He was a well-dressed gentleman, the sort who would carry a nice wallet, but there wasn't one. There was nothing in his pockets to help us determine who he was. He had a train ticket from Treorchy, and he may have driven to that station because there was a set of car keys in his jacket pocket. It was Carol who discovered the photograph so I'll let her tell you about that.'

Carol Mullen got to her feet. 'It was tucked into the small

outside pocket on his jacket and folded in half. When I opened it up I didn't realise Ellie Bevan was standing next to me, and I certainly wasn't anticipating her reaction. PC Davies was quite shocked. She'd been as cool as a cucumber up to that point and a great help with the old lady. However she freaked out when she saw the photograph and I only just stopped her snatching it from me. She wasn't making much sense but that was when DS Matthews arrived, quickly followed by you, and we handed over.'

Matt nodded and held up the photograph, now in an evidence bag, and then picked up another evidence bag that contained an identical item.

'This was the reason for her distress. It seemed highly unlikely that the tale she told us about having a matching one at home would check out – but it did. These two photographs are identical, but on the back of the one we found on the body is written the word "Lizzie". When we took Ellie home she produced the other one and on the back of her copy is written the word "Harriet".'

There was a general buzz of conversation, and some puzzlement. DS Shaw got to her feet.

'Has any other connection had been made between the victim and Ellie Bevan?'

Matt realised that he had forgotten to introduce Shaw to the full team and did so before responding to her question. 'At the moment the only person we have interviewed is Ellie Bevan, and she swears the first time she saw the dead man was last Monday. Apparently he was on the train every morning last week but she'd never seen him before that. She didn't speak to him, although she said she'd noticed him looking at her on several occasions. I suggested that his staring must have made her feel uncomfortable, but she said it wasn't like that, he seemed like a kind and gentle man but that his eyes were sad.

'When we spoke to Ellie we weren't of the opinion that the man had been murdered, so I need to get her to think harder about that train journey. Did she notice anything suspicious – anything different to the norm? Were all the other passengers

63

regular users of that service or did she notice any strangers? She's going to be a key witness.'

'Unless she's our killer!' suggested Maggie Shaw.

Matt nodded. 'Not out of the question, of course, but I go back to what I said earlier – if you had just killed someone would you bring attention to a possible connection between you and your victim?'

Carol Mullen felt the need to emphasise what she had previously said. 'Ellie Bevan was genuinely shocked when I unfolded that photograph. Up to that point she had been incredibly composed given that her usually routine journey to work had conjured up a dead body. As I said, she was brilliant with Mrs Wiseman but she really flipped when she saw that photo.'

Matt looked around at his first case team and suddenly felt about ten feet tall. He took control of the meeting and ensured that everyone knew what was required of them.

Helen Cook-Watts had already linked up with Carol Mullen and the two women headed for Canton to interview Hilda Wiseman. It was Helen's turn to feel important as she sat alongside her uniformed colleague. This was the first time she had been asked to play a part in an investigation without a senior officers being in attendance. Helen was still new to CID, but her compassionate and no-nonsense approach to the job was already being noticed. She was the ideal person to interview the old lady, and although Matt had mentally ruled Mrs Wiseman out as a suspect, it was possible she had noticed something that would help with the case.

Carol slowed the car down as they turned into a street of large terraced properties. 'These houses are huge, although most of them have been converted into flats. My cousin studied at Cardiff University a few years ago and had a bedsit in one of them – talk about getting a quart into a pint pot! I'm sure she said there were fifteen bedrooms in that one house alone. The architects would turn in their graves if they knew how their desirable gentlemen's residences were being used today.'

Helen smiled. 'I'm sure you're right, but how many ordinary families nowadays could afford the upkeep of these houses as just a family home?'

'Well I couldn't on my pay, that's for sure! But it sounds as if Mrs Fisher does live in one that hasn't been converted. She gave me directions for parking at the rear of the property and I think that's the blue fence she mentioned so I'll just pull up next to that Volvo.'

Carol brought the squad car to a halt and quickly made the introductions, as even before the two women were out of their seats they were greeted by Gloria Fisher.

'How is your mother?' asked Helen.

'Well, as you can imagine, the incident was one hell of a shock for her. I really did think it was Mum who had caused the commotion – first of all I thought she was dead and then that she must have had a stroke or something. That was before I saw that poor man lying across the seat and I'm ashamed to say I thought, thank God it's not Mum.'

As she spoke Gloria Fisher ushered her visitors along the edge of a beautifully laid out garden and through what Helen thought was more like a front door than a back door. It was almost as if Mrs Fisher had read the young detective's mind.

'We've turned the house back to front and hardly ever use the original front door because it opens out onto the road and many of the houses have paved over their fronts for parking. It's mayhem out there sometimes but this way we have restored some of the original calm to the house.'

Helen nodded. 'It's a brilliant idea. It works, and just walking through that garden is almost like going back to a more gentle time.'

'My mother's through here,' said Mrs Fisher, leading the way through a formal dining room and a fabulous family kitchen, then doubling back into a small lounge. 'We had this part of the house converted into a flatlet for her but so far she's not been persuaded to leave the community she loves in Treorchy. She comes here a couple of days each week but even then she comes by train instead of letting me or Andrew, my husband, pick her up. Still I think after yesterday's episode she may get a change of heart.'

If Helen and her colleague had been expecting the old lady to be resting and recovering from her ordeal they couldn't have been more wrong. She looked somewhat guilty as the three women walked into the room and held onto the side of a wall-cupboard to help herself down from the chair she had been standing on.

'Mum, for heaven's sake! You'll be the death of me,' her daughter scolded.

Mrs Wiseman looked sheepishly past her daughter, and recognising PC Mullen she went towards her and gave her a hug. Not being used to hugs from members of the public, Carol took it as a bonus and gave a gentle squeeze in return.

After further introductions and the acceptance of some tea and biscuits the four women sat down and Helen began her first solo interview, but not before Mrs Wiseman, who insisted she should be called Hilda, had a few questions of her own.

'Did you find out who he is and what he died of? We've all got our money on it being a heart attack but I didn't see him clutch his chest or cry out in pain – nothing like that! I seem to remember I looked at him just before the train pulled into the station because I'd caught young Ellie's eye and she'd been looking in his direction.'

'Did you see anyone else, other than Ellie, taking an interest in him?'

'I don't think so, but then everyone was gathering up their bits and pieces and either standing up or getting ready to dash off when the train stopped. People are in such a rush these days!'

'I understand you get the same train twice a week to come here and so you probably recognise a lot of the passengers,' Helen suggested.

'Oh, I do, and most of them are very friendly. Some of the younger ones are usually half asleep and a few of them actually doze off ...'

Realising how much Hilda liked talking, Helen tried to rein

her in a bit. 'Tell me the first time you saw the gentleman that died?'

'That's easy,' said Hilda. 'I had only ever seen him twice before – once last Monday and then again on Thursday. He got on at Treorchy, same as me, and yesterday he stood aside for me to get on – and as there were only a couple of seats available I sat by the window and he took the seat next to me. I mean, normally I'd start up a conversation but I got the impression that he was lost in his own thoughts a bit, so I let him have some privacy.'

Helen continued. 'When he got on the train did you see the direction he came from?'

'The car park, I think, but I couldn't be sure.'

'I'd like you to think about the other people on the train. You said that you recognised most of them but did you see any new faces yesterday – anyone who took a particular interest in the man sitting next to you?'

Even before Helen had finished her sentence Hilda leaned forward in her chair and demanded an answer to her earlier question.

'You didn't tell me if he did have a heart attack. In fact, young lady, I think you dodged the question of how he died completely. Why are you asking questions about other passengers – surely he wasn't killed by someone?'

Helen swallowed hard and decided not to pussyfoot around the issue. 'We can't be absolutely sure until we get the results back from the lab, but we believe the gentleman was injected with something and that it's likely to have caused his death.'

'Well, who did it? When did it happen? Is there anything I can do to help? What about looking at mugshots of people who were on the train?'

Hilda's enthusiasm was only stopped by her daughter suggesting she had been watching too many thrillers on TV. Helen thought that the revelation would have upset Hilda, but it looked as if she would be dining out on the story for some time to come.

Both Helen and Carol were smiling as they headed for the car.

'I hope I have half her bottle when I get to her age!' Helen hesitated as she remembered that one of the things she should have offered was a counselling service. Carol just laughed.

'I wouldn't worry about it. She'll soon be in touch with her views on everything if she wants to share them. I think we can all rest easy in our beds knowing that Treorchy's own Miss Marple is on the case!'

Chapter Eight

'I'm always being told I should delegate more, so give me a few minutes to find someone gullible enough to take on this paperwork and I'll be with you. I'd like a sneak preview of the new facilities anyway.'

'Thanks, John, I would really appreciate your input. From the procedural notes it looks to me as if large chunks of evidence may be missing so I need someone with first-hand knowledge of what was happening back then.'

Martin cut the call to Sergeant Evans and returned to his new toy. He could still write everything up in his preferred three columns but now he didn't need to stand at a white board. His computer was linked to a large screen on the wall, and Charlie had formatted things so that his preferred layout was ready-made. Martin could type things in instead of having to write them, so there would be no more officers complaining that they couldn't understand his notes.

With Charlie's helpful scanning of the notes from the initial investigation, he had been able to chronologically enter a mountain of information. However he had to remind himself that, although this investigation was new to him, he was seeing a summary of the facts that were available to officers when the case was closed – unsolved. An initial glance had told him that he would never have been happy with this level of detection, and he began posing the questions he would have been asking had he been fronting the case in 1999.

His 'Facts to be Checked' column was already fuller than the nearly empty 'Absolute Facts' one. He could see little evidence of anybody making a real effort to discover the dead man's identity. The post-mortem results described the deceased as a young man, possibly of African origin, and poorly nourished. It gave the usual measurements and a general account of the state of the body, but Martin couldn't even find anything about the cause of death.

There were photographs, and Martin realised that Alex had indeed remembered the moment very well. It did look as if the corpse was wearing a ruby-red necklace, the imprint from his killer's weapon of choice. It had probably been a wire of some sort but there was no indication that the murder weapon had ever been found.

So 'murder weapon' went below 'identity' in Martin's second column, followed by 'location', 'witnesses', and 'motive'. He was already certain that there must have been more evidence than was now available to him. A young man had been brutally murdered, left naked in a relatively public place, and Martin had seen more effort put into solving a robbery. It didn't smell right – but why?

As if responding to its cue the famous nose of Sergeant Evans entered the room.

'Well, I was told this place was something special – love the comfy chairs!'

Martin laughed. 'That's just the comment I would have expected from you, John. It's your tell-it-as-it-is input I need to help me understand what was happening with this case.'

Evans looked at what Martin had projected and nodded. 'For months afterwards the image of that young man's body refused to leave my head. There was a lot going on at the time and some urgency to get everyone geared up for the events of the millennium. The powers that be seemed to think that there was going to be a crime-wave. Something to do with computers not being able to cope with the date change, and things like banks' security being affected. I was no more a techy person back then than I am now but even I remember it had everyone running round in circles.

'An obvious murder like that would normally merit a high-level investigation, but if memory serves it was a newly appointed DI and just a handful of quite junior officers that made up the team.'

'These are the names I've picked up from the records, but I don't recognise any of them. I thought I would talk to them, so if you recall who they are, and what they went on to do, that would be helpful.'

The sergeant tutted and raised his eyebrows as he glanced over the list of eight names and reread them several times before making his comments.

'The DI I just mentioned is the first name on your list. Jonathan Taylor. It was obvious he was completely out of his depth and I made a point of saying so. You won't be surprised that nothing was done to help him when I tell you who was calling the shots at the time. It was our mutual friend, ex-Detective Chief Inspector Norman Austin, now languishing at Her Majesty's pleasure.'

Martin cringed at the very mention of the man who had murdered a number of people – and who had included Martin in his personal list of people to exterminate. 'I haven't seen his name on anything to do with the Roath investigation – are you sure?'

'I'm positive. Now ... I don't really remember you being here as a PC, but I do remember you as a DS, and that must have been a couple of years after this case was investigated. You hadn't been here long when the Vincent Bowen case came up, but as we both know now, Austin had his own rotten reasons for leaving you out of that investigation.'

'I can't believe now how excited I was to be in the CID and come back to Cardiff as a DS working with DCI Austin – he had an awesome reputation at the time.'

'Well, the man was a brilliant detective. If he'd put his efforts into doing things the right way he would have been an inspiration to us all but somewhere along the line he fell in with evil. He saw corruption, revenge, and murder as the means of paying back people he believed, rightly or wrongly, had damaged him.' Sergeant Evans shook his head. 'Sad, really ...'

'You're a much more forgiving man than me, John. I hate

71

the very thought of the man, but probably more to the point I hate the fact that I was taken in by him.'

'You and hundreds of others.'

'But not you?' suggested Martin.

'No, not me, and that's why I suggest that when you take a fresh look at this case you remember that things may not always be what they seem. Not with Austin manipulating the people he chose to conduct the investigation.'

'So, Jonathan Taylor. Where will I find him, and what about the others?' Martin walked into a screened-off area where there was a kettle, a fridge, and a microwave. He made himself a coffee and found a large mug for the strong sweet tea he knew the sergeant preferred.

He had given Evans time to jot down a note alongside each of the names on the list. They pulled two of the comfy chairs up to a small table, and Evans drank his tea while elaborating on what he had written.

'OK, well, Jonathan Taylor was a graduate entrant, and to put it mildly was wet behind the ears. Nothing wrong with the bloke but he was definitely in the wrong job. Of course he would have to have seen bodies and attended post-mortems a part of his training, but I thought he was going to be sick at the crime scene. If anything he was guided though the procedures by the second name on your list. Pat Waring was also new to her role as a DC, but she was much more streetwise and had been a bloody good PC. Shame how she went after she got promoted, but there you go.

'Let me go back to Taylor, though. I couldn't tell you where he is now, but he had a serious breakdown and it happened quickly and during the investigation of this case. Pat Waring took on most of the responsibility, but whereas Taylor knew he was out of his depth, she revelled in taking charge. She was Austin's blue-eyed girl at the time so God only knows what was going on there.'

'Is she still in the force?' asked Martin. 'She would've started in CID roughly the same time as me – but I don't know the name.'

'She was here one day and gone the next. I suspect the only person who knows the details of her departure is Austin and I've no plans to ask him! I may be able to help a bit, though, because my niece Menna was in the same class as Pat Waring's kid sister. I'll ask her.'

He whisked through the other six names on the list and both men expressed concern and disbelief regarding the lack of experience that had been allocated to this horrific crime. John only knew the name of one other person for certain, Ian Baker. Martin was surprised to learn that he spoke to Ian most days.

'I do? I don't think I know an Ian Baker. The only Ian I know is the guy who works for Iris in the staff dining room.'

'That's him,' laughed Evans. 'It must have been the about same time Pat Waring left when he handed in his notice, but for some reason best known to her, Iris took him on and he's become her main helper.'

Martin grinned. 'This place never fails to amaze me. You must know so many secrets about the people here – feel free to tell me anything you think will be of interest!'

'How long have you got?' Evans laughed. 'What I will do is look up the names of the other three constables on your list. I'm pretty sure that the two men had routine transfers, but I can't remember where they went or when it was.

'PC Stella Powell wasn't someone I had a lot of time for. She caused me to lose a very promising officer by backing up an allegation that he'd made inappropriate advances towards Pat Waring. None of us uniformed staff believed a word of it, and I know for a fact that Stella Powell was nowhere near HQ at the time one of the incidents she "witnessed" was supposed to have taken place, but they had the full support of Austin and his cronies.

'Just hope I've been of some use, Martin. Oh, and I've just remembered – I'm pretty certain Alex Griffiths attended the scene as a new boy in Forensics.'

'Yes, you're right, John, he remembered the case. And you've been a great help. One last thing. Do you remember who the pathologist was? There's a signature on the PM notes but I don't recognise it and the report fall far short of what I would expect from Professor Moore.'

Sergeant Evans looked at the report. 'I can't make out the signature either, but around that time if a locum was needed there was a middle-aged woman who stood in. Ask Mrs Williams, she'll remember.' At the door he turned for one last comment.

'I've told you before, Martin, that none of the uniforms had any time or any respect for the CID around this time. I suspect, just as you did with the Bowen case, you'll find that the force won't come out of this smelling of roses. Do you think the chief super is prepared for that?'

When Evans had left Martin took some time to consider what he'd said. Nothing so far had jumped out as police corruption – just shoddy work and poor leadership. He decided to speak to Alex again and see if that had been the norm for the time or if this particular case had been singled out to be quietly sidelined.

He examined the witness statements, starting with the schoolchildren who had found the body. They were quite straightforward and Martin thought that he would have been unlikely to add anything to what they had written.

There were brief statements from local residents, basically saying they had seen and knew nothing. Even the assistant in the shop where the schoolgirl went for help had simply reported the time of that event and the fact that she had immediately dialled 999.

All of those statements were as Martin would have expected, but another batch taken several days into the inquiry were a bit of a mystery. Why, out of the blue, were there statements from members of African support associations and from trustees of charities that raised funds for Somalia and Ethiopia? There were even statements from local MPs. It was the sort of thing he would have expected to see in the newspapers. He could think of no reason why he, if he had headed up this case, would have interviewed these people.

Martin assumed that as Jonathan Taylor didn't have a clue

what he was doing, he used random links to keep his team busy and fill the files. On the other hand the young DI could have had good reasons for following those lines of enquiry and perhaps someone wasn't happy with what he was doing. Martin just wished Taylor had documented things in more detail.

There were two things that took Martin down several flights of stairs to see one of his favourite women. Number one, he was hungry, and secondly he would take the chance to speak to Ian Baker.

The staff dining room was busy, and although Iris looked a bit flustered she managed to ensure that Martin got the best of what was on offer.

'I'm a bit short-staffed today,' she explained 'but the leek and potato soup should hit the spot, and if you're really hungry Ian's savoury scones are much nicer than bread to go with it.'

Martin took Iris's advice and thoroughly enjoyed his meal. Maybe Ian hadn't made it as a police officer but there was no denying he was an excellent chef. There was no sign of him today, though, and after the serving area had calmed down a little Martin approached Iris.

'I'm not sure I should be friends with you today,' she told Martin, but with her eyes smiling. 'Ian's been a bundle of nerves ever since he found out the Roath body, as he calls it, is being reinvestigated. It was bad enough when he heard that it was being looked at, but when he knew it was you on the case he really freaked out and he didn't turn up for work today.'

'OK, well, I don't know what his problem is, but in my experience it's better to talk about these things rather than bottle them up – so if you give me his address I'll pop round and have a chat with him.'

Iris nodded. 'He's been bottling something up for years and he probably won't thank me for giving you his address – but you could get it through official channels anyway. If anyone is going to talk to him I'd rather it be you, so here it is.' Iris handed over Ian's address that she had written on one of her paper napkins. 'If he needs any help please let me know.'

Martin nodded and was trying to decide whether to go back upstairs or take a walk around the Bay to clear his head when his phone rang. He noted that the caller's number had been withheld and so he answered officially.

'Hello, DCI Phelps speaking.'

'So pleased I got the right number. Laura Cummings here. How are you, DCI Phelps?'

The journalist. Martin had sparred with Laura Cummings before. His first instinct was to ask how the hell she'd got hold of his private mobile number, but he knew the question would never be truthfully answered. He would have to get it changed.

'I doubt you're ringing to enquire about the state of my health so would you like to tell me the real reason for your call?'

'Just trying to be friendly, but of course you are right and rumour has it that you are taking an active interest in Geedi.' Ms Cummings paused knowing that the name was unlikely to mean anything to Martin but she didn't wait for him to put his inevitable question.

'Sorry my mistake, you are more likely to know Geedi as the Roath body. It's not that I know his identity, it's just that when he was found the press decided to dignify him with a name, and in the Somali language *Geedi* means traveller.'

'That was a kind gesture, and from what I've seen there was little else in the way of kindness or dignity shown to him. I can confirm that I'm taking a fresh look at the case, but you aren't so naïve as to think I'll give you information that isn't available to all other media sources. When I have anything to report there will be a statement, or if it warrants it, a press conference.'

'Yeah, yeah, I know all that, but maybe on this occasion *I* could give *you* some information. After all, I was around when the story broke eleven years ago, and I was incensed when the case just floundered. Take a look at some of the stuff I broadcast at the time and you'll be left in no doubt re which way I thought the investigation should go.'

Martin started to reply but Laura Cummings cut him short.

'Look, it's up to you. I know you think there's no such thing as an off-the-record meeting with a journalist, but this could be the one time you need me as much as I need you.'

as ... Chapter ... moving ... for ... memoria ... for this ... ... It is ... only ... for you need a ... ... much as ... told ...

Chapter Nine

Even pushing aside all thoughts of Sarah, and the nagging worries he had about his sisters, Matt still had three women on his mind: the major players so far in his first solo murder investigation.

He concentrated his thoughts on Ellie Bevan, Hilda Wiseman, and Elizabeth Ferguson. The first two he'd already met and his gut feeling was that neither of them would have had anything to do with the murder. At the back of his mind he could hear Martin warning him that although gut feelings should never be ignored they were no substitute for hard evidence. He was expecting Ellie Bevan any moment and had asked DS Shaw to sit in with him on the interview.

It was testament to Matt's current state of mind that he had barely recognised Maggie Shaw as a woman as well as a detective sergeant. None of the other men on the team had failed to notice the blonde hair, blue eyes, and slim, curvy figure of the new arrival. The Matt of old would have been just as enthralled, but with another woman central to the 'private life' side of his brain, DS Shaw wasn't going to be any sort of distraction.

Helen Cook-Watts was interviewing Hilda Wiseman, and although he wasn't expecting much from that session he would catch up with her later for a briefing. The person he most wanted to speak to was Elizabeth Ferguson, and he realised that her identification of the body would be pivotal to the investigation. Everything pointed to it being her father apart from the issue of the car – and that made no sense at all. He hoped she would be able to throw some light on those photographs. The one found in her father's jacket was well-loved and his daughter would surely have seen it before and would recognise the woman and baby.

DS Shaw interrupted his thoughts as she came to let him know that Ellie Bevan had arrived and was being given a cup of coffee in one of the interview rooms.

'She looks scared to death, but I didn't see her yesterday so maybe she always looks like that.'

Matt shook his head. 'I'd say she was remarkably level-headed, several of us commented on how together she was considering her ordeal on the train.'

'Well, maybe she's had nightmares about it. Perhaps we should get down there quickly and see if we can put her at ease. Always supposing she's not guilty of something!'

Ellie jumped as they entered the interview room, but smiled as she recognised Matt.

'I'm glad it's you – at least I won't have to repeat everything I told you yesterday. I've spent the whole night going over and over things in my mind and I just want to stop thinking about them.'

Ellie did look scared to death – or guilty? Matt set about putting her at her ease so that he'd get the most out of the interview.

'Thanks for coming in, Ellie. I do understand what you're saying, but sometimes if we talk things through in detail it can help blow away the worries. I'm sorry but I really do need to go back over everything we did yesterday, just in case there's anything at all you can remember that will help us with our investigation.'

As sensitively as he could, Matt told her that it was certain the man had been murdered. 'We're just waiting for the toxicology results. We have no doubt that he was injected with something that proved to be fatal – we just need to know what that substance was.'

At first Ellie looked puzzled and then even more frightened than she had been before.

'You mean one of the people on the train stuck a needle in

that man ... with all the other passengers around! Was the injection meant for him, or could it have been any one of us who ended up dead?'

Matt realised to his dismay that he had not even considered the possibility of the killing being random. Although the prospect was unlikely it would have to be factored in, but for the moment that wasn't a great help.

'It looks to us as if the incident was planned in advance so I think the killer hit on the right victim – I don't think you or your fellow passengers were ever in any danger. Talking about your fellow passengers – that's where I would value your input. You told us yesterday that you take the same train every morning, and I guess applies to most of the people you travel with?'

Ellie nodded. 'I got my current job about a year ago, well, eleven months to be exact, and I mostly see the same people every day. There are exceptions, of course, and Hilda, that's Mrs Wiseman, is one of them, but even she has a routine. She goes to her daughter's house in Canton on a Monday and a Thursday every week. The daughter's been trying to persuade Hilda to move in with her, apparently she's got a large house and plenty of room now her children have flown the nest.'

Ellie was relaxing and Matt let her ramble on. 'Ask me anything you like about Hilda and her family,' she laughed. 'You only have to sit next to her for one journey and you get her full history, and I've been sitting by her at least once a week for almost a year. She looks out for me as she gets on the train before me – she's from Treorchy.

'Yesterday when I arrived, the man that died was already sitting next to her, and I only managed to get a seat nearby because a few people got off at my stop. They were regulars, they always get off at my stop, but I don't know where they get on.' She looked to Matt for help. 'I'm not really sure what else you want from me.'

'You're doing fine, Ellie,' persuaded Matt. 'If you could think really hard about the people on the train yesterday. Eliminate the people you usually see, tell me about any strangers.'

'Well, the poor old man was a stranger, I suppose. The first time I remember seeing him was last Monday morning, and he was in the same carriage as me for the rest of last week – and of course yesterday. He may have been on the train before but that's the first time I noticed him. There are only four carriages on the train and sometimes it's standing room only. I noticed him the first Monday morning because he was a new face and it seemed as if he was looking for someone. I can't be sure, you know, it was just a feeling I had.'

'Did you speak to him at any time?' questioned DS Shaw.

'No, but I really wish I had!' Ellie hesitated. 'There was a calmness about him and I had an uncanny feeling that I knew him … but I have no recollection of ever seeing him before. That's why I was so shocked when the policeman found that photograph in his pocket. Can we talk about that now? Have you found out what he was doing with it?'

'We'll come to that in a minute,' suggested Matt. 'Were there any other new faces on the train yesterday? Think hard, Ellie, it could be really important.'

'I appreciate that,' Ellie said, 'but I can't remember seeing anyone I haven't seen before. There were people standing and one of them was Andy Cox. He plays rugby for Treorchy but it's rumoured he's been spotted by one of the coaches for the Welsh team. He's a very big lad and I wouldn't have been able to see past him anyway.'

'So you could actually put names to some of the people in your carriage?' asked Matt.

Ellie thought for a moment. 'I could give you the names of everyone who gets on at my station – and probably their addresses as well.'

Maggie Shaw sat back in her chair. 'That's amazing! How can society be so different in different parts of Britain? It's quite a small country, after all! In my neck of the woods you could catch the same train as people all your life and then only be on nodding terms with them.'

'It's definitely not like that in the Valleys,' Ellie said. 'Most of the time people are too nosy for their own good. I can't say I'm always comfortable with it. Since my mother told me I was adopted she's also suggested that I'm probably English or something and that's why I don't properly fit in.'

'We've put out an appeal for passengers who travelled on your train yesterday to come forward to help us with our enquiries, but in the event of them being too shy to come forward we may look to you for help.' Matt leaned forward and bit the bullet regarding the identity of the murdered man.

'Ellie, we're fairly certain that we know the identity of the man who died and we are waiting for his daughter to confirm it. She's travelling from Wiltshire but she left some time ago and we're expecting her within the hour. We traced her father through a car parked in Treorchy Station car park but there are some strange anomalies that we need to sort out before we can be sure.'

Ellie jumped in and asked the question that had been burning a hole in her brain. 'I feel sorry for the woman, but if it is her father will she be able to explain about the photograph? Will I be able to speak to her?'

Before Matt could respond the door opened and he was advised by the desk sergeant that the people he was expecting had arrived.

'The sergeant here will show you to one of our waiting rooms, Ellie, and you are welcome to wait if that's what you want to do. I have no idea how long I will be so it's also OK if you want to disappear and I'll give you a call if I have any news I'm able to share with you.'

DS Shaw was having difficulty keeping up with Matt as he made his way towards the reception desk and caught sight of three people who were obviously waiting for him. He stretched his hand out towards the older of the two women, that he guessed was Elizabeth Ferguson, and had an incredibly strong déjà vu moment. He felt he knew her from somewhere, but she made no signs of knowing him so he assumed she must just have one of those faces. Then the penny dropped, as he remembered watching her playing out of her skin in the finals of a grand slam quite a few years ago. But now wasn't the time to talk to her about tennis.

She was agitated and barely allowed Matt to make the required introductions, refusing point blank his suggestion that they clear up a few points before going forward with any potential identification.

'As I said on the phone, you've got it wrong. True, the description you gave me fits my father, but you've definitely got it wrong about his car.'

Turning to Basil, she insisted he show Matt the photo that he'd taken of the car just a few hours before.

'That doesn't look like a railway station car park, does it? Take a close look and you'll see the surroundings are outbuildings to our family home.'

Matt took the phone from Basil and had to agree. He enlarged the image, focusing on the numberplate, and there was no doubt everything was identical to the one found in Treorchy. What a strange case this was turning out to be – was everything going to be duplicated?

Although she was adamant that the dead man was not going to be her father, Lizzie's resolve was fading as they entered the viewing area, and she looked to Basil to support her as DI Shaw carefully pulled back the white sheet.

Lizzie didn't scream, she didn't faint, she didn't even cry – she just stood next to the man in complete silence and then very gently began stroking his face.

Matt took her gesture to be the positive identification he had been anticipating and ushered everyone out of the room. He stood just outside the door keeping a careful eye on the grieving daughter but giving her the space and the time she needed to be with her dad.

When Matt heard her sobbing he suggested that Basil and Della try to give Lizzie the support she needed. Before showing Basil back into the viewing room Matt asked if he could borrow his phone to get a better look at the car that had been photographed at Woodcanton Hall.

He turned to DS Shaw. 'Look after these people and let me know when Elizabeth Ferguson feels able to speak to me. I'm going to get some expert help on sorting out these two cars, but it's the two photographs I'd really like to ask her about.'

A few minutes later Matt sat in his office and put a call through to Alex. 'We've just had the confirmation we were expecting, the victim is Edward Ferguson. His daughter identified him, and although she was adamant beforehand that it wouldn't be her father when it came to it I don't think she was that surprised.

'What's happening about the car he left in Treorchy? You'll be amazed to learn that there's another one, exactly the same, still at his home in Wiltshire.' Matt went on to explain the saga of the two cars and it was obvious he'd grabbed Alex's attention.

'My initial thoughts had been to examine the car at the place it had been left, but the information I got from the local branch is that there's been lots of cars and people coming and going since the car was left there – so there's not much point. They're looking for CCTV around the station and will come back to us on that, but apparently they are frequently vandalised so I don't hold out much hope. I asked them to get the car transported here for me to get a better look at it and I heard just a few minutes ago that it has arrived. If you want to join me in the usual place we may be able to sort out the real from the cloned!'

'Sounds good to me – see you.'

Before Matt left to join Alex he made the call he'd been putting off all day. Although he had wanted to hear her voice he was relieved to immediately get Sarah's messaging service. What did that mean, though? Maybe she was somewhere where there was a poor signal – maybe she was already at the airport …

Although he knew that she wasn't planning on doing anything so quickly, it was the mental image of Sarah boarding a plane that shook Matt out of his uncharacteristic self-pitying mood and into action.

He had rehearsed several times what he was going to say and

left a fairly long message that ended with a first for Matt. He'd never had a shortage of women in his life, but love – that was something new! He knew he had to stop pussyfooting around, as he had been because he knew that Sarah was still smarting from a fairly recent betrayal. She'd been taken in by false declarations of love and he was scared that she wouldn't trust his words. But he knew saying nothing wasn't an option anymore. He'd done what he had to do and hoped it was enough. Determined to himself into work and get some questions answered, Matt met Alex as arranged.

'Between the actual car in Treorchy and this photograph, it looks as if we're looking at the same car. The reg number is certainly the same for both, but I don't believe for one moment that we'll find the same vehicle identification number on both cars.'

It only took a few minutes for Alex to locate the Jaguar's VIN and for Matt to disappear with the information to crosscheck the details with the DVLA. In his absence Alex made a detailed examination of the car. It was in excellent condition, obviously well-loved. Alex had asked the local officers not to open the car or drive it, just to get it lifted onto the transporter. He had the keys that had been found in the victim's pocket and so was able to zap the lock easily. The interior was even more pristine than the bodywork.

He laid the contents of the glove compartment out on a table and was in the process of itemising them when Matt returned and confirmed that everything seemed to be in order with the car.

'The registration number tallies with the VIN and the vehicle has a current MOT and was taxed and insured by the registered owner who is, or should I say was, Edward Philip Ferguson of Woodcanton Hall, Malmesbury, North Wiltshire.'

'Well, he couldn't legally have two cars with the same numberplate! If you look carefully at the photo the cars may look exactly alike but there are marked differences. The man who has clearly looked after the car we have here is unlikely to be the owner of the one in the photograph. There's mud caked on the wheel flaps and bits of debris under the windscreen wipers, and it's a while since the bodywork has received any TLC. What do you make of it?'

Matt looked closely as Alex had suggested. 'I haven't got a clue, to be perfectly honest, but my instinct says follow that car! It's likely to be hours before Elizabeth Ferguson's in a fit state to be interviewed and so I'm thinking a trip to Wiltshire is on the cards. Fancy a journey down the M4?'

Chapter Ten

Martin drove his Alfa Romeo to a part of Cardiff that he didn't know very well, but following Iris's instructions he soon found 29 Bridgley Road, Thornhill, and pulled up outside. It was a quiet side road comprising some semi-detached properties and groups of modern terraced houses and Martin was uncertain about what sort of reception he was going to get.

He had never before called on a member of staff at home without letting them know he was coming. As he approached the house he realised that he should have asked Iris to tell him a bit more about Ian Baker. Did he live alone? Was he a family man?

Oh well, there was only one way to find out and Martin rang the bell. There was no reply and he rang it again. Still no reply and so Martin moved away from the door and started walking back towards his car. With what looked like a casual glance he ran his eyes over the upstairs windows and then caught sight of a faint movement behind one of the curtains downstairs.

Not wanting his journey to be wasted he turned back and tried the front doorbell one more time. Still no reply, so this time Martin walked purposely back to his car. He could hardly insist on being let into the house but he really wished Ian would open the door.

Luckily for Martin, fate intervened and just as he was getting back into his car a woman crossed the road and made her way towards Ian's house.

She approached the door and was struggling to find a key in her handbag when DCI Phelps approached her and introduced himself.

'Ian should be indoors, he's got a few days' holiday from work and he's helping me with some decorating. He couldn't have heard the bell,' she suggested. 'But not to worry, I've got a key ... if I can find it!'

She ferreted around in her bag and finally came up with a single key attached to a piece of blue ribbon. 'Ian says I should wear this ribbon round my neck because I'm always looking for my key. He's a good boy, always thinking up ways to help his old mother, especially now that there's only him and me here.'

Without realising it Ian's mother had already filled in a number of gaps in Martin's knowledge of her son, and he'd noted the fact that she didn't know he was off sick – she thought he was taking a few days' leave.

'Ian!' she called out as she pushed open the door. 'You there? I've got a visitor for you – he's been ringing the bell. Didn't you hear it?' She turned her attention to Martin and pointed to the lounge. 'Sit in there, Mr Philips, and I'll see if I can find my son. Work with him and his second mum, do you? I hope Iris knows that some of the best recipes he takes to work are mine, not his!' She chuckled to herself as she climbed the stairs and a few minute later a rather embarrassed-looking Ian came down.

'As you will now have gathered my mother is somewhat deaf, and so she got your name and title wrong. That's probably just as well, as she's not got a very good opinion of police officers and thinks all detectives are the devil incarnate. On the other hand, if I told her you were the one responsible for locking up Austin she'd turn into your number one fan.'

The comment was light-hearted, but there was no humour in Ian's voice and his whole demeanour was flat. He looked exhausted.

'Have you had some sort of bug?' asked Martin. 'I spoke to Iris earlier and she said it was unusual for you to be off sick and sends her best wishes.'

'Let's cut to the chase before my mother bombards us with tea and cakes. That'll be one bit of this visit you will enjoy, I can promise you that. Clearly you haven't come here on some welfare mission, and I've heard you are responsible for reopening the Roath case – so I've been expecting you'd ask to see me.'

Ian sat on one of the high-back chairs and took a deep breath. 'I didn't think, after all this time, that learning about the reopening of the case would affect me as much as it has. You have no idea what bastards were running the show back then. Austin brought out the worst in them, and there was a DI David Williams and a Sergeant Mick Walker who were definitely on the take. I still think I'd have made a bloody good officer, but there's only so much bullying a person can take. Still, it's only just over a decade but thankfully, even from my lowly position in the kitchens, I can see enormous change.'

Martin didn't want to stop the flow but he did want to gain Ian's confidence so he briefly interjected. 'Well, you've just mentioned Austin, but you may not be aware that lately I've been re-examining a number of his past convictions and I can only agree with your comment that there were some real bastards in senior positions.'

The words had had the desired effect and Ian seemed to relax a bit. 'I didn't know that, but I'm really glad it's happening and I wouldn't be surprised if you found some of the convictions made from trumped-up evidence – it happened. I should have had the balls to speak up at the time. I think that's why I got so depressed – it wasn't so much what was going on as me realising I wasn't strong enough to stick my head above the parapet.'

'Don't beat yourself up on that score, you weren't the only one. It took Sergeant Evans years to come forward with one piece of information, information that has recently helped overturn a conviction. I know he brought it to the attention of senior officers at the time but I guess, like you, he hit a brick wall when what he had to say didn't fit what they wanted to hear.'

Ian nodded. 'The more you spoke out the more difficult they made your life and so in the end you either shut up or got out. I still keep waiting for Vinny Wicks to print some sort of exposé, but maybe he thinks it wouldn't show him in a very good light.'

'Vinny Wicks?' enquired Martin. 'I'm sure I know the name.'

'You probably do, he's an investigative journalist for one on the nationals now, but back then he was a police constable. He had a really rough time. It's probably in the DNA of the guy to ask questions and that's why he's doing so well now, but as a PC he was considered by some to be a right pain in the arse.'

Martin recalled a recent call when another media personality had offered insight into past police procedures. Laura Cummings and Vinny Wicks could both be useful points of contact.

'I didn't see his name in relation to the Roath case,' queried Martin. 'Was he involved?'

'No, he was gone by then, but not long and I know it wasn't what he wanted to do. He was under threat of a disciplinary hearing regarding his alleged behaviour with a female detective, but we all thought it was trumped up. I can't remember exactly what it was that pushed him through the door – you'd have to ask him.

'The woman I just mentioned was DC Pat Waring and she was on the Roath case – not a woman you would want to tangle with. She was new to CID, but was well in with some of them and I'm sure she was having a fling with Austin. She used to bully Jonathan Taylor unmercifully, taking every opportunity to rubbish everything he said and then pressing herself up against him and pretending he had instigated the moves. It was pathetic when I think back and we should all have spoken out … but we didn't. Her relationship, whatever it was, with Austin seemed to render her untouchable, and to my shame I stood by and watched her destroy a good DI. We could also see that her strings were being pulled from above in relation to solving, or more accurately *not* solving, the case, but to this day I have no explanation as to why senior officers didn't want a result.'

The door opened and the predicted tray of tea was placed on the table next to Ian.

'Sort some tea out for your friend and I'll get the cake.' Mrs

Baker went back to the kitchen and Ian managed a smile.

'She does make exceedingly good cakes, and you've probably sampled some of her recipes as Iris is a great fan of my mum's cooking. I'm going to let her go on thinking that you work with me on that side of things if that's OK with you, because I don't want her getting upset again. I suppose I had some sort of breakdown when I left the Force and she bore the brunt of it.

'It's through my mother and her baking that I got to know Iris, although I had seen her in the staff canteen before she came here to swap recipes with my mother. Iris is a lovely woman and a bit of a philosopher! She convinced me that the best way I could get rid of my bogeymen was to face them and offered me a job back in Goleudy, albeit in a very different role.

'Do you know what? The senior officers who had been instrumental in my departure didn't even recognise me as I cleared the tables and served their food. I only expected to last there a short while but I started to enjoy the job and enrolled in a number of cookery classes. Upshot of it has been that I'm finalising arrangements to open a small restaurant in partnership with a friend of mine.'

His mother came back with not one, but two, plates of cakes and correctly caught her son's last words.

'I hope Elaine is more than just a friend,' she teased and turning to Martin added. 'They're getting married next Easter – but I expect you know all about that, he never stops talking about it! Now eat as much of the cake as you like and there's plenty more where this came from.'

Martin felt the desire to put a small Welsh flag on one of the plates of cake, which displayed two Welsh cakes, two slices of bara brith spread generously with butter, and two traditionally shaped slices of teisen lap. The other plate held a selection of small chocolate cakes each individually crafted and Martin looked helplessly from one plate to the other.

'Don't worry, she won't expect us to eat them all, but don't be surprised when you leave if whatever remains gets handed to you in one of the fancy boxes we'll be using in the restaurant.'

Between them the two men did justice to the cook as Ian told Martin all he could remember about the initial investigation. He ended by thanking Martin for coming to see him.

'I'm sure the feelings I've had over the past few days would have been temporary anyway, but you've made me realise that there was a lot I needed to get off my chest. I'd be the last person to tell you how to do your job, but I'll just say don't take anything you see written about that investigation at face value.

'There were two avenues of inquiry that DI Taylor wanted to pursue but he was prevented from doing so. The first one was in relation to a Somali charity and the second was something to do with a Tory MP. I wasn't party to the detail and the case was put to one side without anything being solved – but then you know that.'

'Thanks for talking so frankly. While I remember do you know where I could find Jonathan Taylor? Not even John Evans could help me on that one.'

'He's dead. Committed suicide following a complete breakdown. It started during the case and then he was in hospital suffering from severe depression.'

'I'm amazed John hadn't heard about that – he seems to be the font of all local knowledge.'

'John, as I'm now able to call him, has volumes of data stored away, but when you compare him with Iris, there's no competition – she knows everything, and that's how I know. Jonathan Taylor left a wife and two small children and I have a great deal of sympathy because at one point I think I was heading in that direction.'

'But you're OK now?' asked Martin.

'I'm more than OK now, and if you see Iris tell her I'll be back tomorrow.

He wasn't sure how what he had learned would benefit his investigation but Martin had a positive feeling as he left the house, clutching a beautifully designed box full of cakes.

Instead of heading back to Goleudy, Martin returned to the area he and Shelley had visited on Saturday. This time he left the car further away from Roath Park and walked around, looking carefully at where main roads turned into side roads and trying to figure out why the body had been dumped in that particular place. He was angry when he thought of the investigation files that he had read. There wasn't even a question raised as to whether 'Geedi' had been killed there or murdered elsewhere and the body dumped later. Had there been a lot of blood?

Martin knew that if the body had been discovered today Alex would be able to answer his questions. SOCOs would determine if the young man had been killed there, and how long he had lain on that patch of ground. Even without a murder weapon Professor Moore and Alex, working together, would give him a pretty detailed description of what had been used to kill the young Somali. The issue of his nudity would be considered.

Was the killing racially motivated? Was it some sort of accident or perhaps a fight that had ended badly? Martin mentally answered 'no'. The damage looked to have been deliberately and professionally executed.

The more he immersed himself in the case the more sympathy Martin felt for the victim. Brutal murder had ended the man's life, but what had he suffered before that? Someone, somewhere, must have known him – as a son or a brother or even a lover. Why hadn't it been possible to identify the victim? Martin wanted to see the setting up of a compulsory national DNA database and often cursed the activists who lobbied against it. However, if, as was quite likely, the victim had been an illegal immigrant, then he wouldn't have been on a database anyway. It was highly likely that Geedi had entered Britain unofficially, but was that a good enough reason to leave this case unsolved? Absolutely not, Martin thought. He was charged with a desire to get some sort of justice for this man, and more importantly, to find the bastard that had killed him.

The patch of ground where the body had been discovered looked just as it had done on Saturday, with one exception. The stones seemed even cleaner and more polished, and there were no weeds around the edges. Shelley had suggested that someone was tending this shrine, and now it looked as if that person had been back in the past few days. Martin felt that whoever it was would be the key to solving the case.

After taking one last look around he headed for his car and was soon back at base. He had no idea how often the shrine-tender went to the memorial. The weeds he and Shelley had seen were gone, so there was no chance of guessing the frequency of visits from the plant growth. For the moment all he knew was that the shrine was being visited, and although flimsy it was his best chance of a breakthrough in this case. He pulled out his phone and called Alex.

'Hi, mate, can you spare me a few minutes to talk about the Roath case? I've got the faintest glimmer of hope and I'd like your help to set up some surveillance cameras!'

Chapter Eleven

'Love to help on both counts,' Alex said, 'but at the moment I'm with Matt en route to Wiltshire. We're trying to find out how there can be two absolutely identical cars parked in two different parts of the country at the same time!'

'Sounds fascinating,' replied Martin 'but I didn't know you and Matt had joined the traffic division.'

'Nothing so exciting! Matt's just following up something in relation to the guy who was murdered on the train yesterday. I don't know if there's anything I can add to what I've told you about your case – I wasn't allowed too close to the action in those days. I'm putting you on speaker in case Matt wants to join in.'

Martin greeted Matt before continuing. 'I understand that you were very junior, Alex, but there's one question you may be able to answer. It's to do with the amount of blood that was present when the body was discovered. You wouldn't have had the experience then to determine whether he was murdered where he was found or killed elsewhere. But think back, remember what you saw, and with the benefit of the knowledge you have now, tell me what you believe could have happened.'

Alex didn't take long to consider the request. 'Not something I would have thought of doing but my response is a definite one – he was killed elsewhere. What do you want the cameras for? I'm not going to be around for the rest of the day but Meg in my department will be able to help. I'll get her to liaise with Charlie because she's got some new gadgets I think she acquired off the back of the new investigation unit. It means that single mini-cameras can be remotely linked to specific computer terminals, and activate prompts when defined activities are recorded.'

Matt was driving but gave a heartfelt moan. 'When I think of the number of times I've sat for hours looking out for some random criminal activity and now you're telling me I could have been comfortably sitting at the computer, drinking coffee, and getting a better view.'

Alex laughed. 'Time marches on, old man, and technology at the moment is leaping ahead. I'll phone my lot straight away, Martin, and you can let them know exactly what you want.'

'Thanks, and good luck with your twin Jags.'

Martin rang off just as Matt's car had reached junction seventeen of the motorway and he drove onto the A350.

Alex looked at the directions given by Basil Copeland that they'd decided to use instead of relying on the sat nav. 'Looking at this we can't be more than ten or maybe fifteen minutes away. The note says to look out for a partially concealed left-hand turn a few minutes before the main road into Malmesbury.'

'It's a really nice part of the country but I'll bet there's a premium to pay for houses around here.'

'Not much different to the properties around Cardiff Bay now I wouldn't have thought ...' He stopped in midsentence and indicated what looked like the turning they were looking for just a short distance ahead.

Although Matt had not spoken to Elizabeth Ferguson since she had identified the body of her father, he'd had a brief conversation with Basil Copeland. Basil was able to give Matt the location of Woodcanton Hall, and Elizabeth had authorised Basil to pass on the access code for the Hall's main gates.

The first code worked perfectly and the front gates opened allowing the visitors access to the grounds and they followed the drive around to the front of the house where a rather-the-worse-for-wear Mini looked completely out of place.

'That's Della Pugh's car,' said Matt. 'I can see why Lizzie Ferguson decided to drive herself to Cardiff rather than being driven in that!'

Alex pointed to the key safe to the right of the substantial oak front door. 'I thought those things had been abolished for anything other than holiday homes. They're a good idea if several people need access to a property and the owner doesn't want to have numerous keys cut, but even this heavy-duty one wouldn't be that difficult to get into. Still I guess here they have the added security of the main gates.

'I'd fancy a look round the house but that's not really what we're here for so I guess those are the outhouses we need to head for.'

Alex pointed to a group of buildings and started to walk towards them when Matt's phone rang.

'All hell could break out here!' reported DS Shaw, 'and I thought you should know about it.'

'What's happening?'

'Well, it's probably my fault, because I showed Elizabeth Ferguson the photograph that had been found in her father's pocket. I had been with her for an hour or more and although she was still very upset about her father's death she was determined to find out what happened to him.

'I didn't feel able to lie to her when she asked how her father had died and so I said we were investigating the possibility that he had been injected with some sort of poison. First of all she looked at me as if I had horns growing out of my head and then she went a bit potty and wanted to know why I thought there was someone out there who wanted to kill her father.

'In a funny sort of way I think her letting off steam and shouting at me was what she needed to do and she calmed down considerably after that. So much so that I thought I would ask her about the photograph and of course she wanted to see it. When I showed it to her it had completely the opposite effect to my first revelation. For ages she sat staring at it and then the floodgates opened and she hasn't stopped crying since.'

'That's OK – I mean, we would've had to ask her about the photo sooner or later. I would maybe have given her a bit more time, but I doubt it would have made much difference. So why do you think all hell is going to break loose?'

'Between the bouts of sobbing she's explained the photograph to me. She says she has a vague memory of the photograph being taken, but she's never seen the actual print before and had no idea that her father had kept a copy of it. Apparently the young woman in the photograph is her and the baby is her child that she was persuaded to give up for adoption. She then went on to tell me that she'd called the baby Harriet and my brain went into overload!'

'Bloody hell, I'm with you. Harriet was the name on the photo Ellie Bevan showed me and given that she's adopted and the age gap is about right – I know where this is taking us. Whatever you do keep this information to yourself – we are going to need some advice on how we handle this situation. It's going to be tricky for two ladies and they are both in Goleudy at the moment.

'That's why I had that déjà vu moment when I went from interviewing Ellie to attending the identification of Edward Ferguson. I was moving from daughter to mother, wasn't I? I'm not a believer in coincidences so what's this all about?'

'God knows but I thought you should know what's happening and get some advice on what to do.'

'Well, don't let the two women meet until we've done some preliminary work with both of them – and as I said we will need some professional help with that. It's going to be one hell of a shock for both of them. Is there anyone with Ellie now? Has Elizabeth got any family members who will be able to support her?'

DS Shaw answered that question very quickly. 'There's her mother and her brother, but I don't think there's any love lost between those three. Elizabeth hasn't been able to contact her mother, but her brother is a Conservative backbencher and he's already been throwing his weight around and is apparently on his way here as we speak. I'm really looking forward to that!'

'Don't let the fact that he's an MP panic you – just treat him like you would anyone else. Presumably he wants to see his father, and even if he doesn't get on with his sister I suspect he'll want to comfort her in the circumstances.'

Alex realised that Matt's attention was going to be taken for a while and so he had walked ahead towards the garages. As soon as he could and after giving the offer of support if needed, Matt ended his call. He was walking towards Alex when he realised that Alex was walking back towards him.

'That's got to be the quickest SOC examination on record!'

'There's nothing to examine,' returned Alex. 'There's no car there! Let's have another look at that copy you had taken of the photo from Basil Copeland's phone. These grounds are pretty extensive – perhaps there are more garages or outbuildings towards the back.'

Both men carefully scrutinised the photograph and both came to the same conclusion. They stood facing the garages and apart from the absent car the picture was identical.

Alex confirmed what Matt was thinking. 'This is definitely the spot from which Mr Copeland took his picture. Look, you can see the edge of that bush there and in the image that garage door is half-closed, just as it is now.'

'I was going to suggest that maybe Elizabeth's mother had returned home and then used the car but that doesn't make sense. I presume she has a car of her own so if she had taken the elusive Jag she would have left hers here and there's no sign of it. It's a bloody mystery.'

Alex had gone into full SOCO mode and was crawling around on his hands and knees.

'A car has been driven away from here very recently and although there are no actual tyre marks it is possible to see where the grass has been briefly flattened. I would say that in the same period of time another vehicle has been driven here and then driven away. That was a heavier vehicle than the Jag because the pressure on the grass for both journeys is greater.'

'OK,' said Matt. 'So someone drove a relatively big car here, presumably with another driver, and then they each drove away – one of them driving the Jag. Is that what you're saying? But why? The second Jaguar, if it really exists, is obviously dodgy, but I can't think of any explanation for it being here in the first place and then disappearing.'

Alex had turned his attention to one of the garages. 'There's a fairly substantial padlock on this door but it's not in use and there are no keys – it's not ancient and it doesn't really look as if it's been used that much.'

Neither men had heard the Mercedes that had used the second entrance and parked at the rear of the house, but both jumped at the sound of an angry voice booming from the verge above the garages.

'What the hell do you think you're doing? This is private property, you are trespassing and I'm going to ring the police. I've got a gun and don't think I won't use it – I've shot animals bigger than you, so get your arses up here and we'll wait for the boys in blue.'

When Matt automatically went to take his warrant card from his pocket the stranger fired a shot in the air.

'The first one's a warning, but try any more tricks and I'll show you how good my aim is.'

Matt's mind went back to the time when he and Martin had followed a murder case from Cardiff to France. On that occasion the suspect had been pointing a very lethal weapon at his wife, whereas the gun here was a simple air rifle and it wasn't actually being pointed at anyone. Nevertheless, they had been threatened and Matt just hoped his voice would work when he voiced his thoughts.

'Mr Charles Ferguson? I am Detective Inspector Matthew Pryor of South Wales Police and we are here in connection with the death of your father, Mr Edward Ferguson.'

Matt's words had the desired effect, as Ferguson realised that no random intruders would be armed with that sort of information. However he wasn't going to be made to look foolish and held the air rifle at arm's length.

'It's in the safest of safe modes, and I've just taken it from the locked compartment in my boot. There are only two places where the ammunition is kept, locked separately from the gun, and that's in the study here and in my London flat. There's not much I don't know about gun safety, Inspector Pryor, so you gentlemen have no need to be concerned.'

Matt wanted to remind him that it was criminal offence to threaten anyone, even potential burglars, with a gun of any sort. He refrained from doing so as he remembered that the man had recently had news about the death of his father and had possibly thought his mother was in the house with two strange men stalking the grounds.

'I'm pleased to hear that,' Matt said curtly, adding with a bit more feeling, 'May I offer you my condolences on the death of your father and assure you we will be doing all we can to find the person who killed him.'

Matt watched as Charles Ferguson shrugged his shoulders. 'I haven't had much to do with the old fellow for years now, so I'm not going to pretend a loss I don't actually feel. My mother won't be wearing widow's weeds either – theirs was never a match made in heaven, but each got what they wanted from it!'

'Well, as I understand it, your sister has been really upset by her father's death, and one of my team seemed to think you were heading for Cardiff to be with her. We didn't expect to see you here.'

'That's bloody rich! I think it should be me saying that. Why in God's name are you investigating my father's death here, when for some bizarre reason he died in Wales? I haven't been able to get in contact with my mother and, according to one of your officers in Cardiff, neither has Lizzie. Thinking that she might be here and simply not answering the phone, I thought it sensible to call in.'

'And is she?'

'Is she what?'

'Is she here?'

'How the hell would I know? I haven't been inside the house yet – I've had to contend with you two, and you still haven't explained what you're doing here.'

Seeing that Matt was on a short fuse thanks to Charles Ferguson's high and mighty attitude, Alex stepped in and explained about the saga of the two Jaguars. Suddenly Charles became more subdued and suggested that such a situation was not possible.

'Exactly what we thought,' continued Alex 'and that is why came here to see for ourselves.'

'And now you can see that there isn't a second car and that my demented sister and her, probably high as kites, friends have probably made up the whole thing. Some sort of sick joke – what do you think?'

'Even if I could think of just one sane reason for them to do such a thing, I know from the sequence of events this morning that it wouldn't have been possible. Why are you even suggesting it? Is your sister fond of tasteless practical jokes?' Matt was remembering the woman he had seen in Cardiff earlier and this picture of her just didn't fit the frame.

Alex showed Ferguson the photograph of the car. If he had been subdued by the mention of it he now paled visibly on actually seeing it. Matt picked up on his reaction and watched him closely as Alex went on to explain their presence.

'When you arrived I was examining the area around the garage and I can see that a car was driven away from here earlier.' He decided against mentioning the possible coming and going of another car and just mentioned casually that he would be asking the local SOCOs to join him and help with his investigations.

Now Charles was really rattled and protested loudly.

'What the hell for? You'd be wasting your time and theirs. Go back to Wales and find out who killed my father. That's what you get paid for, isn't it? Not going off on some wild goose chase into areas way outside your jurisdiction.'

He turned and made his way towards the house with Matt following closely on his heels.

'Do you need to investigate inside the house as well, or can I be allowed *some* privacy in my mother's house?'

'At this stage of the investigation I don't need to come inside, sir, but if that position changes I'll be sure to let you know. It would be helpful to know if your mother is at home – you'll find me working with my colleague when you're able to furnish us with that information.'

'Use your brains, detective! Do you think my mother drives

a clapped-out car like that?' He looked disdainfully at the Mini. 'Whose car *is* that anyway, and what's it doing here?'

'Your mother's car isn't here but your mother may well be. She could have been a passenger, dropped off by someone else.'

Matt smiled as he walked back to where Alex was once again crawling about on all fours. They knew nothing for certain, but Matt felt that Charles Ferguson knew more about the second Jaguar than he was letting on, and he took pleasure in rattling his cage.

'Some people just get under your skin don't they? I fancied doing him for offences under the Firearms Act but it would have come to nothing. Have you found anything else of interest?'

Alex looked up. 'Nothing relating to the cars, but I think these outbuildings have seen some curious activity. The one at the end has been cleaned to a level beyond that of any operating theatre. The door's been wedged open, but in the corners the smell of bleach is still strong. From that same garage and the one next door there are signs of heavy traffic coming and going. The direction of the traffic is not the way we came but towards the back of the house. I can only assume there must be a second entrance. Come to think of it, Charles Ferguson must have come that way, because we'd have heard him if he'd driven up the front drive.'

'I'll take a look,' said Matt. 'I can see what you mean – there's a vague track, but not something I'd associate with the level of traffic you mentioned.'

'That's because it's not recent. I'm talking about comings and goings that happened anything up to a year or more ago. And of course there could be a perfectly innocent explanation – even for the excessive use of bleach!'

Some twenty minutes later Matt returned, having walked about half a mile to the rear entrance of the house and back.

'There is another way in and out of this place, and if anything the black metal gates back there look more daunting than the ones at the front. The gates were locked and it wasn't easy to see beyond them but I looked as best I could for a code entrance device and I couldn't see one. That makes it even more secure than the front entrance – those gates must be operated by remote control only. There's a CCTV camera discreetly mounted on a tree. It's excessive security for a family home, wouldn't you think?'

Alex took in the surroundings. 'Not necessarily given the size of this place, and we don't know what works of art they keep inside. I guess they wouldn't get insured unless their security arrangements were of a certain level. I'm just puzzled by the different arrangements between the two entrances – and then there's that key safe in the porch. One almighty blow with a hammer would get that off the wall, and the same hammer would easily split open the casing.'

Matt nodded. 'It seems as if what's in the grounds is more worthy of protection that what's in the house.'

'Your friend Mr Ferguson has been out to say that his mother is not at home, emphasis on the not, and he would appreciate knowing when we're thinking of leaving. He doesn't fancy making his way to Cardiff and leaving us in the grounds of his mother's house. He was not at all happy when I told him I'd spoken to the local CID and they'd agreed to getting their SOC team to help me.'

'And have they?'

'Yes, and with more enthusiasm than I would have expected. I spoke to a DCI Mortimer and he said he'd welcome the chance of having a look round this place – seems it's been on their radar for some time, but he didn't go into details. They shouldn't be long.'

'We should have come in separate cars,' reflected Matt. 'I really should be getting back to Cardiff before the chaos DS Shaw is expecting breaks out – but I don't want to leave you stranded here.'

'I've a gut feeling that I'm going to be here for some time, but what comes to light here may have nothing to do with your case. DCI Mortimer sounded excited so he's raised my professional interest, and it will be interesting to see how the

North Wiltshire SOCOs go about their business. Charlie's got her cousin Enda staying with us at the moment, so they'll be happy to have a girlie night without me and I'll find somewhere to stay locally and find my way back to Cardiff tomorrow.'

'OK, if you're sure! There's plenty of room for you to stay here but I can't see that hospitality being offered. Not even a chance of us setting foot over the doorstep without a warrant.'

If DI Pryor had been allowed inside the house he would have been party to Charles Ferguson warning his mother, in the strongest of terms, to make sure things were watertight her end and to lay off the whisky.

Chapter Twelve

Martin looked back from Charlie's meticulous presentation of the case to the original notes on Geedi, and realised that even if there had been a suspect, he or she would literally have got away with murder. No half-decent lawyer would have passed up the opportunity to rubbish the police files. There were more crossings-out and impossible to read, half-completed reports, than he would have believed possible.

He smiled as he remembered Charlie's recent comments about all police officers writing the date in the top right hand corner of everything they wrote. Even in this mess that was still a constant. The date opened the report of the first officer to arrive at the scene. He was a PC Knight, and his was one of the better reports even though it simply listed the time he arrived, the names of the children who had found the body, and the fact that he had handed the case over to a DI Taylor.

Staring at the date Martin realised that the anniversary of the death was in fact this very Thursday. It struck him that if he had been lovingly preserving the memory of someone he knew, and perhaps loved, he would need to mark the day in some way. Thursday would be the twelfth anniversary of the murder and Martin had a sudden jolt of memory. He pushed the pictures on his phone back to the ones he had taken of the shrine.

Yes, there were eleven stones, and he felt excited as he contemplated the possibility that there was one for each year and that stone number twelve could be waiting to be laid on Thursday. Did he have an over-fertile imagination or was it a possibility? He had already organised the setting up of some covert surveillance cameras, in the hope that someone would attend the shrine soon, but now he really believed he was being thrown a lifeline.

He would have to consider that twenty-four hour observation would be required on the Thursday. Could he justify doing that based almost totally on a hunch? Probably not, but he'd convinced himself that there had never been a better opportunity to find the real identity of Geedi and get nearer to the killer.

If necessary, Martin would do the whole twenty-four hours himself but he knew from experience that pairs of people, working short periods of time, was the best way to undertake detailed surveillance. He'd speak to Sergeant Evans and get authorisation for overtime from the chief super if necessary. Martin was having difficulty managing his expectations and was willing time to speed up so that his plans could be put in place – he had to be right! It wasn't easy to get his mind back on some of the things that needed checking from his visit to Ian Baker's house. The suggestion had been that he take a look at some Somali charity group, and Martin trawled through the documents alongside Charlie's summary to find the references.

There was only the briefest of mentions in the written records, but Charlie had somewhere found a link that Martin was able to follow to the organisation's website. It was a very professional setup and gave a comprehensive history of the conflicts faced by the people of Somalia. It made sober reading, but Martin had to confess that even after reading it a couple of times he wasn't sure who was to blame for what.

Martin had, through his job, met a number of asylum seekers and illegal immigrants, and he thought they had one thing in common with the victims of any crime. They had been abused and their sense of self-worth had been stolen.

The website confirmed this, concentrating on the ways the organisation had helped people escape the conflicts. In particular they focused on families where the father was in danger of being executed for his religious or political opinions and where even the women and children were in fear of their lives. There was evidence of heart-warming success stories, with pictures of happy children at schools in the UK and short videos of the parents expressing their thanks to people who had donated to the cause.

Martin could see that tens of thousands of people had visited the website, and he wondered how many of them had been sufficiently moved to make a donation. Perhaps if the surveillance went according to plan on Thursday, he would make a donation on behalf of Geedi.

Before leaving the site Martin checked out the chairman, chief executive, and the named trustees of the organisation. He couldn't see the names of the people who had been interviewed eleven years ago but maybe they were no longer involved. Nevertheless there would be records of their previous participation and it shouldn't be too difficult to find them.

Nowhere in any information was there reference to a Tory MP being interviewed – maybe it was just the local MP at the time being asked questions about immigration or about crime in general. Yet Martin racked his brain to remember the politics of the time and he couldn't think of a single Tory MP in Cardiff back then. 1997 had seen a Labour landslide and everything had turned red. Surely it would have been a Labour MP whose views had been sought? In any case, there was no evidence of him in the investigation notes.

His phone rang suddenly.

'Martin, it's John Evans. Just a call to say I spoke to my niece regarding Pat Waring, as promised. Not much to go on, I'm afraid. Menna was quite friendly with Pat's sister Vicky and all she remembers is going to school one day and being told that Vicky and her family had moved away. Menna was upset at the time and couldn't understand why her friend had never said anything about moving. The rumours were that it was something to do with Pat's job, which tallies with Pat leaving like she did, but Menna's never heard from Vicky since she left. Sorry I can't be more helpful.'

'Don't worry, John, I don't think Pat Waring would be all that useful anyway – quite the opposite if she was involved with our old friend Austin. Thanks for trying.'

No sooner had Martin put the phone down than it rang again. It was Alex.

'Sorry, Martin, it looks as if I'm stuck in Wiltshire for tonight at least, so do you want to talk through anything further on the Roath case – or will it keep?'

'It'll keep. You answered my main question and thanks to Charlie and Meg I've got state-of-the-art monitoring set up exactly as I want. All I need now is several sets of human eyes to constantly look at it over a twenty-four hour period. Any offers?'

Alex laughed. 'I'm here for the duration. Matt's on his way back, preparing himself to introduce a mother to the twenty-year-old daughter she has never met. Trauma in itself, but put it on top of their father/grandfather being murdered yesterday and it's more than a bit of a powder keg! Poor Matt, he's getting a solo baptism by fire.'

'But he's OK, isn't he?'

'Oh, sure, I think he's enjoying the challenge. There's something going on with him and Sarah and he hasn't said what, but I guess he will when he's ready. I hope they'll have sorted it out by the twenty-seventh because Charlie's got something lined up for the six of us. With it being your birthday on the twenty-third and hers on the thirty-first she's hoping we can all get together on the Saturday that's between the two. I don't know what the plans are, but I'm pretty sure Shelley's in on the scheming and probably Sarah as well. I did suggest to Charlie that it should be me arranging something for her, as it's her birthday as well as yours, but judging by the look I got she's not got a lot of faith in my social planning skills.

'Hold the line a minute, Martin, I've got a caller trying to get through and it might be my Wiltshire opposite numbers.'

Seconds later Alex reconnected and confirmed he had been able to give the Wiltshire team the entrance code to Woodcanton Hall, allowing access to a car and two vans.

'I don't know what's going on here but this is not the level of support I was expecting. I guess these local guys have been looking for an excuse to get inside this place and they're using me as their reason to do so. Whatever! It promises to be interesting so let's see what I can find out.' Alex signalled to the driver of the car and the small convoy parked between the front of the house and the garages. and

Everything was being closely watched from an upstairs window. Charles Ferguson had met DCI Mortimer before and he wasn't pleased to recognise the car and the short, grey-haired man that got out of it. Their first meeting had been several years ago and Charles was still able to feel the grip of fear as he remembered how close the man had got to discovering parts of his life that he chose to keep hidden. Different forms of sexual orientation were becoming more socially tolerated, but for someone aspiring to reach the top of his political career there were definite limits.

Catherine Ferguson had always known that her son had a Jekyll and Hyde personality, and when he was young it excited her to see how far she could push the Hyde side of his nature. He was so like her. He put on a coat of kindness and respectability but his true character was never far from the surface and as he got older he was finding it increasingly difficult to hide.

He cursed the way he'd dealt with DI Pryor and his colleague earlier. What he should have done was played the part of the grieving son, offered them some refreshment, and sent them on their way. But he'd panicked and seeing them looking around the garages had brought back the same terror he'd experienced with DCI Mortimer.

It was probably just as well that the only thing he'd had to threaten them with was an air rifle. If he'd had something with more of an automatic action there could well have been two dead men in the grounds. Charles tried to control his breathing as one half of his brain told him that he wouldn't have shot them while the other half laughed knowing that he most certainly would have done.

Well the Jaguar wasn't in the garages now so that was one thing at least that his mother had taken care of. He must find out what she had done with it. It would be no use just hiding it away this time – it would have to be completely destroyed. For him the loss of that car would be more intense than the loss of his father. The car bound him and his mother together in that secret part of his life known only to the two of them.

She was the only woman of any consequence in his life, and although he was not openly gay there were few people who doubted that was his sexual preference. Only Catherine knew what he really liked, and lately even she had become disturbed by the lengths he was prepared to go to satisfy his desires. Charles had a preference for males, yes, but it was youth that really turned him on. He had a predilection for underage teenage boys.

The use of his father's car had started out as a bit of a joke and happened when Charles still lived at home. Charles had used it to kerb-crawl around some of the less salubrious parts of his home county. He was careful and most evenings went back to Woodcanton Hall with Mr Hyde's desires unfulfilled. There was no way he could satisfy his needs with anyone who didn't bear at least a vague resemblance to the boy who had introduced him to a sort of love that one man could have for another.

Sometimes the need to discharge his cravings clashed with his father's need to use the Jaguar himself. Charles had his own car, of course, but the added excitement he got from putting his father at risk by using his car had risen to unbelievable heights with 'Mr Hyde'. The Jaguar had become an essential part of the foreplay he needed, and things came to a head one evening when he was desperate to use the car and his father had already driven off in it.

Catherine couldn't bear seeing her son so distraught and first of all as a joke and then very seriously they put a plan in place. It wasn't that difficult to find a car that was the same make, model, and colour as his father's and Catherine had connections that made the acquisition of false numberplates an expensive dawdle. It was yet another secret they shared. Nothing like the biggest one that would have seen them both locked up but the one concerning the car gave Catherine some personal pleasure.

114

She had come to hate the man she had married and loved the idea of making a fool of him behind his back. When Charles's Jaguar was ready for delivery she ensured that the furthest of the garages in the grounds had acquired a new padlock and that there were only two keys. Charles used the car but initially there was not the same thrill. That came when he had put one of his father's old wallets embellished with his sister's silly logo, together with one of his father's coats, with nametag, on the passenger seat of the car. The first night that he used it after that saw him handing out more than a hundred pounds but getting the sort of young, lean body that satisfied him.

It was a long time since Charles had felt so disturbed. He made his way to his mother's side of the house where there would inevitably be a good supply of whisky. Her lounge was one of the largest rooms in the house and, like the rest of her side of things, the interior design was ultramodern and sophisticated.

It looked as if his mother had been entertaining, as there were a number of plates and glasses dotted around. Charles and looked at his watch. In about half an hour Avril and Tom Shepherd would be arriving and he didn't want that to happen. Avril spent a couple of hours each weekday cleaning the house and her husband worked in the grounds. They did their respective jobs well, but Charles knew they were inclined to gossip and didn't want them going back to the village with stories of police crawling all over Woodcanton Hall. Their phone number was alongside the telephone and Charles rang and told them of the death of his father. He suggested they take a week off unless his mother called them with different arrangements.

They seemed genuinely shocked by his father's death and Charles wondered how they would react when it became known that he was murdered. It would surely be on the news, but then it had happened in Wales, so maybe there'd be a time lag. His father was not well known in his own right but his wife was no stranger to the media and his son was an MP. Add that to the fact that his daughter still held a place in the hearts of the

British tennis fans then sooner or later the press would put those things together and come looking for a story.

Charles thought better of that whisky he had been seeking and went through to the kitchen to settle for some strong black coffee. He was going to have to play the part of his life over the next few days and act even more than he was used to doing politically. The only one who wouldn't be convinced that he was a grief-stricken son would be Lizzie.

Chapter Thirteen

'Fill me in on what's happened,' said Matt, 'and if anyone's going to the canteen will they pick me up a sandwich? Anything, I don't care what filling, and a packet of salt and vinegar crisps, please.'

Matt was starving. He hadn't eaten during the Wiltshire trip and it was way past lunchtime. He wasn't sure if anyone had heard his request but five minutes later a ham salad sandwich arrived together with the crisps and a coffee. In the meantime he'd been briefed more fully by DS Shaw and DC Cook-Watts.

'Well, as you know I was keeping an eye on Elizabeth Ferguson and I told you over the phone about explaining to her the possibility that her father was murdered and showing her the photograph.' Maggie Shaw hesitated. 'It seemed like the right thing to do at the time.'

'Yes, and I'd have probably done the same,' replied Matt. 'So what's happened since then?'

'Not a lot, really, as far as Elizabeth Ferguson is concerned. She was obviously shocked when I showed her the photo, but then it was as if a valve had been released, and she poured out years of wondering what had happened to her baby. Her friends had known nothing about her pregnancy; Della wasn't even born at the time, but they've both been very supportive. She's been speculating about what her father was doing in Wales and if it had anything to do with finding her daughter. I get the feeling she's not going to be that surprised to hear Ellie Bevan's story.'

Matt turned to Helen. 'So what about Ellie – where is she with her understanding of the situation?'

'Oh, I think she's streaking ahead. She knows that the name written on the victim's photograph is Elizabeth but the name meant nothing to her. Now she believes that the photographs are of her as a baby in the arms of her mother and that one of them is called Elizabeth and the other Harriet. She thinks it must be her that was named Harriet because that's what her adoptive father was calling her before he died.'

'I think she's got that right, don't you?'

Both the women he was speaking to nodded in unison. Helen continued.

'She's been demanding to know the identity of the victim and to know if he was in some way related to her. Knowing that his identity would soon be public knowledge, I told her that the gentleman was a Mr Edward Ferguson. Not surprisingly, the name was unfamiliar, and then for some reason she wanted to know if he was Welsh. It seemed like a strange question to me!'

'Let me get this straight,' said Matt. 'We are all of the view that Ellie Bevan is the baby that Elizabeth Ferguson gave up for adoption twenty years ago. The victim, Edward Ferguson, is Elizabeth's father and therefore Ellie's grandfather. My instinct is to put Elizabeth in the picture – pardon the pun – and see how she reacts to what we tell her.

'Maggie, you come with me and Helen please stay with Ellie and make sure she's OK. See if there's anyone she'd like to be with her, and if she asks any questions don't hesitate to answer them truthfully. Her thoughts may be streaking ahead but she's going to have more than thoughts to deal with before today is over.'

Lizzie's first thought when Matt entered the room was to ask about the Jag but there was something about his demeanour that stopped her short. 'You know who killed my father – is that it?' she asked.

'No, not yet, but we will find out.'

'OK, Inspector, but at least you saw that his car was at Woodcanton Hall and not where you thought it was?' The second question was more like an accusation but Matt didn't bite.

'We can talk about the cars later, but for the moment I want to tell you about something we have discovered as a result of our investigations. It's of a rather personal nature, so how do you feel about your friends being here?'

Lizzie gave a feeble laugh. 'So far today they have learned that I was raped by my tennis coach at fifteen and that I had a baby girl that I was persuaded to give up for adoption. You can't get much more personal than that, can you?'

Matt spent the next quarter of an hour telling Lizzie about the circumstances surrounding her father's death. Lizzie was surprised to learn that her father had been on the same train every day the previous week.

'But why?' she asked 'What was he doing there?'

By the time Matt had finished talking Lizzie knew the answer to that question. There was silence in the room for several minutes before Lizzie broke it.

'So this young woman – this Ellie – is my daughter. Does she know about me? Does she want to see me? Are you sure about this?'

And then Lizzie had an horrendous thought. 'Surely she had nothing to do with my father's death? Oh, please God don't tell me she was involved. Why was he killed anyway? Did she know he was her grandfather?'

Questions. questions … and there would certainly be plenty more to come. Matt tried to take them one at a time.

'First of all, Ellie doesn't actually know about you yet, although she's adding everything up and suspects she was related to your father. As I said earlier, we don't know as yet who killed your father but I have no reason to suspect Ellie was involved.'

Lizzie interrupted. 'Will I be able to speak to her? Do you think she will want to see me? Oh God, I wish my father was still here. Has anyone been able to get hold of my mother yet? I've given her number to dozens of people. I did speak to my brother and he was supposed to be on his way here. Not that either of them will be bothered about my father, but bloody hell, will they be furious to know that he probably found me my

119

daughter.'

'Why furious?' Matt asked. He thought they'd be overjoyed to welcome Ellie back into the family?

'When my father had rescued the family business he set about putting his affairs in order, and out of the blue he instructed the family solicitors to name my daughter as one of the main beneficiaries of his will. It contains a clause whereby she is entitled to live at Woodcanton Hall for the duration of her life if she chooses to do so.

'My mother went ballistic when she heard what he'd done, but the family solicitor said he was within his rights to decide who could use the house that had been part of his family's estate for generations. She calmed down when I told her that I'd no intention of ever looking for my daughter and it's not been mentioned since.'

Lizzie hesitated. 'Until now I had always believed it would be wrong to disrupt whatever life she'd made for herself – now I'm not at all sure … and I really want to see her. I guess none of us imagined my dad would go off to look for her. I'm sure my mother would have done anything to stop him if she'd known what he was doing.'

Matt silently wondered if the 'done anything' would include murder.

Lizzie's eyes re-filled with tears. 'I hope he saw Ellie – I'll have to get used to calling her that, she's always been Harriet in my mind.'

'From what Ellie described, he did see her, and what she also said was that he seemed like a kind and gentle man but that his eyes were sad – and she told me that she wished she had spoken to him.'

'She's described him perfectly.' More tears welled up in Lizzie's eyes and Matt turned to DI Shaw.

'Stay here with Lizzie while I check on a few details, and then I'll decide how we should proceed.'

'She's here, isn't she? My daughter's here! Don't lie to me, Inspector Pryor – I know she's here!'

Matt was completely taken by surprise by Lizzie's outburst

but quickly regained his composure.

'I don't know where you got that idea from, but I won't lie to you. Yes, Ellie is here – but she doesn't know that you are. There are some things I need to talk to her about and as you can imagine your presence is going to be one hell of a shock for her. It will be for her to decide if she wants to see you or not. I can't and won't make her do anything she isn't comfortable with.'

A few minutes later, with Helen Cook-Watts in attendance, Matt was having a very similar conversation with Ellie Bevan.

'Thank you for being so patient, but there were things I had to be sure about before coming back to speak to you. I was hoping you would have phoned someone to be with you – did you do that?'

'Well, to be honest, DI Pryor, I've never really got on with my adoptive mother, and my two best friends work for the same company as I do. Our boss is already cheesed off with me taking so much time off this week, and I don't want to annoy him further by getting one of the others to take time off as well. I'm saving every penny I earn for a deposit on a place of my own so I can't afford to get the sack at the moment.'

Matt wondered how Ellie would react when she knew that there was a very spacious property in Wiltshire, and the opportunity to turn at least part of it into a home of her own.

'But I've been in touch with my Auntie Julie and she's making her way here. She was my father's sister and I've kept in touch with her since he died, but she lives in Swindon so she may be a while yet.'

'I'm happy to wait until she gets here if you think you need her to be with you when we talk.'

'No, please, let's just get on with it – my brain is working overtime and I'm way beyond making one and one make two … I've got it adding up to six at least.'

Ellie smiled, but she looked tired and Matt knew he would be adding to her burden with some of his revelations.

'I understand DC Cook-Watts has told you the identity of the gentleman on the train. We don't know yet who committed his murder or what possible motive there is for the crime but

121

those are things we will find out. What we do know is the connection that exists between you and Edward Ferguson.'

'Is he my grandfather?' asked Ellie, almost in a whisper.

Matt simply nodded and then went on to fill in all the gaps in Ellie's understanding of the situation. Helen grasped the young girl's hand and provided countless tissues as the truth of what was being said sunk in and Ellie began mourning the death of a grandfather she had only fleetingly encountered.

'The woman in both photographs is Elizabeth Ferguson, his daughter, and as you have been suspecting the child is you – and she is your mother.'

The words brought a fresh flood of tears from Ellie and Matt could see that his DC was struggling to fight back a few of her own. He could barely imagine the emotions that Ellie was facing. Suddenly, for the first time in her life, she knew who she really was.

In the last week she had met but not spoken to her grandfather, and then watched him die. Now she would be getting the opportunity to meet her real mother.

Matt was about to broach that subject very gingerly when Ellie asked, 'Does my mother know I was there when he died? Has she been to see her father? Is she still here?

'Yes, Ellie, to all three questions. I know it's a big thing to consider at the moment, but do you want to meet her?'

'With all my heart – yes.'

It was Matt's turn to fight back the tears as he saw the emotion in Ellie's eyes, but he spoke resolutely.

'We'll make the arrangements, but I'm afraid nothing can happen until your aunt arrives from Swindon. I can't let you face this situation without support, so you need to sit tight for just a bit longer.'

Matt left Helen with Ellie and made his way to the incident room where all known details of Edward Ferguson's murder were available. He looked at the board and was pleased to see some of his questions already answered.

He highlighted the word 'motive' on the board. Someone on that train had a reason to kill Edward Ferguson and the murder must have been carefully planned. Matt had momentarily considered Catherine Ferguson as the killer, but only because had a possible motive. Catherine actually having been on the train, having injected her husband personally was impossible – but would she have been able to arrange his death?

Matt didn't know enough about the woman yet, but he highlighted the need to interview her. Whoever *had* done the deed would have had a syringe already primed, and known the best time to administer the injection and then be able to exit the train anonymously.

Sitting at one of the tables, Matt wrote down everything he could think of regarding possible motives for murder. Eventually he discarded most of what he'd written and ended up with three things that seemed feasible.

His team had already gathered a lot of information about the victim. There was even a family tree that showed Edward's ancestry back to Tudor times. None of the family held peerages, but they would certainly have been classed as landed gentry. Fortunately for the family their ancestral home wasn't that big, in comparison to many that had been too expensive to maintain, and Edward himself had amassed a considerable fortune. He'd rescued the family business from collapse and had made it an extremely profitable concern.

The first possible motive on Matt's list was money. Lizzie had already mentioned her father's contentious will, and Matt made a note that he needed to see it. He assumed Edward's wife and children would be the main beneficiaries, and as such they would all have to be considered as suspects, even Lizzie, although Matt didn't really see her as a likely candidate. He would need a verified alibi of all their whereabouts at the time of the murder ... though even then there was the chance that they'd arranged for someone else to commit the murder.

Having met the son as well as the daughter, Matt struggled to keep his personal dislike of Charles Ferguson from influencing his judgement. Logically Matt could see no reason for Charles wanting his father dead. His political career appeared to be blossoming, and judging by the car he drove and the suits he wore he was no pauper.

The murder had happened at approximately 08.30 yesterday, and members of his team had already interviewed more than twenty people that had been on the train. So far the rugby player that Ellie Bevan had mentioned was their strongest lead. Andy Cox had told DC Cook-Watts that there was someone in the carriage who had caught his attention.

'There aren't many blokes bigger than me,' he'd told Helen. 'But this feller was way above my height, quite dark, and he didn't seem to know where he was – kept looking through the train window. Must have been a stranger to the area.'

Sadly, when pressed for a description of the man Andy Cox wasn't that helpful, and the only additions to the fact that he was tall and big, but not fat, was that he didn't smell too sweetly, and had very big feet.

'It wasn't body odour exactly, more like he'd been eating garlic or something peppery. I'm sure other people in the carriage would have noticed. This man had his back to me most of the time, and to be honest I was nursing a bit of an 'angover so I wasn't feeling sociable. I had my head down, I was avoiding eye contact with a nosy neighbour of mine, and that's why I can describe his shoes in detail but can't tell you much about his face!'

He'd made a statement confirming what he'd said to DC Cook-Watts and Matt scanned it and then looked through all the statements to see if any other passengers had remembered the man.

Matt reined himself in from thinking that this man was probably a trained assassin hired by Charles Ferguson to kill his father, but he had to admit that he desperately wanted to interview him.

Any further deliberation was halted as Helen Cook-Watts came in followed by a woman she introduced as Mrs Fletcher.

Ellie's Auntie Julie.

Chapter Fourteen

Charles Ferguson redialled the number and this time, to his relief, his mother picked up. For years Catherine had insisted that in public, her son called her by her first name, but she knew that when he was particularly worried he reverted to 'Mother'.

'Mother, thank God! Did you get my message? I hope you're sober because we're both going to need our wits about us to get out of this mess.'

'Of course I'm bloody sober! I had lunch with some friends, I must have fallen asleep for a bit – but I'm absolutely fine. And before you start the lecture, yes, I know what time it is. What are you banging on about – what mess?'

'Where are you?'

'That's none of your bloody business. I'm not at home and that's all you need to know.'

'Has anyone told you about Father?'

'I picked up a message from your sister saying something about her having to go to the police station in Cardiff. It didn't make a lot of sense, she was prattling on about his car having been found somewhere in Wales.'

Charles listened carefully to his mother's voice and tried to decide if she was indeed reasonably sober before telling her what he knew.

'Things have moved on a bit since then. It would appear that he died on a train in Cardiff and that the police are treating his death as suspicious.'

He waited for a response from Catherine but she couldn't trust herself to speak and so there was only silence.

'Mother, Mother, are you still there? Remember, it's me

you're talking to so there's no need to pretend you're upset.'

The silence was broken by peals of laughter that even to Charles sounded distasteful. 'You need to tell me where you are so that I can pick you up and take you to Cardiff. Did you hear what I said about the police treating Father's death as suspicious?'

He suddenly remembered the Jaguar and asked about it.

'You know what's happened to that!' she snapped. 'I arranged to get it picked up before daylight this morning because of the business with Lizzie bringing that girl to train at the Hall. I assume it was gone before I left.'

'You assume wrong! Those idiots you hang out with couldn't organise a piss-up in a bloody brewery.'

Charles told her that Lizzie's friend had photographed it in situ and had shown the photograph to the Cardiff police. 'At this moment I've got some scene of crime expert from bloody Wales here and he's enlisted the help of the local lot. That bastard DCI Mortimer was grinning like a Cheshire cat at the chance of setting foot inside our door.'

'So the Jag's still there and they're looking at it? Fuck, you're right, this is a bloody mess!'

'The car has gone, so I guess your friends couldn't get out of bed this morning and eventually picked it up *after* Lizzie had seen it. Do you know where they've taken it? It needs to be destroyed properly. We can't risk these SOC people getting their hands on any part of it.'

'But, darling, you love that car. Maybe when everything has settled down you'll be able to use it again.'

'Mother, have you *completely* taken leave of your senses? Part of the pleasure for me came from imagining I was using Father's car for activities he would consider disgusting – that was a big turn-on. And knowing that if I'd been caught on camera anywhere, he would have taken the rap.'

Catherine listened to her son sharing his secrets with her, as he had always done. She would always protect him, but deep down she knew that one day he would press the self-destruct button and she would only be able to stand and watch. They shared one horrendous secret that for years neither had spoken about, but she knew that at this time of the year it wouldn't be far from his mind. There was little about her son that Catherine wasn't aware of and nothing she couldn't forgive him for.

Catherine looked around the hotel room, and rather longingly at a fresh bottle of whisky, but any thoughts of opening it were dashed by her son's next words.

'Get your public face on and make yourself presentable. If you won't tell me where you are then you'll have to make your own way to the police station. It should take me an hour and a half tops to get there and I don't want you getting there before me. We need a few minutes together before going to see Lizzie and viewing Father's body. It's important we present a united front. We don't have to seem devastated, but we *do* have to show dignity and lend our support to grieving little Lizzie.'

After Charles had ended the call Catherine circled the bottle of whisky several times before deciding that one drop wouldn't do any harm.

Much as he was curious to know what was going on, Charles decided against talking to Alex or DCI Mortimer and within seconds of leaving the house he was driving his gunmetal-grey Mercedes through the main gates and making for the motorway. He was a born politician and was mulling over ways to get some positive publicity off the back of his father's murder. Maybe he would spearhead a campaign to increase the safety of public transport – that was always a vote winner.

He knew that in the past there had been some seriously dodgy activity going on in the grounds of Woodcanton. His luxurious flat in central London had been partly paid for out of the proceeds, but that was years ago and had all stopped when … Charles refused to let his mind conjure up the moment that still bound his mother and himself together in a conspiracy of silence.

He tried to imagine how his sister would be feeling about their father's death. Lizzie had always been as thick as thieves with her dad, and Charles anticipated that she would be in pieces. He knew that Lizzie had her own little secret, but although it would prove an embarrassment to him if it came out, it wasn't quite as potentially ruinous as his was.

Charles drove his car over the Severn Bridge into Wales. If he had been a fly on the wall in Goleudy at that moment he may have decided not to make the crossing.

Auntie Julie hadn't found Ellie sitting in a pile of shredded wallpaper this time, but she could sense that her adoptive niece was in a similar state of uncertainty and she hugged her tightly.

'Inspector Pryor's told me everything that's happened over the last couple of days: no wonder you look exhausted! Your mind must be on a rollercoaster ride. Try not to worry, Ellie, I'm a great believer in fate and from what I've heard I believe you were meant to be with that man when he died.'

She accepted a cup of coffee before sitting down and then depositing her cup on a low table she took both of Ellie's hands in her own.

'I've always respected my brother's wishes that you should be brought up as his own daughter. He loved you so much – you know that, don't you?'

Ellie nodded. She had no control over the tears that welled up in her eyes and escaped down her cheeks.

'When Gwyn died I should have spent more time with you, but my life was complicated at the time and you lived too far away for me to just pop in. Not that Joanne would have taken kindly to my interference anyway – we never got on! But that's no excuse and I should have made it my business to be there for you.'

'I've always known you were there if I needed you.'

'The thing that I feel most guilty about is not telling you that you were adopted. Before Gwyn died he told me that he was making efforts to find your birth mother and so I knew he was gearing up to talking to you about your real family. Knowing that, I should have given you the information he found, after he died, but it just never seemed like the right time and then life just took over. I'm so sorry, Ellie, you shouldn't have found out the way you did.'

Ellie smiled at her. 'That's all in the past now, and to be honest it's only very recently that I've really thought about it. I've always been happy to think of myself as Gwyn Bevan's daughter and I just wish he was here now.'

Julie smiled back and handed her a large brown envelope. Inside was a set of typed sheets, clipped together, plus a letter.

In the letter, written when she was nine, Gwyn explained to Ellie how he had been suffering from the same symptoms that had preceded his own father's death from a coronary thrombosis, and so, worried that he wouldn't be around to watch her grow up, he had found out all he could about her birth family.

The envelope also contained the reports from Porter Investigation Services, the private investigators he'd employed. Michael Porter's last report was dated on Ellie's ninth birthday, and she suddenly remembered going to a block of offices with her dad and waiting in the lobby while he picked something up on their way to her birthday trip to the cinema.

Ellie began to shed fresh tears as she read the reports. Porter had discovered that her birth mother had been raped by her tennis coach when she was just fifteen, but had kept the rape and her subsequent pregnancy a secret from her family until well past the time when termination was an option. The name of her mother had a series of exclamation marks written after it – as well it might, for Elizabeth Ferguson, better known as Lizzie, was one of the top British tennis players of the 1990s. Ellie gasped as she realised she knew exactly what her mother looked like, having seen her many times in the newspapers. She looked very much like Ellie herself.

Other members of the Ferguson family were in the spotlight, with Lizzie's brother being one of the youngest Conservative MPs and her mother a respected fundraiser for Third World charities. Porter had produced his trump card in the form of a photograph. A photocopy was clipped to the file – an exact copy of the photograph Ellie had discovered inside her dad's book. It had come from Edward Ferguson. He'd been the only member of the family prepared to speak to Porter and to even acknowledge the possible existence of a child. He'd said that his family was in no position to have the ghosts of the past brought back to life, but that his own hope was that one day his granddaughter would have the courage to come looking for her mother.

Gwyn's letter finished with, '*Although you were registered as Harriet Elizabeth Ferguson, to me you will always be Ellie Bevan, my daughter, and I love you. I hope that one day you will be able to meet your birth mother and to feel as happy with her as I always have with you.*'

Ellie placed the envelope down on the table and sat quietly for a while. Julie sat with her, her arm around her niece's shoulders. After a few minutes Ellie said, 'I'm ready. I want to meet her.'

Matt suggested that one of the small seminar rooms in Shelley's training department would be a suitable place for everyone to meet.

'There are easy chairs, tea-making facilities, and most importantly, peace and quiet. I've checked and there's nothing going on today so you can take all the time you want. I'll just ask DS Shaw if Elizabeth Ferguson is already there.'

'I'm really scared,' said Ellie.

'You don't have to do this now,' emphasised Matt. 'If you need more time, then take more time. I'm sure everyone would understand.'

'I want more time and I don't want more time and to be honest I don't really know what I want! What if she doesn't like me? What am I supposed to call her?' Ellie started to get up from her chair and the sat down again.

To Matt's relief Julie came to the rescue.

'I can't even begin to think how you feel, Ellie, but I know for sure that it was your father's wish that you get to know your real mother someday, and if he was here now I think he'd be thrilled for you.'

A very different reunion was taking place on the other side of the Bay. Charles Ferguson had arranged to meet his mother in the car park behind the Techniquest science museum. It was an area both had visited in the past, when Catherine had hosted charity events at the prestigious St David's Hotel. He arrived first and picked up a pay and display ticket from the machine.

After waiting ten minutes he started to dial his mother's mobile number when he saw her car approaching. He got another ticket and took it over to where she'd parked – rather badly. The familiar scent of Jean Patou's Joy, heavily applied, together with a strong smell of peppermint, failed to completely cover the whisky fumes. Charles turned purple with rage.

'What kind of bloody idiot are you? We are supposed to be going to the police station and you turn up half-cut! You can't even park properly so God only knows how you drove here. What would have happened if you'd been stopped and breathalysed?'

'Darling! I wasn't, was I? So don't get your knickers in a twist. You wouldn't have wanted me here sober, believe me. All my demons are coming home to roost at the moment and I need a bit of help to deal with them.'

Charles knew from experience that it was no good trying to reason with his mother when she was in this state, and after locking her car and putting her keys into his own pocket he led her towards the nearest coffee shop in Mermaid Quay. He ordered two flat whites, one with a double shot of espresso, and two triple chocolate muffins.

'Don't even think about saying you're on some sort of stupid diet, because I'm not in the mood to listen. You need some food and some strong coffee to soak up the booze.'

Catherine didn't argue but she did wince as she took her first mouthful.'

'Shit! This is much too strong.'

She pushed the cup towards Charles and he pushed it back. His mother's language had already caught the attention of a young woman with a couple of kids.

'You'll drink it whether you like it or not. We won't be leaving here until you're full of coffee and cake and smell a bit less like a bloody distillery.'

Charles drank his own coffee and as he watched his mother sipping hers he realised that she really was becoming a liability. She'd had a drink problem for many years but never allowed it to show publicly. Just lately she didn't seem to care how she behaved and he knew that a whisky-soaked Catherine wouldn't be able to keep her mouth shut.

Three-quarters of an hour later she looked and sounded more like the Catherine Ferguson that her public would recognise and Charles was able to agree a few things with her.

'We'll say as little as possible and as she's already there Lizzie will have identified Father and so we don't even need to see him – unless you want to.'

'Good God, no! I wasn't keen on seeing him alive and I sure as hell don't want to see him dead.'

'Well, as long as you don't express those thoughts to the police. Just say you can't bear the thought of seeing him dead and they'll assume it's grief. You could try giving Lizzie a hug – it's what most mothers would do in the circumstances.'

Catherine raised one of her perfectly outlined eyebrows but made no reply.

'They're bound to ask about the Jaguar so we both need to say the same thing. The detective who came to the Hall showed me a photograph of the Jaguar and said it had been taken this morning outside the garages. I didn't say too much, just indicated that the existence of two identical cars was ridiculous.'

'And that's exactly what I'll say. I could swear on a stack of Bibles that there aren't two cars.' She gave a girlish giggle. 'At least, there aren't any more!'

Despite her poor attempt at humour, Charles was satisfied that his mother was as near to sober as she would ever be, and escorted her down a side road. He knew exactly where he was, and Catherine couldn't help suggesting that he had used the car in question on those very streets.

Charles gave his mother a look of disgust though didn't deny the allegation. He pointed out the unusually shaped building

132

that looked out onto the Bay and was the home of the Welsh Assembly Government.

'I've been there several times when we've been looking at joint policies, so that's how I know the area, and *not* in the way your warped mind is suggesting. I've even been to the police headquarters we're going to. There was an official function there some years ago and I have to admit it's very impressive. It's just around the next corner, so get your grieving widow's expression in place and keep your mouth *shut*.'

Chapter Fifteen

Matt walked with Ellie, Julie, and Helen Cook-Watts to the seminar room where Lizzie and her friends were waiting with Maggie Shaw. What was about to take place wasn't a police matter and he had decided not to be a participant. He was satisfied that from his side Helen and Maggie would give all the support that was needed. They would also be his eyes and ears in the unlikely event that something of relevance to the investigation came up.

He was suddenly exhausted and put it down to the strain of this being the first time he had taken the lead in a murder investigation. The killer was still at large, but at least there were a few names to consider under the heading of motive and his team were working really hard with interviewing potential witnesses. There was plenty to do and he recognised being at the point of a case that Martin frequently referred to as peddling. He could see why because activity was ongoing and the scene was constantly changing but progress was just that bit too slow.

'Penny for them,' called out a familiar voice from the end of the corridor. Matt smiled broadly.

'Well, to be honest, guv, I was thinking about you!'

Martin caught up with his colleague and laughed. 'Nothing too romantic, I hope! How's it going? I take it Alex is still in Wiltshire?'

'I'm not really sure – it seems we may have opened a real can of worms, starting with that *Jonathan Creek* situation: the same car magically in two different parts of the country at the same time.'

Martin raised an eyebrow. 'As I remember it, Jonathan Creek always found a logical explanation in the end.'

'Yes, and the logic is that there are definitely two different cars of the same make, colour, and model, with the same numberplates. What I don't know is why and what, if anything, they had to do with the murder!'

'What are you doing now?' asked Martin.

'I'm just going to find a quiet spot to think. Everyone working on the case is fully occupied and for the moment I'm just waiting for things to come together.'

'If you want to think aloud I'm happy to be a sounding board. Don't worry, I don't want to steal your case, and you could return the favour as I'd like to bounce some thoughts on the case I'm looking at.'

Getting the agreement he was looking for Martin led the way to his end of the top floor and put the kettle on while Matt admired the new setup. He got to the place where Martin's famous columns were boldly displayed on a large screen that he could see was linked to a nearby computer. He laughed out loud.

'Well I never thought I'd ever see the day – you've been allowed into the twenty-first century!'

'Less of the bloody cheek, DI Pryor, but putting my columns aside what do you think of the new facilities?'

'Brilliant. I'm not sure I'd know how to operate everything but I'd love to be shown the ropes.'

'Charlie's the woman to ask for a demonstration and she's determined that we are all going to use everything to its maximum potential.'

Matt latched on to one of Martin's comments.

'You said "all". Does that mean these facilities are going to be opened up? I heard that the chief super wants to use them for high-profile cold cases.'

'The jungle drums are spot on. If he got funding on that premise then good for him, but I want to persuade him that they shouldn't just be kept for that purpose. I've been working on one of those cases, and whereas I've benefitted immensely from some of this new technology it would be even more useful in current cases. A sophisticated programme like this one here will sort out all the new data faster than we can. Anyway, want to do that thinking out loud we spoke about?'

Matt talked his way through the detail of his case without interruption, and was surprised at the order it had brought to his thinking.

'It sounds like your first case is turning into a bit of a cracker. A murder *and* a double-double mystery.'

Matt nodded. 'Hopefully! Both Elizabeth and Ellie seem really nice and I hope something good'll come out of this for them. It would've been better if their lives had come together at a different time, but there's no arguing with fate, is there?

'I think Ellie will come to terms with things quite quickly but I'm not so sure about her mother. She's kept the existence of her daughter a secret for more than twenty years, and now she's struggling to cope with its exposure within hours of being told that her father's dead. Not just dead … murdered.'

Matt's phone rang and he answered to the familiar voice of Mrs Williams.

'I've got the professor with me, and he wants to talk to you about the toxicology report on Edward Ferguson. He's got some things he thinks you would like to see.'

'I'm with DCI Phelps at the moment but I'll come straight down.'

'If you're on the top floor, get the DCI to switch on our link and we'll come up to you – metaphorically speaking.'

Mrs Williams gave a nervous laugh and turned on the connection from her end. Matt told Martin what Mrs Williams had suggested, and he did the same.

Matt was impressed. 'That's the speediest visual linkage ever!'

As always, the Prof was enjoying enthralling his audience. 'Our gentleman was killed by a *dendroaspis polylepis*.'

'By a *what*?' asked Matt and Martin in unison.

There were several screens in the Prof's favourite post-mortem room that were mainly used for training purposes, and

137

on one of them was an image of a deadly looking snake.

'If you know this beauty at all you'll recognise it by its more common name – it's a black mamba. I could entertain you all day with the stories that surround it in Africa. It's sufficient to say that if one was making for me I'd be running away as fast as these old legs could carry me, and even that may not be good enough. These killers move at up to sixteen kilometres an hour when targeting prey, and their venom is deadly. Without the very specific antidote, no human being could expect to live more than about, oh, an hour – possibly less than twenty minutes.'

'Bloody hell,' interjected Matt. 'Are you saying there was a deadly snake loose on the train? Could the puncture wound on the leg be where it bit him, and not from a needle at all?'

The professor laughed. 'Don't get carried away, young man, there's not a deadly snake on the loose in Cardiff! Unfortunately the killer is human, and rather more dangerous than the black mamba, who after all only kills for the food it needs to survive. Mr Ferguson was injected with a syringe full of its venom, and that's why death was so swift. I doubt even if there had been an antidote immediately to hand it would have worked on that level of poison.'

'Would he have died instantly?' asked Martin.

'Well, not quite, and that's the clever thing. Even though the content of the syringe was lethal and the dose was excessive, it wouldn't have worked straight away unless it was administered intravenously. A substance has to get into the bloodstream first of all but once it's done that the process of absorption is usually rapid.

'I said the dose was excessive, but that doesn't mean a large amount of fluid was injected. There are all sorts of ways to concentrate toxicity into a small dose which makes it quicker to administer by injection. The killer wouldn't have wanted to spend even a second more than he had to pushing fluid into the muscle and possibly attracting attention.'

'If someone stuck a needle in me I'd jump,' suggested Matt. 'But we've asked witnesses if they saw any strange behaviour before Mr Ferguson died and there was nothing. Still, from what you say he could have been injected some minutes before he died so we need to wind their memories back a bit.'

'You do indeed. I've made some enquiries about this particular snake venom and it's likely that respiratory paralysis was a prime mover in the death. It's probable that our man just sat there until his lungs, and then his heart, were fatally compromised, and your killer was in a far corner of the carriage waiting to make a speedy exit.

'Now that I know about the venom I'm going to re-examine my post-mortem findings. I don't expect to be able to give you any further information but I need to see if there is anything I should have picked up – for future reference.'

With the video link severed, Matt reiterated what had been revealed and went back to sharing his thoughts on the case.

'If the syringe had been found there'd have been a faster route to its contents,' stated Martin.

'So far Alex has got dozens of fingerprints and all the other things people leave behind on public transport. In the event of me finding the killer I may be able to prove he travelled in that carriage. Problem is, I haven't even got a suspect to match things against. I've ruled out a random killing, and I'm convinced that the motive will turn out to be some sort of gain. My second thought is that maybe he was silenced. From speaking to his daughter I get the impression that Edward Ferguson was an astute businessman, who didn't suffer fools gladly, and it's likely he made enemies in the City.

'I've got people trawling all over his business dealings and his personal finances, and speaking to members of his golf club. We're still at that stage of information-gathering when what I really need is a breakthrough.'

'It'll come,' replied Martin. 'Have you engaged with the media at all?'

'They've been given a statement and I've appealed for passengers on the train or in Cardiff Central at the time to come forward. Someone must have seen something! There *is* one man in particular that we're looking for and he shouldn't be that difficult to find. Several passengers noticed a stranger, and factoring out the usual differences in observation they seem to be describing the same man. Unfortunately people's powers of observation can leave a lot to be desired, and basically all I know is that he's big, probably not from the area, and has very large feet! I guess I'm pinning all my hopes on him coming forward, but if he's the killer I'm not holding out much hope of that happening.'

The two men laughed.

'Feel free to use the new facilities that have been set up here,' Martin offered. 'You can feed in all the interviews your officers do and ask for the word recognition programme to select any witnesses who mention the same feature – for example a ginger-haired man or a young woman wearing a short skirt. The words you've just mentioned, "big" for example, are freely bandied about but there could be more interesting common threads surrounding them.

'It would take you forever to go through every one of those statements with a microscope but this programme will throw up any relevant details in a flash. As we both know, the devil's in the detail, and more than often it's some small detail that solves a case. I don't need to tell you that it's still really early days for your investigation, and you're likely to get more and more frustrated before the end. We've all been there but I'm sure you'll crack it. Pity me, trying to find the identity of someone murdered eleven years ago!'

Matt grinned. 'I don't know where I'd start with that one! Alex told me what he remembered about the case but I've no recollection of it being on the news at all.'

'Let me tell you about what I think could be my big break and you can tell me if I'm in with a chance or need to see a shrink!'

Martin told Matt about the shrine he and Shelley had found the previous Saturday.

'I think someone must be laying a fresh stone at each anniversary of the young man's murder.'

'I guess Alex would be able to tell you if the stones were all placed there at the same time or if there's a period of time between each new arrival.'

Martin acknowledged Matt's suggestion. 'I thought about that, but until Thursday is over I don't want anyone going near the shrine. It looks to me as if the stones are rearranged with the arrival of each new one, to keep the appearance of the petals of a flower carefully placed around one central stone. It's not just a once-yearly thing, either, because the stones are regularly polished and the surrounding area kept free of weeds. Alex's people have already set up some well-hidden CCTV cameras, so all I can do is wait.'

'And if memory serves you're not very good at that,' laughed Matt. 'Anyway, I hope you get a result. Obviously someone has had good reason to remember the victim all this time. If it's one of the kids that found the body or one of the local Somali groups we'd have heard about it. The press love that sort of thing, but there's a very strong Somali community in Cardiff so it could just be someone that wants to see a fellow countrymen regain some respect.'

'And that's my biggest worry. If it is just a fellow countryman, he'll know as little about the victim as I do. I can't believe it's the killer, and my hope is that it's someone who knew the victim, maybe even a relative. I've tried to think about what was happening with new arrivals from Somalia around that time, and my main memory is of the "boat people". We hear stories from all over the world about asylum seekers fleeing war zones, and I guess any country with a coastline is a potential destination. I'm just hoping that my victim came here with someone who still remembers him.'

'Good luck with that,' said Matt and without warning changed the subject in a way which answered questions that had been concerning some of his friends.

'Sarah's going to Australia and I'm bloody fed up,' he announced.

'Do I take it from your tone that she's not just having a once-in-a-lifetime holiday?' asked Martin cautiously.

'No, it's been in the pipeline for some time – she's got

relatives there. To be honest, I think it's to do with a relationship she had with a senior doctor. He turned out to be married with kids and she felt very publicly humiliated. She swears she's over him, but before we met she'd put the wheels in motion for Australia and I don't know if I've done enough to stop her.'

Chapter Sixteen

Wednesday was almost exactly as Martin had predicted. Both he and Matt were immersed in the collation of detail for their respective cases. It was boring and frustrating, but often proved the most revealing and productive part of an investigation.

For the umpteenth time he checked on the arrangement for the monitoring of the shrine. He kept changing his mind regarding his own involvement in the operation. He wanted to watch the monitors Charlie had set up, and at the same time be in one of the unmarked cars that were to be parked on street corners near the site of the shrine.

He wouldn't be going back to his cottage in Llantwit Major – that would be too far away from any potential action. Of course, there was no guarantee there would be any action, and he reminded himself that the whole operation was a long shot. He tried to narrow down the most likely time, and marked up the time the body was discovered as one possibility. Maybe the person who was visiting the shrine knew the time the body had been left there and so he or she would be visiting earlier.

He worried that the whole thing would be a total waste of time and tried to concentrate his mind by reviewing some of the original documents. The post-mortem report was every bit as sketchy as he'd remembered, and a closer examination showed that there was at least one page missing altogether.

The usual preamble was there and helped Martin get a much better picture of Geedi. All the body measurements were in metric, but Martin made the victim five feet seven in height, with a weight of just six stone six pounds. He was hardly the size of a full-grown man, more like a lanky adolescent, but

Martin didn't have the knowledge to be able to factor in things like ethnicity and poor nutrition.

He studied the photographs carefully and noted a lack of facial hair. There was pubic hair, but it looked to be relatively early in its development. The DCI referred back to the front sheet, where the estimated age of the deceased was recorded as between 20 and 25 years.

No way!

Martin though back to some of the sometimes painful processes that took place during adolescence. To the best of his recollection, he would have been about twelve years old when his body was at the stage of development shown in Geedi's photograph. He wouldn't have been as tall, as his major growth spurts had come a bit later – and he would have been much heavier, as he was going through what Aunt Pat had called his 'chunky phase' – but even allowing for the differences in ethnicity and way of life Martin could not see Geedi being more than fourteen at the time of his death. He would have been tall for his age, but everything else put him as being much younger than previously recorded.

Martin thought hard. He might come up with an age by a process of deduction, and still be years out – but the pathologist had had all the tools of her trade at her disposal, so how, or why, did she get it so badly wrong? It made no sense whatsoever.

Martin walked over towards the window with the case notes in his hands and stopped short as the change of light caused him to notice some alterations. He could see very clearly the estimated age, but until that moment he hadn't noticed that the writing had been superimposed on some other figures.

He knew Charlie had scanned in the post-mortem report and so Martin systematically went through the index she had made until he found it. It was easy to enlarge the image of the part that had captured his interest and bingo – there it was!

The pathologist's original figures agreed with his belief that Geedi was between twelve and fourteen years old at the time he was murdered. An attempt had been made to erase the original figures and it was only with the help of the computer enhancement that Martin could see that the new estimation of age was written over the previous entry.

If there had been a simple clerical error a line would have been drawn through the original entry and a new one written alongside. This looked like a deliberate attempt to turn attention away from the fact that this was the body of a boy and not a man – but why? What difference would that have made?

Martin remembered Ian Baker's warning about not taking anything about this case at face value, and now he had found something to support that thinking. He looked at everything with the fresh pair of eyes that Chief Superintendent Atkinson had indicated the case would need. Martin enhanced all the files, and began a page-by-page trawl through all the previous reports to see if there were any more 'errors'.

The daylight that had helped Martin pick up the first irregularity was disappearing fast and, just as he realised that he was struggling to read the lights came on. It was Shelley.

'Your smile's the second thing to light up the room.'

'I know you're not coming home tonight, but I thought you'd like to fill in the time between now and midnight with a meal and some company.'

'I know how I'd like to fill in the time,' suggested Martin. 'But it may not be considered the best use of police facilities.'

Shelley kissed him but quickly pulled away as she realised that he was more than a little serious about his preferred activity.

'You need to keep your mind on what could be a different sort of amazing night,' she teased. 'Let's get you fed. I wasn't thinking of going anywhere special – maybe somewhere where we can get some half-decent pasta. Then it's off home to bed for me. With any luck you'll join me before tomorrow, but I won't hold my breath.'

For a couple of hours Martin pushed almost all thoughts of the case aside and enjoyed his time with Shelley. He told her what Matt had said about Sarah going to Australia and she shook her head.

'Men! What are you like? It took you yonks to even notice my existence, and now Matt's letting what he wants slip through his fingers. He doesn't want her to go, does he?'

'I get the impression he very much wants her to stay.'

'Then he needs to tell her! She's not psychic. Contrary to popular belief we women don't spend all our spare time talking about the men in our lives – though of course you do get a mention – and past relationships are fair game! I know Sarah was devastated when she found out some surgeon she was in love with already had a wife and kids. I think she felt the humiliation more than anything, because from what she says he'd had a string of affairs and everyone but Sarah seemed to know about them. She and Matt make a great couple but she's scared of making another mistake. He needs to tell her exactly how he feels about her or she'll feel she's got no option than to follow the plans she's put in place. Talk to him!'

'I didn't know I was in love with an agony aunt,' laughed Martin. 'But you're right, we men aren't always good at expressing our feelings. OK, yes, I'll talk to him.'

It was just after 10.30 when Martin got back to Goleudy, having settled on a chicken and spinach lasagne that he would've liked to have washed down with a large glass or two of Chianti – but in the circumstances he settled for mineral water. He'd decided to do the full night shift. There was no point considering anything else as there was no way he was going to be able to sleep.

Martin checked the rota he'd been given and yet again satisfied himself that all the arrangements were in place. There was nothing else he could do and so impatiently waited until almost midnight before joining the first team of officers in the monitoring room.

Almost instantly the screen showed a man walking his dog and the sound system even picked up the scraping of a poop-scooper as the dog owner cleared up after his pet.

Shortly after midnight a young couple decided to stop directly in line with one of the cameras, and after a few passionate kisses just couldn't keep their hands off one another.

'I feel like a pervert,' laughed one of the officers. 'I don't really want to watch their antics but I can't look away in case what we're really looking for pops up on the screen. Oh come on, kids, give it a rest.'

His blushes were saved as the man with the dog returned and the couple moved on. Soon after, something more interesting caught the officers' attention and all eyes were on the monitor as a lone male figure was seen approaching. The man was unsteady on his feet as he walked over some uneven ground, but he managed to hang on to the vodka bottle he was holding and didn't even look in the direction of the shrine.

Throughout the night officers handed over to colleagues and were in regular contact with those that were manning the cars in the streets surrounding Roath Park. Nothing at all happened. Martin drank more coffee than was good for him and by 6 a.m. he was feeling punch drunk. His longshot was getting longer with every passing minute.

As the night disappeared Martin stretched his legs and looked out of one of the windows. The traffic was already building up and he'd always had concerns about getting from the Bay to Roath in rush hour. Not that he would need to be first on the scene when the target appeared, as there were officers close by, but he would like to be the initial contact. He still believed that it had been necessary to mount a twenty-four hour operation, but he'd always considered that if a stone was going to be placed it would be at the time the body had been discovered. That time was approaching and he had everything crossed.

He splashed his face with cold water and then walked away from the building and towards his car. It was a clear, dry morning but there was a chilling wind and he didn't hang about in the car park. It was unusual to see the place so empty. The clock on his dashboard showed 07.38 and he reminded himself that barely a third of the operation time had been covered so there was plenty of time for the desired outcome.

Cardiff was by now very much awake although some of the drivers still looked half asleep. The cold morning air and the cumulative result of so much coffee had achieved the desired effect of waking up all his senses. Although the roads were busy there were no holdups and he was soon parked in one of the side-roads near the shrine.

Groups of schoolchildren passed his car, as would no doubt have happened eleven years ago to the day. As nine o'clock approached the general bustle subsided, with just a few hurrying kids still around, obviously already late for school. There was still nothing to report and Martin had his first real low of the night. The timeslot he had pinned his hopes on had passed, and he knew that the other officers were aware of that fact. It was up to him to keep up the morale of the team and not let their attention to detail drop with more than half the surveillance time still ahead.

He realised that he was really hungry and got out of his car and walked in the direction of the nearby shops, making sure everyone knew of his whereabouts.

A familiar voice greeted him when he made contact with the monitoring team back at base.

'What are you doing there?' he asked.

'Sometimes it's easier to do something yourself than make more complicated arrangements,' Sergeant Evans said. 'Two of my staff on your rota called in sick, and then there were another two calls from officers who should've been on other duties. They've all got the same symptoms so there's probably some bug or other doing the rounds. So I'm filling this slot for the next couple of hours or until I can get a replacement.'

'You will have heard that nothing's happened so far.'

'I have but I'm still with you in thinking that today could be the day – it makes sense.'

Martin suddenly felt much more confident as he ended the call. He knew that the operation was now in the safest of hands, and set off on a quest to satisfy his rumbling stomach. He could almost taste the hot buttered toast as he set foot in the café but at that moment his phone sprang to life and he could see two calls waiting.

'Is something happening, John?'

Evans was looking at the screen in front of him as he answered Martin's question.

'Could be nothing – but I don't think it is! I've just picked up someone walking, slowly but very deliberately, towards the area where the shrine is. I'm watching him as I speak … I say "him" but it could be a woman, they're wearing a hoodie and not once have they looked up towards any of our cameras.'

All thoughts of hot buttered toast melted and now the feeling in Martin's stomach was one of nervous anticipation. The second call was from the officers in the car nearest the shrine. They also reported a sighting and were pretty sure that it was the person they'd all been waiting for.

'I'm no more than ten minutes away on foot, so I'll be there as quickly as I can. Do absolutely nothing to make him think he's being watched, and don't interfere with anything he does. You needn't move in too close because everything is being captured on camera, but if he appears to be moving off before I get there then you'll have to stop him.'

After only a few minutes Martin stood with his back against the side wall of one of the nearby houses, watching the activity at the shrine. He'd had a vague idea of what might happen and the reality almost perfectly matched it.

The stones had all been stacked carefully and a new one had been placed to one side. The creator of the shrine was altering the design to accommodate the extra stone, taking care not to disturb the central one.

He was kneeling on the cold, damp ground but there was no sense of hurry. Were they following ethical or religious rules, or was it a personal ritual? Martin felt he was intruding on something sacred, but he had no choice. Not wanting to disturb the moment he ensured his phone was on silent and waited. The hooded figure stood up and stepped back, then knelt back down and made some further adjustments. Finally he bowed his head slightly before getting up again and turning away from his handiwork.

Martin didn't move until he was face to face with the person he had been watching. As the two of them made eye contact

Martin introduced himself.

'I'm Detective Chief Inspector Phelps and I would very much like to speak to you.'

Martin was surprised as the mourner removed their hood – revealing the face of a young woman.

'Of course – I've been waiting for you!'

Chapter Seventeen

There was no fuss as the woman accompanied Martin to the nearest unmarked police car. She had introduced herself to Martin as Basra Shimbir, but had added that she would say nothing more without her solicitor being present.

Martin assured her that she was not under arrest and as far as he knew not even in any trouble. He explained that all he wanted to do was speak to her in the hope that she could help him find out the truth behind a young man's murder.

'If it's the truth you want, I can give it to you, but first I need to know that you are different from the men who wanted anything but the truth eleven years ago. Over time I've convinced myself that if anyone ever came looking for answers then I'd be able to trust them – but now I'm not so sure. The woman who has been like a mother to me here was treated dismissively by the police and warned off from contacting them again. The people involved with my brother's murder left her in no doubt what would happen to her if she spoke out. Does that make you understand why I'm finding it difficult to trust you?'

Martin recognised the turmoil that was in the woman's eyes and made a simple suggestion.

'Why don't we just talk? I can tell you what I think happened and you can tell me as little or as much as you want to. It would be easier if we went to the station but if that makes you uncomfortable then anywhere of your choice will be fine with me.'

Martin didn't know if Basra heard the genuine feeling of concern in his voice or had recognised a real desire for the truth in his eyes, but whatever it was she accepted the lift to Goleudy and got into the car with the uniformed officers.

Walking back to his car and driving to the Bay gave Martin time to think of how he would handle questioning Basra. What had she meant when she said she had been expecting him? There had always been the possibility that the person he had hoped to see would be a woman although conceptually he'd only ever imagined a man. He tried not to speculate about her relationship with Geedi and just briefly wondered if she would be able to reunite the youngster with his real name.

Not wanting to scare her with the formal setup of the interview rooms, he agreed they should use his substantive office and asked the PC who had travelled in the car with Basra to sit in. Ideally Martin would have liked the interview taped, but he was walking a fine line with this woman's trust and couldn't risk it.

They sat down on the two comfortable chairs at the far end of the room, with just a small coffee table between them, whilst PC Woodland made herself at home behind Martin's desk.

Martin needed have worried about adopting the best way of finding out what he wanted to know because almost without pausing for breath Basra got years of stifled emotion off her chest.

'Dalmar! That was his name … Dalmar. He was my baby brother and when we left Somalia, nearly twelve years ago, he was just thirteen and in every way he was still a child.

'He wasn't really my brother – he was taken in by my parents when his family were wiped out and he'd been left for dead. But I will always think of him as my brother and I was his big sister. My role was to look after him, but I didn't do a very good job, did I?'

Martin knew the question wasn't meant for him. He could see the effort Basra was making to keep her emotions in check and silently willed her to continue.

'You have no idea what it was like growing up in my country. It was tolerable for families who simply accepted the corruption, but my father was constantly being locked up, and worse, for speaking his mind. One day we were told that our

152

mother had met with an accident, and after that our father became concerned for the safety of me and my brother. He wasn't worried about his own life, and he was still adamant that nothing was going to stop him standing up for what he believed in.

'I come from a very large extended family and there was enormous support for my father and a shared concern about the potential danger to his children's lives. A man who represented a British charity organisation offered the chance to get me and Dalmar to a place of safety. They offered the same chance to my father but he didn't want it. The offer didn't come cheap and our whole family sold property and possessions to secure a passage for us. We had to leave the country with false papers to hide who we really were.

'I know now that our final destination was somewhere on the coast in the south-east of England but I have no idea what route we took to get there. I remember a relay of boats. We were put ashore several times and then after a few days, and once after several weeks, another boat showed up and our journey continued.

'We had precious little to eat and our numbers dwindled. There were about twenty people, of all ages, on the first boat that took us from our country, but just eight of us at the end of the journey.'

Martin wanted to ask if she knew what had happened to the others but he dreaded the answer; it would have to come later. Instead he offered her a drink and she accepted some water.

'Please take your time,' he told her. 'You were right when you started by saying there are things I couldn't imagine – it must have been terrible for you.'

Basra bit her lip hard and then continued. 'If you think what I've told you so far is terrible then …' she hesitated. 'I'll let you be the judge on the rest. I was approaching my fifteenth birthday when we left, and so it may even have been on the day of my birthday that I was raped for the first time. I cried for days but that didn't stop it happening again. When I tried to resist it was suggested that if I didn't make myself available

153

then Dalmar would be at risk. I couldn't let that happen so I accepted my fate.'

Basra shook her head as if to shake away the memory and her mind went back to Somalia.

'I doubt if there are many members of my family still alive, as my father was always too outspoken for his own good and attracted what my mother once called "the wrong sort". Some people that stayed with us were really nice, and for almost a year we had two Australian businessmen living with us. They spoke English to one another and taught me a bit. I wasn't proficient but I could pick up the gist of what was being said on the boats. The people responsible for moving us always spoke in English, and from some of the things I heard I didn't think any of us would make it.

'Then all of a sudden everything changed and it seemed as if the eight of us had actually got to the end of our journey. But only six of us were allowed off the boat and I've no idea what happened to the two women who were kept on board. It left me and Dalmar, a young child with her mother, and a couple who were probably no more than sixty but looked much older.

'We were transferred to a truck and driven for what seemed like hours. I remember being able to hear the noise of heavy traffic initially but then there was only the occasional passing vehicle and finally a short period of silence. The driver and his mate, who reminded me of one of my uncles, seemed to have taken over responsibility for us. We stopped outside a large building and were quickly ushered inside. Strong metal doors were closed behind us.

'We were in a bleak room. There were six mattresses on the floor at one end, with empty buckets and bowls of water for our personal use. Sounds primitive, doesn't it? But compared with what we had endured it was almost luxury, and our spirits were raised even more when we started getting regular meals and some fresh fruit and vegetables.

'After we'd been in our new "home" for a few days we were given fresh clothes and toiletries – even toothpaste! We all speculated that at last we were going to be taken to the homes of people we believed were ready to take care of us, but all that happened was photographs. A woman with her head and face wrapped in a scarf pointed a camera at us and told us to smile. She was obviously looking for particular shots and was keen that my brother and I held hands and looked happy. The man who looked like my uncle was in fact originally from my country and could speak to us in our own language, so he passed on her instructions. I wanted to ask him what the photographs were all about but instinctively I didn't trust him.

'I constantly though about escaping but I didn't know where we were and I had a definite feeling that any attempts to make trouble would be severely dealt with by our minder. The first time I'd heard him speak I'd been filled with the joy of any traveller hearing their own language in a strange country, but his words were never kind and I was so right not to consider him a friend!'

Basra gulped down a mouthful of water as if she was trying to get rid of a nasty taste in her mouth.

'The metal doors were kept slightly ajar during the day as there was no other light source but all I ever saw outside was trees and very grey skies.' She managed a faint smile. 'I've learned since that grey skies are the norm in the UK at this time of the year. We occasionally heard a car being driven from somewhere close by and returning hours later, often in the middle of the night. One afternoon when our guard was standing near the door, he was confronted by a younger man who started shouting at him. I could only understand a bit of what they were saying, but it was clear that the man didn't know who we were or what we were doing in that place.

'He forced his way into our living space and just stared at us – that is until he saw Dalmar. I followed his gaze as it rested on my brother who I then realised was growing into a very handsome young man. He was far too skinny, of course, but he had dark eyes and an air of innocence that was completely enchanting.

'The guard had also noticed the gaze, and I guess he made some derogatory remark because the man stormed out and we heard that car drive away. The following day the woman who had previously photographed us returned and the man was with her. I can only assume she had explained about us and he seemed to have accepted the situation. I don't really know, but after that he was a regular visitor. My stomach churned whenever he appeared. I didn't really know anything about homosexuality or paedophilia at that time but I did know that this man had a strange attraction to my brother and I could see it made Dalmar uncomfortable.'

Basra suddenly stopped and covered her eyes with her hands.

'I wish it was as easy as that to blind myself of the images that I'm now going to tell you about. Maybe when I have told you I will be able to start laying the past to rest – God, I hope so!'

Martin could see that PC Woodland was perched on the edge of the chair he normally swivelled on and already looked horrified by what she had heard. How would she cope with what was to come?

'The man's obsession with my brother became more obvious with every visit and he became very tactile. He'd take Dalmar's hand and stroke it across his own face and he'd caress my brother's shoulders and neck. I could see Dalmar squirming but he was afraid to say or do anything. It only took a few visits before things got really out of hand.'

She stopped to regain her composure.

'Between visits Dalmar had asked me about what I thought the man wanted from him and I was unable to give him an answer. It sounds incredible that I was so naïve at fifteen but you can't compare my upbringing with that of a fifteen-year-old in Wales today. All I knew then was the baby brother I'd been asked to look after was in the sort of danger I didn't have the experience to help him with.

'I could only watch on the next occasion that the fondling started, and you must remember there were four others, including a child, witnessing this unwanted attention. The man was clearly becoming frustrated with getting no response from

156

Dalmar and he became more forceful. I saw him stroke my brother's buttocks and then slide his hand down the front of Dalmar's trousers. I freaked out!

'I leapt at the man and clawed at his face. He lashed out and with one huge blow he knocked me to the ground. Dalmar tried to defend me – I don't know where he got his strength from, he was like someone possessed by the devil, but I will never forget the way he fought the man who had dared to hurt his sister. He managed to get his hands around the man's throat, and despite their huge difference in strength Dalmar was almost squeezing the life out of him. Then the big guard intervened, and suddenly my brother was lying at my feet with his throat cut.'

Basra was now calm and rested her head on the back of her chair. Martin quietly asked her if she knew which of the men had killed her brother.

'The big one, the guard. When he was minding us he used to shave blobs of paint off the walls with this thing that looked like a cheese wire with wooden handles – I guess he was bored, it seemed to amuse him. I'm sure that's what he used to kill Dalmar. Although there are two others who are not without responsibility in my brother's death.'

'Two?' questioned Martin.

'Yes, the man who wanted to possess my brother – and me.'

'You can't possibly hold yourself responsible. You did what anyone would've done in the circumstances.'

'It would have been agony to watch the trauma and humiliation of my brother being sodomised, but he would still be alive. I shouldn't have intervened.'

Martin realised that she had been living for eleven years with that thought, and he wasn't sure if anything he said would be of any help, but he had to try.

'I would have done exactly what you did. There's absolutely no doubt in my mind. And your love for your brother may be the thing that finally brings his killer to justice. Your memorial stones demonstrate how much you care, and they're what brought us to this point.'

Martin suddenly remembered something. 'What did you

157

mean when you said you'd been waiting for me?'

'Not you personally.' Basra smiled sadly. 'I just knew that if someone found me, wanted to talk to me, they would be looking for the truth.'

'What happened to you after your brother was killed?' asked Martin.

'I discovered that charities aren't always all they seem. It's not unusual for families in Somalia, and other desperately poor countries, to pay large sums of money, usually to unscrupulous people, so that their relatives can have the chance of a better life. Some people are the ones you read about in the news, hidden in trucks … others are transported by more devious means, like the charity that was supposed to help me. It's not unusual for people to get … lost … in transit. There are bad apples everywhere, DCI Phelps. The people who brought me into the country had no compassion for the people of Somalia – even though many of them were Somalis too. They use the organisation to fill their pockets. It makes me sick to think of how many of their own people have suffered for their financial gain. They are evil and have to be stopped.'

DCI Phelps could barely comprehend what he was hearing and asked Basra to go back a bit.

'After Dalmar was killed I was too shocked to really know what was happening, but I do remember the veiled woman arriving and taking control. The other Somalis were taken off somewhere immediately, and I've never seen them since – although I've seen some of their photographs in the charity's campaign leaflets.

'Nothing else happened for a while and I know I just lay on the floor and sobbed. Then a small van arrived and after the woman had spoken to the driver I was bundled into the back. By then I thought I was prepared for anything, but not the fact that my brother's body, stripped naked, would be thrown in alongside me.

'I had no fight left in me, and in the darkness of the van I couldn't see Dalmar's mutilated body so was strangely comforted by his presence. God knows how far we travelled and from time to time I heard raised voices from the front of the van. They were not speaking English but arguing in Somali. Cardiff was mentioned several times, but it wasn't a place I had ever heard of, so it meant nothing to me. Quite suddenly the van stopped and the front passenger got out and opened the back door. As if he was handling a piece of meat he lifted Dalmar up and just dumped him on the ground, and I know it's bizarre, he was already dead, but I remember thinking it was so cold and yet he had nothing on – I was still in shock. The place Dalmar's body was dumped is where I go to think of him and, as you know, where I've placed a stone every year in memory of his life.

'I was dumped with only a little more dignity than my brother, outside a block of flats in Cardiff, but at least I was alive. If I'd been them I would have killed me immediately following my brother's murder, but they must have panicked and decided that the only course of action was to follow the original plan and at least get one of us to Cardiff.

'I was outside the home of a woman called Elmi, and although she and her husband were expecting both me and my brother, they didn't seem surprised that only one of us had arrived. I told her what had happened to Dalmar and she just shook her head.'

'Almost immediately knew I was with some good people. Days and possibly weeks went by before I was in any fit state to get my head around everything that had happened to me. I guess it was some sort of post-traumatic stress and I'm pretty sure I was being sedated.'

'Why didn't she go to the police? There would have been a lot of media coverage at the time your brother's body was discovered.'

'Elmi and her husband, Amiin, they are good people, but ... DCI Phelps, you know the sort of people I have been talking about. Dalmar wasn't the first person not to make it. Nevertheless, Elmi did attempt to go to the police, even though things were going on at the time that made it an unsafe option.

'I've learned since that her efforts to bring the circumstances of Dalmar's death to the attention of the police resulted in threats to her and her family and eventually she gave up. Even now she won't tell me everything that went on, but she says it changed her whole perception of the police. I'm afraid she doesn't trust you at all now and some of that has rubbed off on me.

'Elmi seemed to think I would've been sent back to Somalia, and any bad publicity would have been a disaster for the charitable organisation she was involved with. The whole transport of people to the UK ... although there are charities which do that legitimately, my papers were false and the fact that I was an illegal immigrant might have counted against Elmi and her organisation's work. Then one of her sons was beaten up and told that his mother should keep her mouth shut. And who knows what other kind of threats were made?

'Would you be able to identify any of the people involved with what you have spoken about? You say the woman initially had her face covered but was there anything about her you can remember. Was she tall or short? Roughly what age was she? Anything at all!'

'Her voice,' replied Basra. 'It still rings in my ears when I think about it. Certainly not the Cardiff accent I've come to know and love! She sounded ... well, posh, but her voice was hard – almost brittle.'

'I know it's a long time ago, but we do have a voice recognition unit here, and our staff could help work out which part of the UK she comes from. It could help.'

Martin knew he was clutching at straws but he wanted to give Basra some hope. He asked her the same question regarding the men who had been involved.

'I could draw you a picture of the man who killed my brother. I've only got to shut my eyes and I can see every detail of his face. I've never seen him from that day to this. That is not the case with Dalmar's abuser.'

For a moment Martin thought he had misheard.

'Sorry, does that mean you've seen that man?'

'Yes.'

160

'Actually seen him here in Cardiff?'

'No, Chief Inspector, I haven't seen him walking around the streets – I've seen him on the television. I think you will have too.'

Chapter Eighteen

Following her revelation that she could identify the man who was present at the time of her brother's death, Basra told Martin about her life in Wales.

She'd lived initially with a family in Grangetown and had been immediately accepted by the Somali people living in the area. Not all of them were refugees or new immigrants, many of the elders had been seamen, with their families, who'd stayed on after their working days in Cardiff Docks had ended.

Basra's education in Somalia had been basic, and to begin with her English wasn't very good, but she'd been determined not to let her family's sacrifice be in vain. Grangetown was quite a poor area, but it hadn't taken Basra long to realise that there were amazing opportunities in the city. Many of the local kids her age had gone to university, and some of them were now working as solicitors, dentists, and in other professional jobs. Basra had missed out on that opportunity, but she did have one more year at school and there realised her talent for art. She told Martin proudly of the well-paid job she had in an advertising company, and of the Welshman who had recently proposed to her.

'Does he know about your brother?' asked Martin.

'Not the whole story, no – but when I leave here Craig's picking me up. Then I'll tell him everything.'

She looked questioningly at Martin. 'I guess this is only the start of things, and I will be expected to tell others what I have told you – in court?'

Martin nodded. 'Hopefully that's where we're heading, but it's a long way off and I need some advice on handling this appropriately. You said earlier that you had no idea where your brother's body had been left, so how did you find out?'

'It was all over the newspapers at the time, and although I was shielded from it Elmi kept copies of everything and when she thought I was ready to know she told me. It was years before I plucked up the courage to go to that place, and it was such a cold and desolate spot that I knew I had to bring something perfect there as a tribute to Dalmar. Those first few years were amazing, and although English wasn't spoken much at my new home I was keen to learn and used every opportunity to talk to local people. The Somali people were initially up in arms regarding what had happened to my brother but no one was prepared to speak out publicly.

'The family were unbelievably kind to me and did everything to help with the times when my feelings of loss for my home and family were almost unbearable. I was taken to the coast a few times and St Mary's Well Bay became my special place. It's not a busy beach, even in summer, and I often sit on the rocks there and look out over the Bristol Channel.

'One day when I was sitting there I found a particularly smooth stone that had been washed into a perfect shape by the sea and that's when I thought of creating a special place for Dalmar. It would be a place for me to think of him and my family – somewhere only I knew about. I knew where Dalmar's body had been left, but I'd never been there until I found three perfect stones and carried them there.'

'Three?' questioned Martin.

'Yes, three! You see the first time I went there was on the third anniversary of his death and I had decided to place a new stone there for every year – so I had to catch up.'

Martin grinned broadly. 'I'm really glad you did because I'd never have made the connection if there'd been two less stones. It was the fact that the number of stones related to the number of years since your brother's terrible murder that made me hope you'd be back to place another one.'

Basra returned the smile and nodded. 'There's a reason for everything, don't you think?'

'Yes, I do, but I still don't understand why Elmi didn't make more of a fuss. You told her what had happened to you and your brother and to the other people who left Somalia with you. I know she'd been threatened, but if the press had got hold of your story at the time there'd have been intensive media coverage and your brother's killer may have been brought to justice.'

Basra shook her head slowly. 'With respect, Chief Inspector, yours is a common but very naïve understanding of the situation for people like us. I don't think the plan had been for my brother to be killed – I believe we were meant to be amongst the lucky ones. I believe the six of us who made it to Britain would be the poster people – Somalis that the charity could claim to have helped, while keeping quiet about the illegal side of the proceedings. They have that kind of good news story on their website. Can't you see how the powers that be would prefer that type of story?

'There are some excellent charities that support the resettlement of my people into other countries, but the one we experienced is not one of them.'

Before leaving Goleudy, Basra made detailed drawings of the man who had killed her brother. She sketched his face from the front and both sides, and finally produced a full body image.

'Have you ever made these drawings before?' Martin asked her, and for the first time in the interview Basra lost control, a torrent of tears that streaming down her face.

'I've wanted to, as a means of getting him out of my system, but there was never a good enough reason to give the devil substance. Whilst he was just in my head I could somehow keep him contained. But if you're worried that I may not have remembered him well enough to be drawing him for the first time after all these years then don't be. At the risk of sounding boastful I'd say my drawings are as good as any photograph you could take of that monster.

'I don't know if he's dead or alive, if he lives here or somewhere else – and remember he will be older but that's him.' She handed the drawings to Martin.

'He's the killer, and I have given you the name of the other man who was involved so at last I feel able to hand them both over and whatever happens from here on is for you to decide. I know I'll have to be involved but for me those four sketches have released my demons and I feel I can cope with anything now.'

DCI Phelps couldn't even begin to imagine how Basra was feeling as he watched her drive off in the car that she'd arranged to pick her up. He hoped her Welsh fiancé would give her the support she needed when she told him the account of her journey to Wales. It had brought tears to the eyes of PC Woodland and had left Martin feeling angry. How dare these people pose as paragons of virtue when preying on the misery of others – and pocketing a fortune to boot? He reminded himself of people he knew personally who were involved with charities and doing a bloody good job, but as he knew from the recent Austin case, there were bad apples in every barrel – even the force.

The surveillance operation couldn't have had a better result and Geedi could now be given his real name. Realistically, Martin thought, there would be little chance of catching his killer – men like that usually remained anonymous, and were often protected by the people who used them to do their dirty work. But the other man Basra had mentioned was a very different kettle of fish, and Martin headed to the top floor hoping that Chief Superintendent Atkinson would be in his office.

'In a rush, mate?' asked Alex who was coming down the stairs. 'Charlie tells me you got a result from the Roath Park stakeout – well done! She says you picked someone up, so did you get any leads from him?'

'Not him – her! Turned out to be the victim's sister.'

'Bloody hell, that is a result! So after all these years we now know who that poor sod was – the first victim of crime I'd ever seen. Was I right about him not having been killed there?'

'Absolutely right, and I'll be briefing everyone who was

166

involved later, so join us if you want to.'

'I'll be sure to.' Alex noticed the drawings that Martin was holding. 'Matt's dragged you in to finding his killer, has he?'

'Sorry?'

'That sketch looks very like the ones our people have constructed from the memories of people on the train from Treorchy to Cardiff on Monday morning. Let's have a look.'

Martin showed Alex the drawings and explained how he'd got them.

'Hell's bells! I thought getting the identity of the victim was a scoop, but a detailed sketch of his killer – that's something else.'

Alex stared at the drawings in his usual analytical way and then laughed.

'I'm in danger of doing what we try to persuade all our witnesses to avoid. We've all got some stereotypical images of people from different parts of the world and conjure them up as soon as that country is mentioned. I'd guess this man is from somewhere around the Horn of Africa, possibly Djibouti, Ethiopia, or Somalia, but although I get that from his features my mind conjures a much smaller, thinner man when I think of those areas.'

'Yes, I know what you mean. I tend to think that the Japanese people are short and neat but then you've got sumo wrestlers and I wouldn't like to tangle with one of them. So Matt's looking for a lookalike to my man, is he?'

Alex studied the drawings and asked a few questions about height and build before deciding he'd probably got it wrong. 'I think it's just me seeing double again! First there were the identical photographs and then the identical cars, and now I'm suggesting you've come up with an almost identical drawing. I'm cracking up!'

Martin grinned. 'Well, I don't know about that, but tell me – how did Matt get the picture of what I guess is his prime suspect?'

'There were four people on the train who could give vague images of a stranger, but none of them could really describe

167

him. They're all people who make the same journey on a regular basis and none had ever seen this guy before Monday.

'Individually what they remembered was absolutely useless, but after a few hours with the guys in the Identification Suite they came up with an image between them. They all realised they'd seen him even though they hadn't stored the memory – didn't think they had reason to.'

Alex handed the drawings back to Martin. 'These are really good, the detail is amazing, but they're definitely of a younger man than the one Matt is looking for.'

Martin had a quick response to that. 'What if the staff in the Identification Suite were able to age him by eleven years – would he come even nearer to Matt's killer?'

'But what's the connection, mate? There's nothing to link the victims. The first one was a young Somali and the second an elderly English gentleman. How likely is it that they'd both be killed by the same man, and eleven years apart? Nothing is impossible in this business, but there'd have to be a very strong link, and from what I've heard there's nothing even vaguely likely.'

'No, but you know me, Alex, I think that cases are often solved by the most unlikely pieces of – for want of a better word – luck. Do me a favour, ask Matt if we can all meet up later and examine any possibilities of a connection. It'll probably just be to rule it out, but now the thought's in my head I'll have to follow it through.'

Alex nodded. 'I know that Matt's going to release his image to the press, ask the man or anyone who knows him to come forward. He may have done it already, actually. When do you want to get together?'

'I've got to see Chief Superintendent Atkinson before anything else, but I'll let you know.'

'I'll fit in with whatever suits Matt, and we can sort out some social arrangements at the same time.'

'Yes, birthdays are looming, and I want to do something special for Charlie, but she's hell-bent on sorting something out for you and I think she and Shelley are in on it together. Has she said anything to you?'

'All I know is when I said a quiet night in would suit me fine, I was told it had nothing to do with me! Don't you just love bossy women?'

Martin continued up the stairs and focused his mind on the report he was going to make to Atkinson. He was used to working with senior officers who were good at managing the wider political scene but didn't have a clue what was going on under their noses. This man was different, and it came as no surprise to Martin to learn that the chief super already knew about the successful surveillance operation.

Atkinson had been leaving for a meeting when Martin showed up. He apologised, saying he could only spare a few minutes, but changed his mind when Martin told him whose name had come up during the interview.

The superintendent requested two coffees from Jackie, and instructed her to give his apologies for absence to the meeting.

'Certainly, sir, but remember, you requested the meeting. Some of the senior officers would expect you to be there.'

'You go!'

'What do you mean?'

'Take the presentation – you know as much about how it was put together as I do, and my commentary is there to go with it, so it's just a question of setting it all up and letting it run for an hour. I don't need to sit and watch it, and by the time it's finished I'll be with you to answer any questions. Perfect solution – could become a regular thing!'

Atkinson knew that Jackie wouldn't be fazed by the great and the good at the meeting, and would conduct the presentation more professionally than he would have himself. He watched her pick up all the paraphernalia she had set aside for him to take, and smiled as she headed for the door with a look of determination – leaving the two men to pour their own coffee.

'Martin, John Evans had told me about the round-the-clock surveillance op you mounted, but why did you choose that particular timeslot? I can't believe you're just a lucky sod!'

Martin explained about the number of stones and the date the body had been found. Although he said nothing, Atkinson increased an opinion he already held – that DCI Phelps was a born detective.

Martin gave a full but concise account of events leading up to his meeting with Basra and the subsequent interview.

'What an ordeal. It's easy to say we can imagine the pain and humiliation she went through – but we can't, can we? Some people are real bastards.' Chief Superintendent Atkinson's face was hard. 'And she's sure about being able to identify the man who had designs on her brother and who was present at the time of his death?'

Martin nodded.

'What about the woman that she mentioned a few times?'

'Nothing much to go on there,' replied Martin. 'Basra could tell me the woman had green eyes and was able to give me an idea of her height and build but she never saw her face. She did say she would recognise her voice.'

'OK, let's look at where we go with this. What do you want from me?'

'Well, I know you were keen to get a result from this case but I think there's a bigger can of worms to open than just bringing in Dalmar's killer. If we open up an investigation into the charity that Basra identified, then there could be political repercussions as some of the trustees as public figures.'

Atkinson sat forward in his seat. 'I don't give a damn about naming and shaming, but I do know from experience that if we go down that road we must have all our facts absolutely right. These people always have the best lawyers, and more often than not get off on technicalities rather than due process.'

'That's why my answer to your question re what do I want from you is – time. At the moment there are only five people who definitely know about the dark side of this charity.'

'Five?'

'Oh yes, sorry. There's Basra herself, the two of us, and PC Woodland, who sat in on the interview – and I forgot to mention that Basra was going to speak to her fiancé when she left here. We can rely on PC Woodland and I don't think Basra is going to endanger herself or her fiancé after all this time.

'There's a lot I want to ask Basra regarding the place where her brother was killed, and the man and woman who in one way or another witnessed the murder. They didn't actually commit it, and even if we were able to bring them both in now we would only get them on perverting the course of justice. I thought about false imprisonment, but lawyers could probably argue that the Somalis were there willingly, under their protection. I'm keen to re-examine all the facts and don't want to go public on any of this until I'm absolutely sure that what we've got will stick.'

Chief Superintendent Atkinson got up and Martin followed.

'It's been eleven years since the body was discovered, so waiting a bit longer for the right result isn't a problem. As long as the people involved with the crime have no idea of the progress we've made, then they're going to continue to believe they've got away with murder. It'll be worth it when we can finally make them realise that although the young man was killed eleven years ago his case was never dead. Brilliant result so far, Martin, and yes, take your time, get every bit of evidence watertight, and nail the bastards!

'I also understand that DI Pryor is making good progress with the unexplained death on the train – now most definitely a murder case. It would be a brilliant boost for him if he could bring in the killer. Look out for his debut on this evening's TV news.'

Chapter Nineteen

'I'm telling you, I've just seen his ugly mug plastered across my TV screen. Don't tell me to calm down … don't you dare tell me to calm down … you're all a load of fucking idiots! What the hell are we going to do? If they find him he'll tell them everything – you know he will. Where is he now? Has he joined you? Wasn't that the plan after Monday's job? Come to that, where are you?'

Catherine's onslaught was unrelenting. So was her stranglehold on the whisky bottle she clutched.

'I've had a bloody awful time of it already today – desperately avoiding my daughter's desire to reunite me with my granddaughter!'

'What granddaughter? I didn't have you down as a granny.'

His attempt at warped humour fell on deaf ears, and Catherine screamed more obscenities into her phone. More followed as Samatar Rahim told her that neither he nor Omar were planning a return to the UK in the immediate future.

'You *bastards*! Leaving me to pick up your fucking pieces! Why didn't you take Ahmed with you? What if he gets picked up – he won't keep his mouth shut, will he? Someone will recognise him from this photo-kit that's being broadcast on just about every channel. I'm bloody *scared*, Samatar, and I'm getting a flight out to join you before the shit hits the fan and lands all over me.'

Catherine could barely contain herself and re-filled her glass.

Samatar realised that she was in danger of pressing the self-destruct button and taking them all with her.

'OK, I'll sort something out. Just stay where you are and try to get some sleep, you sound exhausted. I'll take care of Ahmed – he was getting to the end of his usefulness anyway – and if the police find him dead from his own poison they'll stop looking.'

Catherine was surprised at his newly caring tone, but she recognised the risk in his soothing words.

'It's as easy as that, is it?' she howled. 'When someone is no longer any use to you ... you just get rid of them. Where the fucking hell does that leave me?'

Samatar had no compunction in arranging murder and other heinous crimes, yet he had a real hatred of women swearing. He cringed, but continued in what for him was a sympathetic vein.

'Catherine, we go back a long way, and as you've constantly reminded us you've got an ace card up your sleeve. If we got rid of you the police would have access to that little black book of yours and that's something I want to avoid.'

The mention of her secret insurance policy did a lot to improve Catherine's mood. 'There's not a detail left out, and don't you forget it! True, it wouldn't do me any credit either, but if I was dead ... well, it wouldn't be my problem then, would it?'

After agreeing that she would do nothing until Samatar came back to her with the results of his promises for dealing with Ahmed, Catherine collapsed on the bed. She thought back over the past few hours and was pleased that her son had decided to drive her home and then go straight to his London flat.

They had abused one another to the nth degree on the journey, and if Catherine had been looking for support and sympathy from her son she now knew there would never be any. She knew that it was her drinking that had alienated Charles, but surely at a time like this he could cut her a bit of slack.

It had been a lot to take in. They'd been expecting to go to the Cardiff police station and offer some simulated sympathy to Lizzie. They both declined the offer to see Edward's body and Charles didn't even make any pretence at showing a sense of loss over his father's death. He'd already made it clear to DI

Pryor that he and his father were estranged, and so any show of grief would have been absurd. He had however used the opportunity to score some political points regarding crime rates, but they were cut short by his sister's announcement.

At first Catherine had failed to grasp what was being said, and the story that Lizzie related about the photograph in her father's pocket being the same one that Ellie had made no sense at all. They didn't know anyone called Ellie! Lizzie must have flipped from the knowledge that her father had been murdered.

When she realised the import of her daughter's words Catherine had almost fainted. She'd been taken to a quiet room where Charles insisted that he'd deal with the situation. When they were alone her son had taken control, and now in the quiet of her own home she remembered his words.

He'd basically told her to shut up and say nothing. It hadn't been difficult for him to explain to the police that his mother was in shock and he needed to get her home. Lizzie had realised that Catherine had been drinking and agreed that it wasn't a good time for her family to be introduced to her new-found daughter.

Catherine was suddenly feeling wide awake, and her thoughts darting off in every direction. There was only one way to stop them and she wandered into her kitchen to find another bottle. Although she was more than used to the effects of the alcohol, there were always times when it took her by surprise and this was one of them.

The first gulp sharpened her brain and she felt able to see her situation as if for the first time. She even remembered her husband taking the photograph of Lizzie and the baby, but had never seen a copy of it. She hadn't given the child a thought from that day to this and had already made up her mind to have nothing to do with the grown-up version.

The second mouthful she swallowed more slowly, beginning to giggle like a schoolgirl. She looked through the window at the sprawling grounds of Woodcanton Hall – it was all hers now! Edward would have made provisions for Lizzie in his will but there was no way that Catherine would give up the Hall.

She would contest anything that didn't allow her to live like the lady of the manor.

Charles would be happy to accept any financial benefits from his father's estate but he wouldn't want to live there – there were too many bitter memories.

There would be no place for Lizzie and her tennis cronies, and certainly no place for Lizzie's daughter. Catherine suddenly remembered the will Edward had brought to the family's attention some time ago. She wished she could remember the details, but felt sick as she recalled something about the wretched girl being able to consider Woodcanton Hall as her home.

With a third large measure swallowed, Catherine started to panic. How would Samatar deal with Ahmed? She was certain he wouldn't get his own hands dirty. During the years that she had known them it was always Ahmed who had done the dirty work – there'd never been anyone else. So who would they get to do the job? They were still in America, so it would have to be someone already in place. Someone she didn't know about … the thought chilled her. What else didn't she know about them?

She thought she should eat something, but couldn't be bothered and poured another drink instead. The phone rang and somewhat unsteadily she walked over and picked it up.

'Hello … Hello, who's there? Hello!'

She swore into the phone and the line went dead. The call had unsettled and vaguely scared her, and she sat at the kitchen table trying to think who'd called. Thinking was too difficult and she collapsed into a drunken sleep.

At the other end of the telephone line the caller carefully replaced the receiver. He was satisfied that Catherine was at home, and by the sound of it she was well down the road to being incapacitated. That suited him well.

Before they'd left Goleudy, Charles had insisted his mother give her car keys to Lizzie and get one of Lizzie's friends to drive the car back to Woodcanton. The girl Della would have to collect her hideous old car at some point so it seemed a sensible arrangement.

Their journey back had been fraught, and with every mile Charles became more and more concerned that his mother's drink problem was getting out of hand. His disquiet was not fuelled by love, but by fear for his own position. There would be questions regarding his father's death, and of course there would be an inquest. There'd be no legal reason for the family to attend, but Charles was a stickler for protocol and believed that someone in his position should be seen to be doing the right thing. Whereas his mother wouldn't stand the ordeal without extra rations of liquid malt, and that would loosen her tongue. She was getting to be a liability

Getting her into a clinic could be an option, but when he'd dared mention it she'd lashed out at him and almost sent them crashing into the central barrier of the M4. She'd threatened him with the secrets she believed would ruin his political career, but for the first time ever on this subject he'd laughed at her.

He'd told her in no uncertain terms that if she revealed the big secret she held over him, it would do as much damage to her, and if her only remaining trump card was to out him as homosexual then she had nothing. Charles laughed again as he told her that being gay could almost guarantee him a job at the top of his profession these days.

By the time they reached Woodcanton Hall their relationship was in pieces. Charles didn't even go into the house. He told her to lay off the drink and to stay put until he returned. He knew that his mother's first task would be to find a whisky bottle, and it made him feel sick just to think of what she was turning into.

He was his mother's son all right. As she did, he put self before anything else, and so as soon as he had dropped her off he made a phone call. The recipient assured him that plans were already in place to put things right.

Very briefly he pictured his mother draining glass after glass of her favourite tipple. She was a beautiful woman and had always enjoyed the admiration of men, so she wouldn't handle growing old at all well, especially not once the booze ravaged her looks. It was a comforting thought.

Hours later, Catherine stirred. It was still dark. Her head thumped and she noticed for the first time that her hands were shaking and for the umpteenth time she vowed to stop drinking. She wasn't even kidding herself because she knew it wasn't going to happen. She struggled to her feet, but the room spun round, causing her to fall back onto the chair.

This degree of hangover was something new, but looking at the empty bottle on the floor she realised that even by her standards she'd over-indulged. Her unsteady legs carried her to the kitchen and she managed to sort out some coffee and drank several cups in quick succession. The caffeine was helping, and when followed by a few glasses of water her body was, for the moment, recovering. She reached for a packet of Panadol, swallowed twice the recommended dose, then contemplated taking a shower.

Her mind went back over the journey she'd had with Charles coming back from Cardiff. They'd both said some pretty awful things but she was having difficulty making sense of why he'd been so angry. The two of them had always been so very close, and she'd proven over the years that there was nothing she wouldn't do for him.

She couldn't really remember what he'd said when he left her outside the house. When was he coming back, and when were those people Lizzie knew bringing her car back? It would be easy enough to call him, but knowing they hadn't parted on good terms she wasn't going to be the first to hold out an olive branch.

Temptation was already knocking on the door of Catherine's mind, but with caffeine and Panadol on side she resisted and took a shower. Afterwards, drying her hair in front of a long mirror, the thought that she was getting old struck home. She still had a figure that most women would die for, but she could see that the signs of ageing were increasing and it depressed her.

Quickly covering up with a silk robe she sat at the dressing table and began applying makeup. Mirrors had always been her friend, but now this one was highlighting lines and age spots that she was sure hadn't been there yesterday. In a fit of temper she swept bottles of face cream and perfume off the dressing table and onto the floor.

She made her way back to the kitchen, settling for some toast and another cup of coffee – generously laced with whisky! There was only one more bottle left and she made a mental note to ring her suppliers for some more.

Catherine heard the intercom for the main gates click and poured yet more whisky into her coffee before putting the bottle back in the cupboard. Whoever it was had used the entry code and it was only the family and her 'special' colleagues who knew it. They also had their own keys to the house, so there was no need for Catherine to let anyone in.

She decided that whoever it was she would greet them perfectly presented, finishing the make-up job she'd started and teased her expertly cut hair into shape. From her lavish wardrobe she took a pair of white linen trousers – and then changed her mind. Even if she didn't feel like a grieving widow, she should probably look like one. The white trousers were swapped for a long black skirt and a deep purple sweater topped it off. This time when she looked in the long mirror she was pleased with what she saw.

It suddenly occurred to her that she hadn't heard much sound from her visitor, but she could suddenly hear drawers being opened and closed in the room just below – the one she used as her office.

Why would anyone be in there? It was her domain and was where she kept her personal stuff.

She wanted to see what was going on before giving the person time to cover their tracks and so quietly she walked down the stairs and opened the door to her study.

'*You*!' she shouted. 'What the fuck do you think you're doing?'

Chapter Twenty

'This is just perfect,' announced Charlie. 'It's strange to think I've never been to the cottage. Alex often talks about the weekends he's had here before but I guess you won't be using the wetsuits tonight. It's cold enough on land, but if you set foot in the sea it'd freeze your balls off!'

'Ever the lady!' laughed Alex. 'I hope you're not going to teach our daughter such common Irish expressions.'

Charlie protested that she'd probably picked that one up from him, but it wasn't that which Shelley had homed up on.

'Daughter! You're having a baby girl – did it show up on the scan? I thought you said you didn't want to know.'

Alex looked a bit sheepish but Charlie's smile lit up her face and he knew he was off the hook. She detached her handbag from the back of her wheelchair, fished out a pink leather wallet, and handed it to Shelley.

'We didn't think we'd want to know and when we had the twelve-week scan we told the sonographer that she wasn't to tell us. When we went for the twenty-week scan it was supposed to be the same, but the baby was lying on her back and when eagle-eye here couldn't see any extra bits between the legs he said it had to be a girl!'

Alex looked over Shelley's shoulder and pointed out the various parts of the baby that could be seen in the scan photograph.

'My God, this is amazing! The last time I saw a scan picture was years ago when a schoolfriend got pregnant and we all looked at it in the classroom. Some kids reckoned they could make out arms and legs but I just thought it looked like something from outer space. This is so clear – and what's this?'

Shelley had taken a DVD from the other side of the pink wallet.

'It's my birthday present from Alex. Margaret, the sonographer at the Heath, was brilliant and when we told her that we'd changed our minds about not wanting to know our baby's sex she made some suggestions. We kept the image where it's obvious she's a girl, but then I wriggled around a bit to get the baby to move and she came up with a picture where the baby's leg is raised and you can't see the area that shows what sex she is.'

'And it was that photo you showed me and everyone else in the dining room at work.' laughed Shelley. 'But you didn't mention a DVD.'

'Well, that's my birthday present. Margaret told us that although the hospital wasn't able to provide a DVD of the scan there were private clinics that did and she gave us a few contacts. It wasn't that expensive and we came out of the session with this pink leather case and the most amazing film of our baby. You can see her heart beating. Oops, there I go again! I get emotional just talking about it. It's the best birthday present I've ever had, I could just sit and watch it all day.'

Shelley hugged her friend. 'Is it just for you and Alex, or do we get a look?'

'I want to show it to the world – even put it on YouTube – but I'm restraining myself. Of course you can see it, but should we wait for Sarah and then have a girlie session without the men?'

'Talking about Sarah,' said Alex, 'are they coming? Is everything OK with the two of them?'

'I spoke to Matt, and he told me Sarah is thinking of moving to Australia and that he didn't feel able to stop her. Apparently Sarah's auntie lives in Perth and she's been trying to get Sarah to take a job there for ages.' Martin hesitated. 'I think Sarah's really good for Matt and I for one would be sorry to see her go.'

Shelley interrupted. 'When Martin told me what Matt had said I'm afraid I couldn't let it rest.'

'What do you mean? – you haven't said anything to me.'

Shelley blushed slightly. 'I don't tell you everything! And, well, as you'd already labelled me as an agony aunt I thought I'd stick my oar in.'

'Sounds like something I'd be guilty of,' said Charlie. 'What happened?'

'Well, I hope it's more of a question of what's happening, but let's get some drinks and nibbles and then I'll tell you my guilty secret.'

Shelley stepped into the kitchen and moments later returned with a tray of appetisers and glasses. She asked Martin to get the drinks while she explained the origin of some of the things she'd prepared.

'I'm not a natural cook like you, Charlie, and generally I only get it right if I stick to a recipe – and not always then! But things are on the up. Martin got me a one-day cookery course at Llanerch Vineyard and opted to do a curry thingy. You remember Llanerch? We had that fab evening on my birthday. Well, I didn't stop at the one session, and I've done two more short courses and got myself booked onto a few more.'

Martin sorted out the drinks and suggested they all sit around the fire and sample some of Shelley's efforts.

'I was a bit embarrassed at the start of the day, I thought everyone would be better than me, but to be honest we were all pretty useless to begin with. It's amazing how much you can learn in just one session. Still, as they say, the proof of the pudding is in the eating – so tuck in and tell me what you think.'

Alex helped Charlie get out of her wheelchair and settle herself into three large cushions he'd moved into an armchair shape.

'As I said just now, this is just perfect. It's really good sometimes for me to lounge around at the same level as everyone else instead of having people towering over me.'

Alex leaned over to kiss his wife and the four of them watched as the fire gave a cosy glow to the cottage.

'There's something magical about an open fire. Though the

magic dies a bit when you have to clean out the grate in the morning!' said Alex.

Charlie crumpled a paper napkin into a ball and threw it at him. 'Trust you to spoil the moment! Anyway, Shelley, these samosa-type things are scrummy – can I just keep eating them or do I have to leave room for a main meal?'

'Keep eating if you want! I've got a series of small dishes that we can have as and when we like during the evening – nothing formal.'

'Getting back to where we were about ten minutes ago, perhaps our self-appointed agony aunt would like to tell us what she's done with Matt and Sarah,' teased Martin.

Shelley poked her tongue out at him. 'Well, none of us know Sarah that well, but Martin said that Matt was smitten from the off.'

'I did and it's true. I've lost count of the number of women he's gone out with over the years, but with Sarah I could see from the beginning that it was different. It wasn't the most auspicious start to any relationship – you remember, we were in the middle of that case, the care home patients where Sarah worked were being killed for their money – awful case, but I'd never seen Matt so happy!'

Charlie interrupted. 'So has she ditched him or what? I agree with what everyone's said – they just seem so right for each other.'

'It's all to do with the fact that when they met Sarah was on the rebound. She was besotted with some guy she worked with at the Heath Hospital, and although I'm sure Matt has more than taken his place in her heart he hasn't been able to heal her pride.

'I've been shopping with Sarah a few times, and whenever we've met people she used to work with they've all said how much she's missed and what a great senior nurse she was. She wouldn't have walked away from a job she loved unless she'd reached an all-time low. Maybe Matt came on the scene just that bit too soon. The Australia thing has been on the cards for years, and in fact if it hadn't been for her affair with that bloke she'd have gone last year. Ironic, isn't it? If that had happened she and Matt would never have met.'

'Not only that!' interrupted Martin. 'It would have meant she'd never have worked in the Parkland Nursing Home. It was Sarah who suggested to Matt that some deaths there were worth looking into. If she hadn't been working there who knows how many more would have died at the hands of that doctor?'

'So maybe we should be grateful to Sarah's cheating doctor – not sure she'd see it that way, though! I know I wouldn't, I'd want to kill him! Matt and Sarah are great together but I don't think she's got faith in her judgement of men any more. She's been here before and I can understand her dilemma.' Charlie snapped up the last of the small parcels filled with spicy chicken. 'These are really good.'

'Ta.'

'What she really means,' laughed Alex, 'is are there any more?'

'Well, I'm not soaking mine up with alcohol like *some* I could mention, so I've got room for more food and I'm eating for two.'

'It was forever so!' Alex laughed. 'I didn't think you'd have the cheek to blame your love of food on your pregnant state, but I can't say I blame you for trying.'

Shelley picked up on the banter and placed plate two of her offering, chicken pakoras and dips, on the centre of the rug. Martin threw a few more logs on the fire.

'This is just perfect,' Charlie said again, causing a wave of companionable laughter.

'No, I mean it! Eating out is great but you can't beat a night in with friends and in such a warm cosy setting – it's …'

'*Just perfect,*' finished all four of them in unison.

Shelley made herself comfortable propped up against Martin. 'Anyway, to cut to the chase, when Martin said that Sarah was practically on the way to Australia I decided to find out if it really was what she wanted. We met for coffee and at first she seemed upbeat about the thought of a new life Down Under but there reached a point – after the second cappuccino –

when we both realised that she was trying too hard.'

'So she's not going?' asked Charlie.

'It's not that simple. There are two issues really, but although Sarah worries about the first I don't really see it as a problem. This is the second time her aunt has made arrangements for Sarah to live in Perth, things like a job and all the necessary paperwork. The first set of plans were axed when Sarah met the infamous surgeon and believed that her life would be here in the UK with him. She doesn't feel able to let her aunt down again, and especially as her reason sounds so much like the last one – she's found a man and wants to be with him!'

'And does she?' asked Charlie. 'Does she want to be with Matt?'

'We eventually agreed that although her aunt might be cheesed off with having to cancel another set of preparations, it wouldn't be the end of the world and it was her second issue that really mattered.'

'So she does want to be with Matt?'

'She told me Matt is the best thing that's ever happened to her. His sisters have welcomed her with open arms and made her feel part of the family – apparently something she's not known before. Contrary to what men think, not all women go into details about our love life, but I got the impression that the physical side of their relationship is A1.'

'So what's the problem – sounds to me like she wants to be with him, doesn't it?'

'We need to remember how badly she was treated and what that's done to her confidence. She can't trust her judgment anymore when it comes to men. On top of that, Matt isn't helping! She says he seems to have just accepted that she's going and hasn't once said he wants her to stay or will miss her or anything.'

Charlie looked exasperated.

'Bloody men – brains in their trousers as usual! When will they realise we need to *hear* how they feel? Actions don't always speak louder than words. Someone needs to tell Matt

186

before it's too late. Martin you've known him the longest – why don't you have a word?'

'One agony aunt in this house is more than enough, and to be honest I've always steered clear of Matt's romantic entanglements.'

'I hope there'll be no need for any of us to get involved, as when I left Sarah she was determined to find out exactly where she stands with Matt.'.

'Matt got a call from Sarah just as I was leaving work so hopefully they've sorted something out. He's doing OK on his case and his first media conference went well. Did you see it?'

'Yes,' replied Martin. 'He looked to be taking it all in his stride. And I absolutely agree that his potential killer looks remarkably like mine. I hope it gets good coverage and he gets some results from it.'

'Me too! But as I was saying, he got a call from Sarah and the last thing I heard him saying was he'd pick her up in ten minutes.'

'That was hours ago! They were supposed to be coming here tonight, weren't they? Charlie fidgeted as she spoke and Alex pulled her forward and put an extra cushion behind her.

'Yes, I happen to know she'd bought a birthday present for you and Martin – she had them with her when we met for coffee. We laughed over them because they both will have been a nightmare to wrap but she said they were Matt's idea of a joke. Can't tell you any more or I'll ruin the surprise.'

Martin refilled everyone's glasses and looked at the clock.

'It's getting late, so it's looking unlikely that they'll be handing out gifts tonight. I can't make up my mind if the time gap is a good or a bad thing but on balance I think it's good – they'll have a hell of a lot to talk about.'

They'd all been so busy talking, eating, and drinking that they hadn't heard the car that had parked a little way down from the cottage and were startled when the doorbell penetrated through their chatter.

Martin jumped up and the others waited anxiously.

'Come in, Sarah – is Matt with you?'

187

'No.'

Sarah struggled through the cottage door carrying two strange shaped parcels that she handed to Charlie and Martin.

'Happy birthdays! Next year it will be books for both of you or else Matt will have to wrap his own strange presents.'

Not all the four people hearing her words were detectives but they all picked up on her words: 'next year'.

'Matt may or may not get here later. He got a call from someone in Wiltshire and said he'd no option other than to follow it up. Don't ask me what it's all about because I've no idea. But, anyway, I don't want to get you all talking about work so open your presents and give me a drink – looks like I've got some catching up to do!'

Seeing Shelley's quizzical look, Sarah smiled.

'Don't worry – things have a way of sorting themselves out!'

Chapter Twenty-one

'I asked you a question.'

Catherine got the same stony silence as before. It was as if her visitor didn't even know she was there, until without warning he turned. Suddenly she felt less able to shout obscenities at him.

'Where is it?' he demanded.

'Where's what? What the hell are you looking for?'

'Not even *you* can be that thick! How long did you think it would be before Samatar sent me to look for it? Even your own son thinks you're a disposable commodity, but we've got to tie up a few loose ends before the fun starts.'

Catherine was now terrified, knowing only too well that Ahmed's idea of fun was not likely to be hers. She desperately wanted to make use of that last bottle of whisky, and it was as if he'd read her thoughts.

'Go ahead.'

He knew she wouldn't call the police, and if she phoned her beloved son he'd be disappointed because he was anticipating never hearing from her again.

Catherine didn't even bother with a glass, and took a large swig directly from the bottle. It immediately made her feel she had a friend and after a couple more mouthfuls she felt able to go back to her study. She still believed that she was more use to Samatar and the organisation alive than dead – and anyway, Ahmed was looking in the wrong place for her insurance policy. If she just told him that he'd go away – wouldn't he?

She hardly recognised her study when she returned, as every drawer had been ransacked and every movable piece of furniture turned upside down.

'You know what I'm looking for, so why not save yourself from any more aggro and tell me where it is? If I don't find it I'll give you the same treatment as I've given this lot.' He kicked the upturned desk to prove his point. 'Come to think of it, that would give me a great deal of pleasure.'

Catherine froze as she thought of something she should have anticipated before. He wouldn't have to kill her to satisfy his sadistic ego ... She shivered as she remembered stories of rape and torture that had been inflicted on some of the refugees. Ahmed would have been responsible for some of it, and there'd never been any love lost between the two of them ...

She thought he was an ignorant lout and he'd made it plain he hated women of her type – 'rich and toffee-nosed'. Over the years there had been countless times when she'd looked at him disdainfully, spoken to him like a dog. She'd made her contempt for him clear, and she could see from his face how much pleasure he was getting now from watching her cringe in fear. Not even the whisky was taking the edge off.

She desperately tried another tack.

'I could tell you where it but that would leave me vulnerable ...'

Ahmed's cruel laugh stopped her words.

'You're even more of a stupid bitch than I thought if you don't think you're already vulnerable. But I'm getting pissed off so let's move on.'

Moving quickly for a man of his size, he leapt forward, grabbing Catherine's right forearm with one of his hands and using the other hand to force her wrist back.

The bones cracked.

She screamed, her knees buckling as she fainted. Sadly for her, the oblivion was short-lived, and to her disgust she found as she came to that she'd wet herself. Her humiliation excited Ahmed and he teased her about it.

'Had a piss, have you, sweetheart? Not very ladylike!'

Catherine stared at her hand, half-expecting it to be detached from her arm. The pain was almost unbearable. She looked towards her whisky bottle, but it had smashed on the floor when she fainted.

Catherine staggered to her feet, but fell back down as Ahmed kicked her in the shin.

'This time when I ask the question I want you to rethink your answer, get it? Where is it?'

There was no hesitation as Catherine answered quietly.

'It's with my solicitor.'

'Your solicitor? Speak up. Are you saying the document Samatar needs is not here? You've given it to your solicitor?'

'Yes.' Catherine tried to speak louder but her words were choked by her tears. Maybe if she gave Ahmed a bit more information he would leave her alone. 'It's the family solicitor.'

She didn't know what to expect but something she'd said was making Ahmed think.

'What does that mean?'

'William Everton and Sons have been solicitors to Edward's family for decades, and when we were married I automatically used them.'

'So they're your son's solicitors too?'

Catherine winced as Ahmed pushed past her and made for the door. At first she thought someone else had arrived and he was talking to them. Surely if it was her son he'd forget about the row they'd had and get her out of this mess. Her hand was swelling at an alarming rate, and as the skin stretched the pain increased and was becoming unbearable. She realised that it was only Ahmed's voice she could hear, so he must be on the phone – but why had he left the room to make the call?

Thoughts of escaping fleetingly crossed Catherine's mind, but only long enough to be dismissed. She wouldn't have a hope in hell of getting anywhere. Even if she could have driven one-handed, she didn't have a car, and Woodcanton Hall was miles from anywhere so even without her leg injury running off was not an option. She'd have to brazen it out and for once in her life try not to wind up someone she detested.

When he returned to the study his sneering smile made new waves of abject fear race through Catherine's body. She had no idea who he'd spoken to but whatever had been said had pleased him.

'Didn't really think the Fergusons' family firm would stand by you, did you, bitch? Oh, by the way, that was Charley boy.'

'What? No one has *ever* called him Charley – he's always been Charles,' said Catherine with as much dignity as she could muster. '

Ahmed laughed and spat in her face.

'Think you know your boy, do you – stupid cow! You've got a lot to answer for. He was messed up even before he tried it on with one of your refugees. Watching me deal with the situation made him turn the final corner. Believe me when I tell you he's a bigger psycho than I've ever been. It's amused you to think you've been in the same league as Samatar and Omar and thinking your little black book would keep them in order. It would never have been that difficult to get hold of it, but now it couldn't be easier.'

Catherine used the back of her undamaged hand to wipe her face and looked down despairingly at her bleeding leg. Ahmed grabbed a handful of her hair and yanked her head up so that she was looking directly into his face. His eyes were pure evil, but it was his voice that confused Catherine. He'd always been the silent one – the one who walked a few steps behind the others and spoke when he was spoken to. She'd never heard him say more than a few words and hadn't expected him to have such a good command of the English language.

'The replica car you set up for *Charley* may have started as a bit of fun, given you and him a laugh at your husband's expense, but it gave your boy a real opportunity to be creative with his dark side. And when I say dark side I mean *jet black*! We all knew about it. I've personally cleared up some of his messes. Not that I mind – each one has put darling Charley more in our debt, and he's willing to make certain like-minded officials in certain government departments look the other way. Useful when a reputable charity is fronting a drugs distribution network.

Catherine could barely move but her eyes widened at the

mention of drugs.

Ahmed laughed at her reaction and let go of her hair.

'You bloody high and mighty English women! You're like snakes at the bottom of a pit. It's OK for you to make money from the misery of poor Africans, but not to soil your manicured hands with drugs. You've no idea what hell those people are trying to get away from – you wouldn't last five minutes.

'Oh, and by the way, it wasn't to please you that your husband was sorted out, although we were happy to let you think that.' He smirked. 'We'd found out that your husband had been making enquiries about his granddaughter, and passed on the information to Charley. It wasn't in Charley's best interest to have family skeletons brought out of the cupboard, and he didn't want to share his family home with his niece – so we had to put a stop to him finding her. He's under the impression that he can make his father's will disappear. So much so that he's already got the removal van sorted to move into this place.

'Your daughter won't be happy either, because her precious tennis academy is no longer on the cards. I'm sure you remember why your son will want to burn down all those outbuildings and bury his memories in the ashes. No, *Mrs* Ferguson, nobody but your precious Charley will be benefitting from your husband's arranged death. And you'll be joining him much sooner than you'd have imagined.'

Catherine had already been trembling from a mixture of cold, fear, and the need for more whisky, but Ahmed's last words caused a more erratic surge of the shakes. She was petrified, and although she knew it was useless she had one final desperate try at using her insurance policy.

'My little black book –'

'You stupid fucking cow! Didn't I just tell you I was talking to Charley boy on the phone? Your family solicitors would have handed over your husband's stuff to you as the next of kin, wouldn't they?'

Catherine nodded.

'In the same way they'll hand over your stuff to Charley, as your next of kin … get it?'

Even in her current state of mind Ahmed's words left her in no doubt about her fate. She would never know how long he would have played with her before her execution, because, unexpectedly, his hand was forced. The intercom to the main gates picked up the sound of an approaching car and he knew he had to act fast.

With his hands around her throat he squeezed until her eyes were ready to pop. Her tongue protruded in search of air. With his brute strength the whole thing was over quickly. He threw her to the floor in a final act of disgust.

Ahmed thought that luck was on his side as he could hear the voices being transmitted from outside the main gates.

'Mother, are you there?' asked Lizzie. 'Sorry it's so late. Has the access code been changed, or are the gates jammed? Nothing's working and I can't get in!'

Ahmed smiled. He'd been given the new code by Charles Ferguson and was delighted that Charles hadn't shared it with his sister. There was no need for him to rush now and he took a last look at his handiwork. Catherine Ferguson looked much prettier dead than alive, and just for the fun of it he picked up the broken bottle and poured what remained in the bottom over her head.

There was no need for him to cover his tracks as he knew for certain that neither his DNA nor fingerprints were on record. Not in the UK or anywhere else. He ambled out to his car and before getting in he made a phone call as he'd promised.

'All done. You can expect a call from your sister soon as she's looking for someone to give her the code for Woodcanton Hall.'

'It looks like she's already ringing me. Are you still on the premises? How long do you need?'

'In less than a minute I'll be out through the rear entrance, and then I plan on being out of the country for some time.'

Charles ended the call and accepted the one that was waiting.

'What's the panic, Lizzie?'

'I can't open the gates at the Hall!'

'I thought you'd be staying in Cardiff tonight – catching up with your darling daughter. That was a bit of a turn-up. Not sure Mother fancies herself as a granny!'

'Neither you nor Mother wanted to know about her when I had her so I'm not expecting any family bonding now. Look, Charles, I'm not in the mood for small talk – I couldn't sleep and I've come back to get some things together. I just want to know if you can help with the code.'

'The code had to be changed because too many people knew it – but I gave it to Mother and she should be there to let you in. She must be there because I dropped her off earlier and her car's in Cardiff.'

'Well, either she's not here or she's asleep or drunk. Whichever it is, she's not answering the intercom, and all I want from you is the new number.'

'Hold on. The number's on a pad in the car.'

He kept Lizzie hanging on while he pretended to get it for her. She was getting frustrated with the delay, and so Basil got out and stood next to the keypad, waiting to punch in the numbers as Lizzie called them out. Della was asleep in the back. Who would have thought, when he and their young protégée arrived at the Hall, that they'd end up having had one of the strangest days of their lives? Lizzie looked done in, and he'd make it his business to see she had something to eat before going to bed. She needed a good night's sleep and even this hiccup with the code was more hassle than she should have to deal with – enough was enough.

Finally, believing he'd given Ahmed more than enough time to exit via the rear gate, Charles gave his sister the number. Realising that her friends were still with her, he acted the caring brother and told her she should try to get some sleep.

In reality he knew that wasn't going to happen and just for a second he wondered how she would react to finding their mother. She was definitely at home. Not drunk or asleep … but dead.

Chapter Twenty-two

'Sorry to drag you back, guv, but I know DCI Mortimer very well and he seems to think you'd want to hear first-hand what he's got to say. It's not often that he sounds animated but he was! I'll get his office to put you through to him.'

Maggie Shaw spoke to a few people she knew from the Wiltshire force, and when she was through to DCI Mortimer she handed the receiver to Matt.

'Matt Pryor here – how can I help?'

'Hello, Matt – this is Graham Mortimer. I've got some news from Woodcanton Hall. I don't quite know how it links with your investigation but there has to be a connection.'

For a moment Matt cursed the man for dragging him back to work and away from an evening with Sarah and his friends. Surely what he had to say could have waited until the morning?

'Did you find something in the garages or those out-buildings?'

'To be honest, we didn't expect to find anything because the people we want to lay our hands on are experts in their field. People trafficking and drugs are on their list of activities but so far they've kept ahead of us.'

'So how do you think I can help?'

'I understand from Maggie Shaw that Catherine Ferguson was interviewed by you earlier today.'

'I wouldn't call it an interview – she was here because, as you know, her husband was found murdered in Cardiff. She's not a suspect, and it was her daughter who identified the body.'

'Yes I've heard all about it, including the fact that Lizzie Ferguson has been reunited with the daughter she gave up for adoption. Lizzie had a rollercoaster ride with you, Matt, but it was nothing when compared with what she came home to.'

'Did she go home? I was under the impression she was taking her friends back to collect their car that was left at Woodcanton Hall.'

'Sorry, I was talking about the family home, not her flat. It's a good job her two tennis friends were still with her when she got there. She found her mother dead, and this time the murder wasn't even made to look like a natural death – it was quite brutal.'

'Bloody hell! So both her parents have been murdered – *and* her daughter's just come back into her life. You've obviously seen her – how is she?'

There was a moment of hesitation before the DCI responded.

'I've known the Ferguson family for many years and Edward was well-respected and will be mourned. His wife … is a different matter. Catherine Morris was something of a local beauty, but she was always selfish to the core and as a young woman she was frequently found on the edge of trouble. She had all the men in Wiltshire eating out of her hand, but she had her eyes set on being the mistress of Woodcanton Hall. It's rumoured that when she became pregnant there were a few men in the pipeline, but she claimed that Edward was the father and they were married.

'I have no idea if Charles is really Edward's son but he is certainly Catherine's. You probably know that the man is earmarked for a bright future in politics but I wouldn't trust him any further than I could throw him.'

'Quite a family!'

'Yes, and the only reason I'm telling you this is to explain that Elizabeth may be shocked by her mother's death – and in particular by the nature of her death – but she won't be heartbroken. I'm not at all sure how Charles will react other than that he'll get all the political mileage possible from the situation.'

'How was she killed?' questioned Matt.

'We think it's likely that she was knocked about a bit before

198

being strangled, and our thinking is that someone was after something she had. Possibly money or jewellery, possibly drugs, but an initial check shows the safe hasn't been tampered with and there are a lot of valuable things still on show.

'I'm not a great believer in coincidences, Matt, and in my mind there has to be a connection between the two murders.'

Matt gave a short laugh. 'You remind me of someone I know, and he absolutely doesn't believe in coincidences! How do you want to proceed?'

'There's no rush as far as I'm concerned. I'm going home to my bed. My people will be turning this whole place over and looking at all the CCTV footage they can lay their hands on. There are obvious routes in and out of the county and traffic cameras may be helpful. The one positive thing is that we know the time of death, probably to within five minutes.

'My suggestion is that we both sleep on it. I'll give you a ring mid-morning tomorrow and see if we can make some sort of picture if we put our pieces together. Meanwhile, give my regards to DS Shaw. If you want to know more about Mrs Ferguson and her son Charles, Maggie will tell you why we've been interested in them for some time.'

Matt sat down and rubbed his face. He was tired and more than a bit emotionally drained. He gratefully accepted the coffee handed to him by Maggie Shaw, and really noticed her for the first time. She was quite a looker, and he was amused as he realised that her eyes were flirting with him and probably had been since her arrival. He hadn't even picked up on her signals! Not like him at all. It could have been the case, but he was focussed on Sarah, and struggled to think of anything else.

DS Shaw interrupted his thoughts and brought him back to reality.

'I only heard your end of the conversation with DCI Mortimer, but do I take it that someone's been killed at Woodcanton Hall?'

'Yes. I'm told you know the setup there quite well. What about Catherine Ferguson? You must have seen her when she was here earlier. What did you make of her then?'

'Well, I've seen her many times before and she's always looked like someone that's just stepped out of the pages of *Vogue*, but today I thought she looked rough. She reminded me of times when I've used extra makeup to hide my hangover from the public. I'm sure that most people thought she was shaky because of her husband's murder, but I think the woman's got a serious drink problem.'

'*Had* a serious drink problem.'

'Good God! You mean she's the one that's been murdered? Now that does surprise me. I always had her down as a member of some sort of self-preservation society. We've been close to investigating her charity for years, there's definitely something dodgy there, but she's always seemed invincible and I'm pretty certain that people higher up the command chain have protected her. What happened?'

Driving home to Pontprennau Matt thought about families and how complicated they could be. The place he called home was where he and his sisters had been brought up. They'd all married and left, and so he'd re-mortgaged it and given his sisters their due shares. His sisters, their partners, and their daughters were the biggest part of his life outside of work but things were changing and for the first time he was thinking about creating a family of his own. Were men supposed to feel broody?

Matt's mind briefly went back to his case, but he didn't allow it to stay there. If he started thinking about possible connections now he'd be awake all night trying to link them. He was missing Martin and the way they usually bounced ideas off one another. The word around the office was that his DCI had managed to solve the Roath Park murder, and that would be a feather in his cap.

Matt resolved to talk to Martin in the morning and ask him if he had any suggestions re linking the murders, other than the obvious ones. He wouldn't have a problem asking Martin for his views – they'd been a team for a couple of years and he'd be stupid if he let his pride stand in the way of getting another opinion. This was his first solo murder case and there'd be no shame in asking for help.

He didn't bother putting the car in the garage and left it on the road. His thoughts returned to Sarah. She'd been badly bruised by her previous relationship, and he hadn't realised how much that had been stifling her feelings for him. There'd been a mutual attraction from the first day they met, and it wasn't long before they were enjoying each other's company and not bothering to say goodbye at the end of a date.

Matt had more experience with the opposite sex than even he cared to admit, and until tonight he'd lived by one golden rule – never admit to feelings of love and commitment! Instinctively, he'd gone down the same road with Sarah, and so he hadn't told her he loved her and wanted her to share his life.

He had raised no objections when she voiced her plans to go to Australia either. *Who says women are the weaker sex*, he thought. It couldn't have been easy for Sarah to ask him outright if he wanted her to stay. She'd opened herself wide to another possible rejection and it was that look of panic in her eyes that had made Matt realise, and more importantly tell her, that he loved her and was dreading the thought of losing her.

Once that particular genie was out of the bottle it couldn't be put back and he liked the way the words sounded and so said them over and over.

They hadn't talked much after that, although lots of talking would be needed soon. Would Sarah move in with him? There would be no point in her still renting her flat when he had plenty of space for the two of them, but would she want to share a house that had so many of his memories and none of hers? He'd ask her what she wanted to do – share his thoughts and give voice to his hopes for their future. Gone were the days of thinking like a bachelor – and it felt surprisingly good!

Matt was sure he'd never get to sleep and so was amazed when he heard his alarm. He smiled as he texted Sarah another declaration of love – followed by 'There, now I've even put it in writing so you can use it in evidence against me! ☺ Xxx'.

When Matt arrived at Goleudy there were just a handful of cars parked but one of them was an Alfa Romeo. En route to the top floor he grabbed some papers that had been left on his desk and noticed a handwritten note from Maggie Shaw. DCI Mortimer had left a message scheduling a session for 10.30.

'Good morning and happy birthday. I thought you'd be having an extra hour in bed as I doubt you were drinking water last night!'

Martin smiled. 'No, but I didn't over-indulge. I'll catch up on that over the weekend. My birthday is the twenty-sixth, but last night's session fell nicely between mine and Charlie's. Oh, and thanks for the present – Spikeball! I'd never heard of it until Sarah struggled in with it. It's different, I'll give you that!'

Matt laughed. 'I could have just bought a bottle of malt but decided Spikeball would be better for your health. I don't know about you but I could definitely do with a bit more running around.'

'Thanks, I'll give it a try, but it needs two teams – so do I take it you and Sarah will be up for it? You certainly look like the cat that's got the cream this morning. Sorry you couldn't make it – was last night's return to work interesting? '

'I've got an unsolved murder on my hands – but I've never been happier. What are we like? Your could have lost the love of your life by hesitating, and *my* hesitation nearly saw Sarah on a slow boat to China … well, a fast plane to Australia as it happens! She's not going, unless at some time in the future we both decide to take the plunge.'

'Is that likely?' asked Martin.

'Who knows? One step at a time, and the first step must be to be sort out our living arrangements. How has it worked with Shelley moving into the cottage?'

'She loves it, but then it suits her style. Not sure she'd have wanted to move into a modern flat or anywhere on an estate.'

'I suspect Sarah and I'll be looking for somewhere that's ours rather than mine. That should be entertaining – I've never house-hunted in my life.'

Matt changed the subject back to work and as he spread his

papers out on one of the desks he briefed Martin on his conversation with DCI Mortimer.

'Phew! I remember watching Lizzie Ferguson play tennis when I was a teenager. Everyone thought she'd hit the big time – I certainly didn't know she'd had a child, but then it obviously wasn't public knowledge. I read recently that she's coaching a future tennis star.'

'Yes, her name's Della and she was here yesterday. She and a guy called Basil, her fitness coach, were looking at the facilities up at Woodcanton Hall when I phoned to ask about Edward Ferguson. They drove to Cardiff with Lizzie, and to be honest they were a lot more supportive than her mother and brother, who arrived much later.'

'Good God, I hope *someone* is supporting her – but I've got a bloody good reason for suggesting it won't be her brother.'

Martin picked up some of the papers and then sat down as he looked at a photofit image. He wished he'd watched the television news last night or this morning or had had more reason to share the interest shown by Alex yesterday. Now, with the opportunity to study Matt's image carefully, several connections hit his brain simultaneously but he refrained from voicing them before checking out some facts.

'OK, so you've got a man dead on arrival at Cardiff Central. The man's car led to you identifying him as Edward Ferguson. The photo in his pocket was recognised by a young woman on the train who turned out to be his granddaughter – you couldn't make it up, could you? I don't believe for one moment it was a coincidence, and from what you've said I think he was looking for a way to contact her.'

'That fits with what she said about him,' said Matt. 'She told me she caught him looking in her direction several times, but she didn't get the impression that he was an old man ogling a young girl. She described him as looking kind but sad.'

'So, he's on the train and plucking up the courage to speak to the girl he knows is his granddaughter when someone sticks a needle in him. Who and why?'

'I believe the "who" is the person whose image you're

looking at, but I'm at a loss as to the "why". We've had the usual responses from the television appeal, placing him simultaneously at all points from John O'Groats to Land's End. I've got people sorting out the wheat from the chaff on that but I'm not holding my breath.'

Matt explained the mystery of the two cars and the visit he and Alex had made to Woodcanton Hall. Martin absorbed every detail, but Matt could see that the DCI's mind was racing as he'd got up and was pacing the floor.

'What's up? Have I missed something obvious?'

'A few minutes ago I commented that you couldn't make it up in relation to the photograph – well, I think I'm now going to prove that life really can be stranger than fiction. You wanted connections to share with DCI Mortimer and his murder case, but what would you say to some connections with me and mine?'

Leaving Matt looking puzzled, Martin got up and made them both coffee.

'I'll bring you up to speed on the case I've been investigating and then you'll know what I'm talking about.'

Fifteen minutes later Martin finished his account of how he'd managed to find out the identity of the Roath victim.

'Bloody hell! Congratulations on coming up with the link with the stones, but what I don't understand is why this Basra didn't come to us with the account she's given to you. I can see why she wouldn't have done so immediately. With everything that happened to her she'd hardly trust anybody, but surely over the years ...'

'She said she believed that if someone found her then that someone would be looking for the truth. I took that to mean that people with influence and authority may want the truth buried, and she didn't want to risk that happening. This is where I could do with a drum roll as I reveal my stranger-than-fiction connection – the honourable Charles Ferguson MP.'

'Now you've really lost me! Are you saying Ferguson killed the young Somalian and dumped his body in Roath ... and eleven years later killed his father on a train ... *and* strangled his mother?'

'He's not killed anyone that we know of, and he's certainly not personally responsible for the murders we are investigating.'

'So ... I don't get it! What's his connection to the Roath crime?'

'Basra named him as the man who was forcing his attentions on her brother.'

'No way!'

Martin explained the charity connection. 'God only knows what they were up to altogether, but the more I've thought about it the more I think that Catherine Ferguson was the woman Basra described. She never saw the woman's face but the height is right and the plum-in-the-mouth accent fits.'

Matt nodded. 'Well, we can't question her on that now, but surely you can bring Charles Ferguson in for questioning?'

'On what basis? The word of a young woman who has chosen to remain silent for eleven years, and who now wants to ruin the reputation of a politician at the time when his father and his mother have been taken from him in the most tragic of circumstances? I've got no real evidence! The links to the charity would be seen as tenuous, and so it's just her word against his. No prizes for guessing who'd be believed.'

Martin put Matt's constructed photograph alongside the drawing Basra has done of her brother's killer.

'I've no doubt that Basra's given me an accurate picture of her brother's killer, and it's the slightly lopsided nature of his face that makes me think your witnesses saw the same man.'

'I can't argue with that. It's got to be the same man – so where does that take us?'

'He kills Dalmar and then seemingly disappears off the radar until this week, when he kills Edward Ferguson and possibly Catherine Ferguson. The methods of killing are different in all cases, but I don't think we're looking at a serial killer, more like a paid assassin who could adapt his MO to meet any circumstances. It sounds to me as if Dalmar's killing was the automatic response of a trained killer to a situation he thought was getting out of hand. It wasn't planned. Basra has described how that happened and how the body was dumped.'

'You mentioned a paid assassin – paid by who, and for what purpose?'

'Looks like I may have a bit of a breakthrough there. Someone called Michael Porter called following my media appeal, and it would appear that Edward contacted him recently. He's a private investigator and says he went to Woodcanton Hall some years ago on behalf of a client – Ellie's late father. At the time he met Edward and was given a photograph that he handed over to Gwyn, Ellie's dad, so that explains how he got it. I can only assume that Gwyn had been trying to locate Ellie's real mother. Anyway, amongst these papers I've got a note that details how Edward Ferguson contacted Porters Investigation Services in October this year, asking for contact details for one of the company's clients, and against protocol the temporary receptionist just gave out Gwyn Bevan's address.

'I need to interview Michael Porter, of course, but where I'm going with this is that Edward must have told someone he was looking for his granddaughter and possibly that person had a reason to stop him from doing that. What do you think?'

'It's a perfectly acceptable assumption, but it would need to be one hell of a big reason to provoke murder. Let's assume that he'd found her – who could have gained or lost from that situation?'

'Well, I know from investigating his business that he's got money to spare, and some. If he'd found Ellie she'd be in line for a share, as indeed she probably is now anyway. But as he was so keen to find her he could've been considering something more generous – even giving her the lot. That gives his wife and his son a very good motive for wanting to stop him.'

'And his daughter,' suggested Martin.

'I guess so, but she was the only one who showed any signs of distress over his death. Yes, we've seen that used as a cover-up before, but I think her grief was really genuine.'

The two men simultaneously had the same thought and it was Matt who voiced it.

'Looks like we're chasing the same killer or killers. Two heads will certainly be better than one, so I guess the old team is back together and I for one am happy with that. I've got a session with DCI Mortimer at 10.30 so if you join that then between the three of us we should make some headway. I'll get Charlie and her lot to transfer the data on the train murder and collate it with the Roath murder and see what else we come up with. Does that suit you?'

'Yes. I've been told not to rattle Charles Ferguson's cage until I've got evidence that will stand up in court. I'll join you at 10.30, but now I want to call Laura Cummings. Hopefully she'll be able to give us some of the help she promised me.'

Chapter Twenty-three

'The same way as I find out everything else, you fool! We may not be in the UK but we have contacts that keep us informed of everything that's going on. I was bloody furious when I was told to look at the BBC News site and was confronted with your ugly face staring back at me. When did you learn to be so careless? We've spent years ensuring that nothing about you is in the public domain – no fingerprints, no DNA, and certainly no fucking photographs.

'You're no good to us in the UK now so the sooner we get you out of the country the better. You'll have to scrap the original plan of flying straight to the US from Heathrow. Every customs officer and airport official will have a copy of your mug and you'll never get through Security.'

'So what do I do? If the airport is a no-go area then it'll be the same for boats and ferries and international trains. I'll just have to stay put until things blow over.'

Samatar and Omar were enjoying a first-class hotel in Washington. They hid so well behind the façade of a respectable business, and no longer needed to get up close and personal to those who dealt drugs and death on their behalf. It had taken years of meticulous planning and mingling with the right people to reach their level of outward respectability, and now for the first time it was under serious threat.

Ahmed was no longer an asset but a dangerous liability. The two men had no doubt that if he was caught he would sing like a canary, and that was something they couldn't risk. He wasn't the only available killer they had at their disposal, but he was the best – and he spent his life looking over his shoulder and anticipating trouble, so his self-preservation instincts would have kicked in now he knew his bosses were losing patience.

Samatar knew what Ahmed would be thinking and to keep him onside he changed his tack.

'Dump the car. There's the possibility that traffic cameras around Woodcanton Hall may have picked you up and they'll be on the lookout for you. I'll text you details for a number of contacts that will look after you and provide you with a different vehicle and a place to keep your head down. It shouldn't take too long to work out an exit plan for you, so bear with us and keep your line open.'

Ahmed watched the call cut out, and contrary to what had been requested he turned his phone off. He needed to do some thinking of his own, and if he knew one thing for certain it would be that he wouldn't be cosying up to any of the contacts suggested by Samatar. It made his blood boil as he thought how stupid they believed him to be. Did they really think he wouldn't remember that he'd help set up these people?

What they didn't know was that Ahmed had established a few contacts of his own, and they all owed him big time. He guessed they'd all have witnessed his recent notoriety, but two in particular would never expose him to the police – they wouldn't want their own activities revealed. He'd helped them, and now it was payback time. Ahmed worked out who was closest to his current location.

When he'd received Samatar's call he'd been on his way to Heathrow airport, having been told to pick up a first-class ticket in the usual place. They always travelled first or business class, as bizarrely they'd discovered that it was the easiest way to travel. Maybe the airport staff thought people who could afford such expensive comfort were unlikely to be flying for anything but genuine business or pleasure. He remembered many times when he'd loved to have told the stewardess who fawned over him, hoping for the big tip that they weren't supposed to accept, how much killing satisfied him.

Ahmed realised that he was drifting off into random thoughts and was having difficulty concentrating on the importance of planning his next moves. Not surprising really considering he'd had nothing to eat or drink for the best part of twenty-four hours.

Nick Cutler had a setup just off the M4 on the outskirts of Swindon. He ran a huge and very lucrative cannabis farm behind a popular and seemingly respectable children's fun farm. He'd come into contact with Samatar and the others through the underworld connections of people who deal in drugs of one sort or another. When one of his employees had been curious to know why the back of one of the animal enclosures was warm to the touch, she'd found more than she'd bargained for and Ahmed had offered to make sure she didn't talk about her discovery.

It was time for him to ask for a return favour. He got off the motorway and followed the minor roads and eventually an upgraded farm track that was now suitable for the busloads of schoolchildren that often spent the day at 'Farmer Giles's'.

Nick's number was stored in Ahmed's phone and although it was still early he made the call.

The reply he got wasn't what he'd expected.

'What the hell do you want?'

'You owe me a favour!'

'Yes, but you're in deep shit, and I don't want to join you if that's what you're suggesting.'

'Well, I was thinking of joining you, and in fact I'm outside. I need somewhere to dump this car, and a place to stay until Samatar sorts out something.'

'Have you seen the news lately? I'm half-expecting to hear sirens even as we speak.'

'Then open the fucking doors and let's get me off the radar.'

With no other option open to him, Nick released the mechanism to the security doors and Ahmed drove through. He wasn't an animal lover, and hated the underlying smell of the farmyard.

'Don't leave the car here! I'll go through and open the side gates so that it's out of sight until we decide what to do. I'm hoping at the very least that you've got something for me to enjoy in exchange for this hassle.'

Ahmed nodded. He never went anywhere without a supply of drugs, though wasn't a user in the usual sense of the word. He used drugs to buy himself favours and to get others to do what he wanted them to. He felt pleased as he realised that Nick was low on supplies and that would make things easier for him.

He devoured some chunks of bread and cheese, washing them down with watery coffee as Nick told him of the breaking news on the television. Initially Ahmed though he was referring to the discovery of a body in North Wiltshire, but Nick played around with the remote control to an enormous television screen. He found the news programme he'd watched earlier and replayed it.

An excited reporter introduced herself as Laura Cummings of the BBC, and reminded viewers of a body that had been discovered in Cardiff years earlier. She warned the public that they might find some of the images upsetting but that didn't stop her showing several shots of Dalmar lying where his body had been found.

Ahmed almost choked as she continued her exposé.

'Those of you that remember the case will know that my colleagues and I took a personal interest in the plight of this young man and I'm delighted to be able to report some amazing recent progress. Thanks to the insight of DCI Phelps we are at last able to identify the body as Dalmar Shimbir – a Somalian teenager. We are now 100% certain of the validity of this information, and the witness who came forward was also able to tell the police the circumstances surrounding his death.'

After pausing for her information to register with the viewers, Laura Cummings continued.

'Not only was she able to tell the DCI how Dalmar was murdered, she was able to produce a detailed sketch of his killer.'

At this point the cameras zoomed in on a copy of the full-face drawing that Basra had made. Ahmed blanched as he saw an amazing likeness of himself, even down to the shirt he'd been wearing the day he'd cut the throat of the young Somalian.

To his horror there was more to follow.

'In recent news bulletins viewers have been shown a computer-generated image of the man police are looking for in connection with the murder of an elderly man on a train travelling from Treherbert to Cardiff.'

For maximum dramatic effect the camera showed both images side by side, then filled the whole screen with Basra's drawing and ended with the man wanted in connection with the latest murder. The effect was startling, and the cider Ahmed had just swallowed was pushed back into his throat by the involuntary contraction of his stomach.

He looked on in abject horror at the satisfied face of Laura Cummings as she put the final nail in his coffin.

'The wonderfully brave witness who provided this picture of the man wanted in connection with the Roath murder has been able to identify others that were present around the time of his death. We are certain that one such person is a prominent public figure but for the moment we are unable to release any names. Continue watching for more breaking news, and please get in touch if you think you've seen this man.'

The news feature ended with the most recent image of Ahmed staring out at him.

Nick knew what he had to say wouldn't improve Ahmed's mood but it had to be said.

'It's not just on the Welsh news now! The main stations have picked up on this issue of someone who may be in public office being involved. The media love a good scandal, and if it's a celebrity or a politician or anyone like that they'll be in their element. Shit! What am I saying? You obviously know who it is, don't you?'

Ahmed thought back to the murder of the Somali boy, something he'd thought buried long ago. He almost regretted losing his cool. He'd always considered it a waste of time to kill where he wasn't personally threatened, or not making a profit, but in trying to ingratiate himself with Charles Ferguson he had overstepped the mark. He could have rendered the boy unconscious with one blow, but he'd had the wire in his hand … now his indiscipline was coming back to haunt him.

'Here's what you're going to do.'

Nick was in a euphoric state, thanks to the little present Ahmed had provided. The drug made him feel superior and self-confident, and whereas he would normally pussyfoot around the likes of Ahmed he felt able, for the moment, to take control of the situation.

'The animals need tending to, and it won't be long before my staff arrive to feed them and get them ready for the kids that are booked in to visit today. Ever since my little scare – the one you sorted for me – I've had an additional wall of security built between the animal houses and the weed. Apart from my wife and my son no one has access to that area, and there's a small barn at the back for drying and curing the crops. There are times when the plants need constant care and attention and they get more of that from my wife than I do. She practically lives out there and there's a bed and Portaloo you can use.'

Ahmed scowled at the thought of such primitive living conditions but he didn't argue. He was dog-tired, and allowed himself to be led through the security gates and into another world. It was November and extremely cold as they walked through the farmyard, but after entering a few codes and unlocking a steel door they stepped through into summer-like warmth.

Ahmed was shocked by the scale of the operation.

'Why some are some bits in darkness and some in that light?'

'Don't ask me – I'm not the expert. It's what the plants need at different stages of growth. My wife's got it down to a fine art, and all I care about is that the leaves she produces are top quality and bring in big bucks. Here's where you can get your head down.'

Nick pointed to the corner that had been turned into a mini-bedsit. Ahmed walked over, manoeuvred his heavy body onto the low bed, and watched Nick walk away.

Although Ahmed wanted his brain to stop thinking and allow him to sleep, it wasn't happening. He'd told Samatar a hundred times that the Fergusons were a liability but it had fallen on deaf ears. His boss was bewitched by anything to do with English society, and saw Charles and Catherine as a ticket to being accepted.

Well, they were all in one hell of a hole now. It was his face being splashed all over the place, but from what that woman on the news had said the net was closing in around Charley boy too. One way out would be to make sure Charles didn't talk – but someone else would have to do the deed. Ahmed couldn't risk being spotted by some crime-busting member of the public. He remembered that he'd been told to keep his phone on, and struggled between his need to know if any plans had been made and his need for sleep.

Habit took over and he turned the phone on. No signal. What the hell was he doing here? Miles from anywhere and the whole country was looking for him.

He couldn't think straight and closed his eyes. The warmth of the surroundings was working the magic he wanted, and for the next five hours not even the distorted dying face of Catherine Ferguson disturbed his sleep.

Chapter Twenty-four

'What the hell do you mean? Why don't you know where he is? He takes orders from you, doesn't he?'

Samatar held the phone some distance away from his ear, to avoid the loud, sardonic abuse that was being aimed at him. 'If you can't calm down and think this through you might just as well hand yourself in to the police. They've got nothing on you.'

Charles Ferguson started to interrupt but Samatar continued.

'People may have seen Ahmed with me and with Omar, but never with you – think about it. He never attended any of the dinners or meetings, for the most part stayed he in the background. I realise that it was a mistake to allow him to stay in the same hotels as we did, but you've got to admit he's been bloody useful – and he is part of my extended family.'

'*Every* bloody Somalian is part of your extended family!'

Charles Ferguson paced up and down the lounge of his London flat and thought about the scene he'd been called to just after Lizzie had found their mother's body.

'He made a hell of a mess, and I need to ask him exactly what my mother said in relation to the stuff we want to get hold of. It didn't occur to me at the time but it may not be as easy as I'd thought.'

Now it was Samatar's turn to shout down the phone.

'Why the hell not – I thought you had the family solicitors in your pocket? What's the problem?'

'My mother's bloody murder, of course! I rang the solicitors as soon as I got back from the Hall, but that bastard DCI Mortimer had already been on to them and they've been instructed not to release any family documents until he's seen them. If my mother really did write everything down, then we're all done for. That bloody crime reporter also suggested that Dalmar's sister is able to identify others in connection with his killing.'

'I'm surprised you remember his name,' sneered Samatar.

'He was a beautiful boy.'

Something about the way Charles's voice caressed the words made Samatar slightly queasy, and he offered up a prayer of thanks that there was a very big ocean between the two of them.

'Charles, you need to get a grip. Even if the little bitch has told the police that you were involved with her brother's murder, it would come down to her word against yours. Your lawyers would tear her to pieces. Where's her evidence? There's no way she could know where the murder actually happened. You've got to keep your nerve, and at least in the case of your mother you can really act like the bereaved son. Even I thought you had *some* feelings for her!'

'She had her uses. Anyway, what are you going to do about Ahmed?'

'Ideally I'd like to get him back to Somalia, but as I said, I'm having no luck contacting him.'

'Well, he'd better not turn up here!'

'Hardly likely – he hates your guts!'

'Look, just make sure you let me know when it's been sorted. And I do mean sorted … permanently.'

After their meeting Martin had left Matt and got in touch with Laura Cummings. He'd never had such a positive response from the press; she'd practically bitten his hand off. In return for the sort of coverage Martin was requesting, he promised that she'd be the first to know of any breakthroughs in the case.

Matt had moved his team up to the top floor of Goleudy and was determined that a joint effort was going to solve three murders. Charlie mentioned that some emails had been received from North Wiltshire. Just before 10.30 Martin returned with Alex in tow and they all waited for the call from DCI Mortimer, which came through exactly when promised.

'Have you got the videos my people sent?'

Matt looked around, and Charlie winked as with the press of a button the grounds of the Hall sprang to life on the screen.

'We're looking at them now.'

'You and Alex know the setup here, but I thought this would be the easiest way to refresh your memories and for the others to get the picture. Before I forget, Paul from our SOC team wants a word with Alex when I'm finished.

'We were called here last night when Elizabeth Ferguson returned from Cardiff. Fortunately she was with two friends, and it was the man who discovered her mother's body. Sorry! I've jumped the gun on something significant. When they arrived at the Hall the security code for the front gates had been changed and she couldn't get in. She had to call her brother to get the code.'

'Why do you think that's important?'

'I just had a gut feeling that there was some sort of delaying strategy in place – but when I heard that the murder probably happened just minutes before the body was found I was convinced of it. My own reading of the crime is that the killer was given the time needed to drive down the track that leads to the rear gates.'

'So some sort of accomplice – is that what you're suggesting?' questioned Matt.

'When Lizzie – and she insists we call her that – phoned her brother, he told her that he'd kept her hanging on because he was taking another call. When she asked him for the new code he kept her waiting again, supposedly to get the paper he'd written it on was in his car. But given that the new code is his own date of birth I don't see him having to check that out!'

'Do you think Charles Ferguson had something to do with his own mother's death?' Matt looked around for some sign that others were getting the same message.

'I've got absolutely no evidence to suggest he had. I think the man's despicable, but unfortunately that won't satisfy the CPS, and with his political connections I know I'm going to have to come up with something that really sticks. What I've got doesn't even come into the parameters of circumstantial evidence.'

Martin asked if his counterpart had seen the news regarding a possible connection between a cold case he was investigating and Matt's train murder. 'You may remember that the reporter said my witness knew the identity of a man who was present when her brother was killed.'

'Yes, I wasn't sure if that meant she could describe him or if she actually knew him.'

'She doesn't actually know him, but she does know who he is – and I agree with you, he's despicable!'

There was silence at the other end of the phone, but everyone could metaphorically hear DCI Mortimer's brain clicking the pieces into place.

'I was going to ask so why haven't you arrested him for perverting the course of justice at the very least, but hell, wasn't it me just talking about evidence! Still, we're stacking up enough to bring him in for questioning, aren't we? I need to get hold of his phone but he's not going to let me have it without a warrant. If I let him see we think he's anything other than just a grieving son I'll have the best criminal lawyers in the country on my back. Not to mention a political situation that won't go down well with my superiors.

'When we're finished here I'm going to have a good think about what action to take. I'm not normally one to pussyfoot around, but this case could go badly wrong if we don't take a united approach.'

Martin explained that his actions with the media were in the hope of getting Charles Ferguson to run scared and do something stupid that would incriminate him. 'Laura Cummings will be drip-feeding snippets of information over the next twenty-four hours, so if you've got anything at all I'd be happy to share it with her.'

'Well, as you can imagine, the murder of Catherine Ferguson has created a lot of media coverage in its own right. You could give your reporter the nod that both Cardiff police and the locals are looking at it as a joint investigation: both Ferguson murders in fact. That should ruffle a few feathers and make Charles Ferguson realise that life is going to get difficult for him. I'm sure he's not a murderer, not personally, but he knows someone who is and has omitted to pass on that information to the appropriate authorities. Not what we'd expect from a man in his position … or is it? Sorry, I'm getting more cynical by the day!'

The call was about to be ended when Matt reminded the DCI that one of his team wanted to speak to Alex and handed the phone over.

'Hi, Paul. Did you find anything from the tyre marks after I left you?

Realising the phone was still on speaker Alex turned it off and started to jot down some of the information he was being fed. Ten minutes later he put the phone down and pondered over what he'd written.

'Penny for them,' suggested Martin.

'With any luck, this'll be worth more than a penny. I take it we've got the DNA profile on all our victims?'

'Yes, of course – why?'

'As Matt knows, I stayed the night near Woodcanton Hall on the day we went down to look at a car that wasn't there! There was tyre tread activity but nothing conclusive. The local SOCOs were more interested in the garages and the outbuildings, as they'd suspected criminal activity in the past but never had enough to act on their suspicions. Most of the buildings contained the items you'd expect to find, broken tools, garden furniture that was falling to pieces, paintbrushes soaking in jam jars – you know what I mean …'

Matt nodded, thinking that if he and Sarah did look for a house together he'd have years' worth of similar junk to clear from his own shed.

'Anyway, let's watch this first,' Alex suggested, 'and then I'll brief you on Paul's find.'

The video was comprehensive, starting at the main gate with a shot of the intercom system that Elizabeth Ferguson would have used when she attempted to speak to her mother. Some of the officers made comments about the size of the property and its beautiful setting as the camera scanned the grounds before focusing on the front door.

What came next was anything but beautiful.

'Wow! Somebody's really lost it there!' said Helen Cook-Watts. 'And not a weakling either. That looks like a solid oak desk – I couldn't move that one inch, never mind pick it up and throw it.'

She stopped speaking as the focus moved to a figure lying amongst the destruction of the desk and bookshelves that had been torn from the walls. It looked as if the woman had been given some of the same treatment as the furniture. Her leg was bloodied and sore-looking, but it was her hand, bent back in an impossible position, that made her look like a discarded ragdoll.

'Oh, the poor woman. She must have been terrified – what a monster!'

'No one deserves to die like this,' Matt said, 'but we've got reason to believe Catherine Ferguson wasn't the angel of mercy that she appeared. This woman has probably been living off the misery of Somalian refugees for years. There's nothing we can prove as yet, but we're getting there, aren't we, guv?'

Martin nodded. 'At the moment we've got a compelling witness linking my eleven-year-old case to both Edward and Catherine Ferguson: their son Charles. Although he's not the murderer he knows who is. My witness can categorically place him at the scene of the murder, but as things stand it would be her word against his.

'Matt says he's got an alibi for his father's murder, and I'm sure DCI Mortimer will be questioning him closely about where he was when he spoke to his sister and if anyone can corroborate his whereabouts. Of course, he'll be walking on eggshells with the possibility of a political scandal brewing.

'We need a bit of luck here! The images of the killer are excellent, and thanks to Laura Cummings we couldn't have got better media coverage, but where has it got us? True, we've had the usual sightings, but nothing's turned out to be of any use so far and –'

Helen Cook-Watts interrupted. 'There's one woman I spoke to on the phone about an hour ago, and she swears she's seen him before. When I pressed her for more details she became more and more vague, said she simply couldn't remember where or when she'd seen him – but she's adamant that she has seen him, and more than once!

'I'm expecting a return call because she's fairly sure that she was with her husband when she saw him, and she thinks his memory may be better than hers. Her husband's in a meeting at the moment, but she'll ring back as soon as she's spoken to him. It may not be much but it's the best we've had from the public and she's adamant she's seen him.'

'Let's hope her husband's memory is better than hers,' said Martin. 'Alex?'

'Paul was excited at the prospect of getting a good look inside the grounds of Woodcanton Hall. He told me a few investigations in the past had taken his colleagues there – but only as far as that intercom; they'd never managed to get a warrant for the house itself. I asked for help in relation to tracking down the ghost car and he and his colleagues jumped at the chance. Even though they were investigating his father's death, Charles was furious at their presence.

'Paul took the opportunity to have a good look at the outhouses. He was hoping to find some evidence of drugs and became fixated by the largest of the buildings that had been cleaned out. And when I say cleaned out – I mean cleaned out! It could have been used for a surgical procedure. It was so out of place with the other typical storage sheds and we all agreed that the level of cleaning that had been employed could only be to cover up previous activity that someone wanted to remain hidden. Paul practically took it to pieces – he's a good bloke.

'The people who did the cleaning probably thought they'd done a good job, but some things are almost impossible to destroy completely. Blood residue is one of them – it can be recovered thousands of years later. The floor had been boarded over, not recently, but all the other buildings have concrete

223

floors so why was this one different? Paul found the reason when he took up the floorboards and found what he was sure was old bloodstaining. Tests proved him right, and he's been able to produce a DNA profile.'

'Have they tried matching it?' asked Matt.

'Yes, but no luck other than the general DNA profile matches people from the African continent.

'I doubt there's any African blood in the Ferguson family history – so if this type of DNA has been isolated from the blood residue, how did it get there and why have such efforts been made to cover it up? We need to show Dalmar and Charles Ferguson in the same place, but until now I hadn't considered that place could be our politician's home. Could it really be that the Somalis were being kept there when they'd been brought into the country?'

'Makes sense,' said Matt.' From what you've said, they could never have been sure of the number that would actually get here. They'd need somewhere to sort out the documentation for the survivors and to get them dressed in decent clothes, ready for the British public.'

'But,' Martin added, 'Charles Ferguson became involved. I wonder if he'd always known about his mother's activities? I don't know but I suspect not. He's always had serious political ambitions and I don't see him risking them by allowing people-trafficking in his family home. He didn't live there, so the only person who might have had suspicions would have been Edward Ferguson.'

'Lizzie told me that her father was always away on business a lot until he retired, and had lost all interest in the estate for years,' said Helen. 'She was hoping her decision to finally use it for tennis coaching would reignite his enthusiasm.'

'Perhaps that's the motive I'm looking for,' Matt suggested. 'Lizzie said her father welcomed the creation of a tennis academy in the grounds, but that would have meant work being done on those buildings. Maybe Charles and his mother thought that would have revealed what had been happening there.'

Alex shook his head. 'That may well be what they thought,

but it would never have happened. If there'd been a body to discover that would've been a different story! But builders don't usually think they're working on a crime scene, and even if they'd recognised the old blood it's unlikely they would have realised its importance. If Edward Ferguson was murdered to prevent his plans for future Wimbledon stars then he was killed out of irrational fear.

'Anyway, there's only one way to find out if this speculation and hope is justified and that's to compare the DNA that Paul has obtained with what you've got on file for Dalmar and hope –'

Charlie interrupted her husband. 'I'm way ahead of you on that. I've called up the relevant section of Martin's case file but there's no DNA record. There's a note on the post-mortem summary listing the various tests that were requested. DNA is one of them but there's no results on file.'

'Why doesn't that surprise me!' Martin looked furious. 'The bloody idiots who looked at this case initially were either totally incompetent or corrupt – or both.'

It was Matt who suggested what to everyone but Martin seemed obvious.

'We can test his sister! Her DNA profile will give us the proof we need.'

Martin smiled sadly. 'It would, normally – but then she's not actually his sister!'

Chapter Twenty-five

'Yes, of course it's OK for you to exhume Dalmar's body, you have my full blessing. My fiancé has been brilliant in all of this, and Dalmar's final resting place is something we've talked a lot about. Craig's family has a plot in the grounds of a small chapel, and there's space for two more bodies to be interred. It sounds a bit macabre, but Craig asked his family about the possibility of Dalmar being buried there and they've all agreed.

'The problem is, we've hit a brick wall when it comes to getting the right permission for Dalmar's body to be relocated, and Craig didn't think I should be bothering you – so your call was an answer to my prayers. What happens now?'

'I spoke to Professor Moore, our forensic pathologist, before coming here and he's certain that he can persuade the relevant authorities of the need to move quickly. He's making arrangements for the exhumation as we speak. I wanted to make sure you knew, because these things aren't that common and so they inevitably attract the media.'

Basra thanked Martin and asked about the actual procedure and what would happen to Dalmar's remains.

'Professor Moore has suggested that Dalmar is brought back to his examination rooms for DNA profiling and kept there until you are ready to proceed with the final burial arrangements. The whole process won't take that long, and I can't tell you how pleased we all are that at last you'll be able to do the right thing for your brother.'

'Thank you, DCI Phelps, thank you for everything. I just have to ask you one thing. Why is Dalmar's DNA suddenly so significant? Craig says you must be looking to link it to his killer, or to Charles Ferguson, but we can't figure out how you'd do that.'

Martin smiled. 'Perhaps that's just as well, or you and Craig could be after my job! I'll let you know everything in the fullness of time, but for now I have to admit we are processing theories rather than hard facts and I don't want to give you any false hopes.'

Martin got up to leave and to his surprise Basra threw her arms around his neck and kissed him on the cheek. He stood back and smiled as Basra's face turned pink.

'Well, that's not something I get very often during a murder investigation – but very welcome nevertheless.'

'Even if all of this doesn't lead to you finding my brother's killer, or even arresting Ferguson, I'm just grateful that Dalmar will finally be laid to rest in peace.'

'I'll be in touch as soon as there's anything I can share with you. You can go ahead with organising the re-burial for Dalmar as soon as you like. I suspect the professor will be ready either later today or tomorrow – there's no stopping him when he's on a mission.'

When he left the house Martin called the Prof's department and spoke to Mrs Williams.

'It's all arranged,' she said. 'Professor Moore has asked Alex Griffiths to attend the exhumation, and they're just waiting for your agreement to go ahead. I'm preparing for the body to be returned here for examination and storage. I've seen a few of these during the time I've worked here, DCI Phelps, but I can't say I look forward to them. I've heard the Prof give a number of lectures on the reasons why decomposition is unpredictable, and each one makes me more certain that I'll choose cremation as my preferred mode of transport out of this world.'

'I'll second that,' replied Martin.

'I've been asked to ring Alex Griffiths as soon as I've heard from you so that they can go ahead. Oh and just one other thing. Professor Moore has asked if you'd like to attend the examination session when he gets the body back here.'

Martin grinned as he got a mental picture of the Prof making the suggestion with a twinkle in his eye but this time Martin had a trump card.

'May as well put the new technology to use so when you're ready just give me the nod and I'll watch from the relative safety of the fifth floor.'

Immediately after his conversation with Mrs Williams Martin made another call.

'This is DCI Martin Phelps. I'd like to speak to Laura Cummings, please – she's expecting my call.'

Seconds later she was on the line.

'Thanks for the coverage. We're not at the arrest stage yet, but cages are being rattled and we're pretty certain we'll get there soon.'

'That's fine, but I'm running out of new things to say and in spite of my best pleading the news editors will drop the story if I can't keep it fresh.'

Martin sensed the frustration in the crime-reporter's voice. He told her about the planned exhumation and she was instantly back on-board.

'And it's OK for me to take a camera crew there – I won't be sent away with a flea in my ear? I've been on the receiving end of Dafydd Moore's acid tongue more times than I care to remember.'

'Don't worry, they're expecting you. I know you don't appreciate being told how to report a story, but I'd like it to be known that the body is being exhumed for the purpose of obtaining DNA evidence. You can reveal that we are hoping to match Dalmar's DNA with a sample found at a key location in the enquiry. Such a match would lead to the identification of people present at the time he was murdered.'

'Where was it found? What people?'

'That's as much as I can give you until we get the DNA results.'

'Oh, bloody hell – that's like showing a kid an ice-cream and not letting them have a lick!'

229

'You'll get the news before anyone else, and there's always the human interest story of a sister who will now be able to say a dignified goodbye to her brother.'

'Yes, yes, people love that sort of thing but it's not really my area. I'm much more interested in being first to get the name of the killer – speak later!'

She rang off, and Martin could imagine her being photographed at the entrance to the cemetery as she broke the news of the exhumation. He hadn't always seen eye to eye with Laura Cummings, and had good personal reason to remember that she was like a terrier when trying to find out information. It felt good to have her on his side on this occasion.

Having made the two calls Martin started the engine of his Alfa Romeo and drove back to the Bay. He'd barely turned the engine off in the car park of Goleudy when Matt walked towards him.

'I'm in need of some fresh air so I'm going for a walk. Fancy joining me?

The two men walked with no particular destination in mind, but there was a keen wind and the temperature was plummeting.

'Good God, it's freezing,' complained Matt. 'I wouldn't have suggested a walk if I'd realised it was this cold. I haven't got my head around it being so close to Christmas yet, but there's plenty of evidence around here. Mince pie with your coffee?' he asked as they sat down in one of the many coffee shops.

'It always sneaks up on me – first it's my birthday, then in a blink it's Christmas and then it's all over!'

'I haven't even given it a thought,' confessed Matt 'but now I know I'll be spending it with Sarah I'm going to make it a Christmas to remember.'

'Good for you – so turkey and chips for everyone at yours, is it?' Martin teased.

'Watch this space! But don't make any plans of your own, and pass the message on to Alex and Charlie.'

Their relaxation was soon interrupted as Laura Cummings'

face appeared on the television screen above the cake counter. The sound wasn't on, but subtitles were showing and Martin was pleased with what was being transmitted.

'Remember when she gave you such a hard time over the Austin murders? And that press conference when she was after your scalp! What made you bring her in on your case?'

'She offered! And when I went back and looked at her reporting of the case at the time I could see I had a ready-made ally. It was she who got the public to dignify the body with a name, and even Dalmar's sister thinks the name Geedi was respectful and relevant. I think Laura may have got her wrists slapped when she asked political questions about Britain's immigration policy and the role of some charities that were getting government funding. I think she took it as far as she could back then, and she jumped at the opportunity to be part of getting at the real story behind Dalmar's death. I just hope we can give it to her!'

'Well, she looks quite pleased with herself in the absence of any other reporters – and I take it the words she's using may have been prompted by you?'

Martin smiled. 'It's almost word for word what I told her. All I wish now was that DNA analysis was instant – I hate this waiting game.'

'Not much hanging about so far though – I can almost picture the Prof with a spade in his hand when he was waiting for your phone call!'

Both men laughed. 'They've obviously moved quickly and it's probably best we don't know if all the requisite paperwork is in order!' Matt said. The technicians don't hang about with results if Professor Moore is waiting for them, and I bet you'll have them by this time tomorrow.'

'Let's hope so.' Martin paid for their refreshments and they walked back to the station. 'I think we should put another call through to your friend DCI Mortimer and decide how we want to proceed in the event of a positive match.'

'I'll do that as soon as we get back and have you thought about what you'll do if it isn't a match?'

'Yes – I'll cry!'
'Me too!'

The two detectives weren't the only ones to see the news item, but their impatience was inconsequential compared to the fear it had instilled in Charles Ferguson.

He sat in his London flat vainly trying to foresee the future. He'd already ignored a three-line whip on an important government policy decision, but that wouldn't matter as his absence would be seen as perfectly acceptable considering both his parents had been murdered. He'd even had a condolence message from the PM himself and the flat was full of flowers and sympathy cards.

Charles had a really bad feeling about the news item, but there was always an outside chance that the whole thing had been set up to cause anyone with a guilty conscience to show their hand. He wasn't going to do that. He wasn't a politician for nothing, and manipulating situations was something he did rather well.

His first appeal to the family solicitors for his mother's papers had failed. The jobsworth office manager told him that the firm was under strict orders from DCI Mortimer not to release anything they were holding on Mrs Ferguson's behalf. Luckily for him, Charles was an expert in making use of the old boys' network, and contacted the eldest son of the company, who was known to have political aspirations of his own. Later that day they'd met at the golf course, and in exchange for nothing more than some vague promises of future political help he handed over the documents Charles needed.

Part of him had wanted to read what his mother had written but he suspected it would make him angry and there was already enough going on to fuel his anger. So he put them in a drawer to be read and then destroyed when things were back to normal. It was a measure of the man's arrogance that he still believed he was untouchable.

He walked to his study and from a locked drawer took out a pay-as-you-go mobile phone and selected Samatar's number.

Despite the difference in time between the UK and America the phone was answered immediately.

'I've been expecting a call. Did you manage to get hold of your mother's papers?'

'Of course.'

'And was her *insurance policy* worth as much as she made it out to be?'

Charles didn't want to admit that he hadn't had the stomach to read it. 'Suffice it to say that it's better in my hands than being turned over to the police.'

'So the bitch did name names, did she?'

'It's irrelevant now. I'm guessing you're keeping up to speed with the news from here. It was suggested that Dalmar's sister could identify people in relation to her brother's death. That means Ahmed and, more importantly, me! Normally the police would act immediately on that, but if it comes down to my word against hers there'll be no contest. Yes, Dalmar was killed at Woodcanton Hall, but I personally saw to it that every trace of him was wiped clean. I even had new flooring fixed over the concrete. The local SOC were down there a few days ago, trying to solve the mystery of my father's car, but that was all.'

Charles hesitated. 'I think I'm going to take a look anyway, just to be sure. If that side of things is OK then I think I'm in the clear – There's nothing that my lawyers won't be able to sort. What's happening with Ahmed?'

'He's my biggest problem at the moment. He could be staying –'

'Don't tell me where he is! The less I know, and the more distance there is between me and him, the better I like it. Can't you just have him put down?'

There was silence. Charles thought they'd been disconnected until Samatar's cold voice replied.

'That would be the way you English gentlemen deal with things that are no longer useful, but it's not our way. Ahmed is a fellow countryman, a member of my extended family, and unlike you I have respect for my family. I'll make whatever

233

arrangements are necessary to get him out of the country – as you say, he's not your problem.'

'But he would be if the police caught up with him and he opened his big mouth. So make sure you do sort things out – and quickly.' He cut the call.

Samatar marvelled at the arrogance of the man he'd been speaking to. If self-importance and egotism were pre-requisites for a PM then he'd been speaking to a future government leader.

He tried for the umpteenth time to contact Ahmed. The line was still dead, and so he went through the list of names he and Ahmed shared as contacts. In total there were eighteen names, and he'd almost come to the end of the list before he reached Nick Cutler.

'Yes, he's here, much to my wife's disgust. She keeps telling me that every policeman in the country is looking for him, and we've got too much to lose if they come snooping around here.'

'Can I speak to him?'

'There's no phone signal where he is, and I'm not going to risk him wandering about the farm with all the kids and families we've got here just now. I can give him a message.'

'What I want you to do is give him a vehicle, and to make sure it's got a full tank of petrol. I'll ring you back in half an hour to give details of where I've arranged for him to go. Tell him to be prepared to move quickly.'

Nick dodged the nagging questions from his wife about the call, and answered a few questions from farm visitors about why the pigs were so pink. When it was safe to do so he opened the security door and made his way to the rear of the animal enclosures. Ahmed was pacing about and his face was red and blotchy.

'I can't take much more! This bloody weed stinks, and I think I'm allergic to something it gives off. Look at me – I'm pinker than your disgusting pigs.'

Nick had to admit that Ahmed looked very hot and bothered.

'You're on the move anyway so no worries. Samatar has got something planned for you and wants you out of here quickly –

so be ready to go.'

'What the hell do you mean, be ready to move? I've only got the clothes I stand up in and all the documents I need are in the car.'

'Yes, but you can't take the car you drove here in, so get what you need from it and I'll sort out some alternative transport.'

'Where am I going?'

'Don't ask me, I don't even want to know. All I have to do is make sure you have plenty of petrol and tell you to make sure your phone is fully charged. When I get the next call I'll tell you what time you're to leave here.'

True to his word Samatar made a second call to Nick exactly thirty minutes after the first, and soon after the farm had closed for visitors Ahmed was driving away in one of the vans usually used for transporting livestock. The smell in the van was more obnoxious than the cannabis, but Ahmed was in no position to argue.

'Samatar's instructions were for you to drive the first ten miles in the direction I've told you and then to wait for his call. That's all I know and all I want to know.' There were no fond farewells, and it was with considerable relief that Nick and his wife watched Ahmed drive away.

Having just spent over twenty-four hours in the hothouse Ahmed was finding the early November evening very cold indeed. Although he was shivering from the cold his face and hands were burning up and he felt awful.

After driving just over nine miles his phone sprang to life and lots of missed calls and messages flooded in. He ignored them all, but they prompted him to pull over to the side of the road in anticipation of the call he'd soon be getting from Samatar.

Chapter Twenty-six

'Tell your DCI Phelps that his idea was nothing short of brilliant. He's obviously got the measure of Charles Ferguson, and he was spot on with those papers – taught an old dog some new tricks there!

'I'd made sure that William Everton and Sons had been instructed not to release any of Catherine Ferguson's papers, but I hadn't reckoned on Charles having such influence over the "and Sons". Fortunately Martin had foreseen that possibility, and I've now got in my office photocopies of everything taken before the originals were handed over to Charles – and it all make compelling reading. I guess Catherine Ferguson knew the type of men that she was dealing with, and one notebook in particular she must have seen as her personal insurance policy. It's stupid, really, because the contents implicate her as much as anyone else – but that won't worry her now, which was probably always the plan.'

DCI Mortimer paused for breath before continuing. 'Anyway, she makes it very clear that the killer we're looking for is named Ahmed Hassan, and I've got full details of his personal documentation here, as well as a comprehensive list of his known associates. Will you ask Martin to ensure his media friend tells the world?'

Matt found Martin on the phone.

'Tuesday the thirtieth is fine with us, Basra. Professor Moore suggests you get the undertakers to speak directly to him and together they'll be able to make whatever arrangements you want. Sorry? Yes, of course I'll join you and … what? Yes, of course, if that's your wish.'

'So have you had the DNA results?' asked Matt.

'No. But the Prof has told her to go ahead with the funeral anyway and she was just checking with me.'

'Does she want you to be a bearer? Is that her wish? Sorry, I wasn't eavesdropping …'

'No – she just asked if I wouldn't wear a suit!'

'OK! Well what I really came to talk to you about is the conversation I've just had with Graham Mortimer. He's had a chance to read the papers Catherine Ferguson left with her solicitors – well at least the photocopies. Charles did exactly as you suspected he would and has the originals in his possession. I'd love to be around when he explains that away.'

Matt filled Martin in on the rest of his exchange with Mortimer and passed on the request for maximum media exposure. Without delay Martin phoned Laura Cummings.

'A name! You're giving me the actual name of the man wanted for these murders. DCI Phelps, I love you!'

Martin ignored the journalist's last words but corrected one sentence. 'Wanted in connection with these murders is as good as you get for now.'

'Still that's brilliant but my editor may want confirmation from you before he allows me to broadcast.'

'Put him on – I want this this to be aired as soon as possible.'

After giving the required endorsement Martin listened to the rest of Matt's report.

'A positive DNA result would be the icing on the cake, but DCI Mortimer believes he's already got enough to bring Charles Ferguson in for questioning. Trouble is, he's having problems locating him at the moment. His office isn't expecting him and he's not answering any of his phones. His sister's got no idea where he is but needs to contact him to sort out some family matters.'

'Woodcanton Hall?' suggested Martin.

'It's a possibility, but if I were him I wouldn't go near the place. Too many ghosts!

It was a view shared by someone else in a very different type of conversation.

'You're off your fucking head! Nothing would induce me to go back to that place. It'll be swarming with cops! I might just as well walk into the nearest station and hand myself in. Think again – it's not going to happen.'

'Calm down and listen. There are very few options. Getting you out of the country by any of the conventional ways is out of the question. I've spoken to people who would usually help and they won't have anything to do it – not for any amount of money. A helicopter is a perfectly good option, and thankfully I know someone who owns one. More to the point, I know that he uses his prize possession for trips other than the legitimate business that he declares ... and he'd prefer me to keep my mouth shut. He's brought the machine down in the grounds of Woodcanton Hall twice before, so that'll give you a clue about his activities. The estimated time to land, get you on board, and get out again is apparently no more than five minutes. The engines won't be switched off, and it will be for you to get yourself into position to be picked up. No one will be expecting this so you'll have the element of surprise.'

'I'd have to get inside the place first, and the cops are hardly likely to open the doors for me in my pig van.'

Pig van? Samatar didn't bother asking for an explanation. 'I spoke to Charles earlier, and he told me that the two entrances aren't operated on the same security code, so you'll be able to use the usual one for the rear gates. He says he plans on going to Woodcanton later to see exactly what's going on there. I assumed he meant in relation to his mother's death, but he kept harping on about the outbuildings. I think he's losing the plot, so the sooner we get you out and leave him to stew in his own juice the better.

'The police will be focusing on the inside of the house. They probably won't even realise the helicopter was there until it's all over. Even if they do pick up the sound before it lands, none of them will have the legs of Mo Farah and I'm not even sure he'd get there in time. It's a really good plan and it will work.'

Samatar's positivity was rubbing off on Ahmed and he listened to details of timing and logistics.

'Are you sure you can get it all sorted in such a short time?'

'Positive. Just make your way to one of the lanes near the Hall and park out of sight. Keep your phone line open and be ready to move at a moment's notice.

Charles had already reached the front door of the house and was prevented from entering his mother's part of the house by barriers of blue and white tape and an officious young officer.

'You can't go through there!'

Rather more used to giving orders than taking them, Charles gave her a withering look before turning left into the room he'd always used as an office when he was at his parents' home. He knew what Samatar was planning, and he thought it would be amusing to see the police being fooled as the killer the whole country was looking for escaped under their very noses. The thought made him smile and he felt more confident than he'd done for some time.

He fancied a drink but knew that there'd be nothing worth having on this side of the house and so he settled for a coffee. All the time he listened and tried to second-guess what was happening just a few yards away.

His new-found confidence would have vanished instantly if he'd been able to hear the call that was being made to DCI Mortimer.

'He's here, sir! No, he hasn't said anything at all, and he's in the house somewhere. No, that's fine, we won't speak to him or give him any clue that you want to speak to him – unless he gets into his car.'

Armed with the information he'd been waiting for, the DCI put a call through to Goleudy and interrupted Martin and Matt who were enjoying one of Iris's famous hot beef and horseradish rolls.

'We'd love to be there when you arrest Charles Ferguson, but you'll want to do it as soon as you can and it's at least an hour down the motorway for us. Let us know how you get on.

Oh, and there *is* someone who will want to be as close to the action as possible, and maybe she'll have some local media contacts, so I'll give Laura Cummings a call. She's been such a help, and I'd be grateful if you could give her the first shout on whatever happens.'

Martin's mobile rang whilst he was on the phone to Graham and he handed it to Matt to take the call that he could see was from Prof. Moore. Matt gave a thumbs-up and Martin relayed the news.

His next call, to Laura Cummings, was answered immediately. When he told her that police were on their way to Malmesbury to arrest Charles Ferguson MP in connection with the death of Dalmar Shimbir, she gave a screech that almost perforated his eardrums.

'DCI Phelps, I'm going to have you as my personal lucky mascot. Do you know where I am now?'

Not expecting or waiting for an answer she rushed on.

'Amazingly, I'm visiting an old schoolfriend who lives in the quintessentially English village of Biddestone. It's less than twenty minutes from Malmesbury and I'm on my way!'

The information he'd just received from his fellow officers in Cardiff was the icing on the cake for DCI Mortimer. The package of papers from Catherine Ferguson's solicitors was damning, though it was always possible that some clever QC would be able to prove that she'd lied – but there was no disputing the DNA evidence. It categorically proved that Dalmar Shimbir had been killed in the outbuilding at Woodcanton Hall, also helping corroborate the sister's statement.

Mortimer had arrested men like Charles Ferguson before. They presented a public image of total respectability, when in reality they were guilty of every crime in the book. Generally speaking, they didn't resist arrest, but they did protest loudly and wheel in the best lawyers that money could buy. DCI Mortimer was looking forward to ensuring that this particular worm didn't wriggle off the hook.

Three police cars arrived silently at the gates of Woodcanton Hall. Knowing the entry code they drove in and parked at the side of the house seemingly unnoticed.

They were however expected by the team already working in the house and the young officer who had previously spoken to Charles Ferguson came out to meet the DCI.

'I've been keeping an eye on Mr Ferguson, and at one point I thought he was going to drive off. He left the house, but he didn't go near his car. He went down that slope and I think he went into the last building over there.'

She pointed to a building the DCI knew was one Ferguson would be particularly interested in.

'I didn't show myself or speak to him, and I'm sure he didn't even realise he was being watched. He was only there for a few minutes, but I don't think he liked what he saw because his face was a mixture of fury and fear when he went back into the house.'

'And he's there now, is he?'

'Yes, I haven't heard a sound from him for the last half-hour or so.'

A sudden thought panicked the DCI, and he walked quickly towards the front door, going straight through into Charles Ferguson's study. Men like Ferguson were not always renowned for their courage, and in times like this often took a coward's way out ...

Luckily, all that faced him in the study was a man sitting at an enormous oak desk, leaning forward with his head resting on his hands. Charles Ferguson looked like a broken man.

With due formality, Mortimer introduced himself before making the arrest. There was no reaction from his captive, and two of the officers with the DCI moved away from the door and around the desk.

Charles suddenly leapt to his feet and rushed through the front door like a man possessed. He took the officers by surprise yet again as he headed not to his car, but down the slope and towards the open expanse of the grounds.

Until then no one else had really heard the helicopter. Even if they had, it wouldn't have registered as anything significant, but to Charles the sound of the engine and the blades meant only one thing. He was going to be arrested and publicly hung out to dry, while Ahmed was going to get away with it – and he wasn't going to let that happen.

He struggled to get the breath he needed to run, and it was only the element of surprise and his knowledge of the grounds that kept him ahead of the officers. There was no doubt now of the helicopter's presence: the noise was deafening. He could see it hovering above and could already feel the force of the air it was moving.

From where he stood, looking down from the top of the slope, DCI Mortimer was the first to spot another figure approaching the helicopter from the rear gates of the Hall.

Charles was still some distance from the helicopter. He still hadn't seen Ahmed, but knew he must be close, and his one desire was to stop him getting on board.

It wasn't to be, as Charles was brought to the ground by one of the officers who had been chasing him – but at that point he did see Ahmed. He was so close to getting away and Charles tried to warn the officers but his voice couldn't be heard above the now overwhelming vibrations of the helicopter as it lifted into the air and over the treetops.

'Where the hell are my camera crew when I need them?'

Laura Cummings was using the video facility on her phone to capture the comings and goings of the helicopter at Woodcanton Hall. She'd notified her editor about what was happening, and he'd promised her a backup crew of photographers and soundmen as soon as he could round them up from the local stations. Meanwhile she and her friend waited outside the main gates, and waited, and waited.

Twenty minutes later Laura's patience was rewarded as a van pulled up, containing a team of people who quickly started hauling media equipment out of the back. She joined in their banter but was frustrated by the lack of activity from the other side of the gates. It had crossed her mind that there could be more than one entrance to an estate of this size, but she'd been promised a tip-off so she'd just have to keep waiting.

As if he was reading her thoughts, she received call from DCI Phelps.

'The number for the keypad is 1970 – in you go, DCI Mortimer is expecting you.'

'Seriously? We can just go in? Nobody's going to arrest us or anything?'

Martin laughed. 'It's not like you to be so circumspect! Guess I'll just have to watch for breaking news to see how you get on.'

'You've got it … and thanks … I think!'

Laura's friend Tricia was standing by the keypad and entered the numbers as Laura called them.

'You stay here just in case there's any trouble.'

Tricia shook her head and squeezed into the back of the transit van. 'Not on your nelly! This is exciting, and now I'll really have something to brag about at my next WI meeting!'

The van was met by the ubiquitous young officer, who told Laura that when the police cars had left DCI Mortimer would be happy to be interviewed. Laura was about to ask questions when the front door opened and Charles Ferguson was led out in handcuffs. He declined Laura's invitation to 'smile for the camera' and kept his head down. She shouted a few questions relating to his political position, of course receiving no reply.

Laura was so intent on the team getting the best shots of the soon to be ex-MP that she almost missed the second handcuffed person flanked on either side by a police officer.

'Bloody hell – oh bloody hell! What a scoop!

The crime reporter couldn't believe her luck as she watched both men being guided into the waiting police cars and driven away.

'Did you get that? Did you get that, boys? Did you get some good shots?' The cameramen nodded emphatically.

'You know who that second man is, don't you? You know he's the one I've been banging on about for the past few days? Take some shots of the two police cars leaving – it'll make a great ending for my news item. DCI Phelps, I don't just love you – I adore you!'

Half an hour later a much more composed Laura Cummings stood, microphone in hand, in the area where the helicopter had attempted to land.

'I'm here at Woodcanton Hall near Malmesbury with DCI Graham Mortimer of the Wiltshire police. DCI Mortimer, some incredible scenes here in the last couple of hours, and as I understand it you've arrested someone in connection with not only the murders of both Edward and Catherine Ferguson, but also in connection with the murder of a young Somali boy in Cardiff eleven years ago?'

Mortimer answered Laura's questions as far as he could, and he couldn't resist grinning as he confirmed the arrest of Charles Ferguson MP.

'Well, DCI Mortimer, you must be very pleased with the result you've achieved today. I'm sure the public will be equally pleased to see these arrests, to say nothing of proving that the Establishment is subject to the same rules as everybody else.'

DCI Mortimer kept his own counsel in relation to the reporter's last comment, but added a few words of his own. 'I'd like to credit my colleagues from Cardiff, without whom we'd never have been able to obtain some crucial evidence. It's a good reminder that criminals should never rest easy in their beds. We'll get them eventually, even if it takes eleven years or longer – and in this case there can be no truer saying than we've left no stone unturned.'

Chapter Twenty-seven

'Thanks for the public accolades – they were much appreciated. It looks as if we missed out on some fireworks your end, though.'

Martin, Matt, and Alex were having a 'speaker on' telephone conversation with Graham Mortimer, and both forces were basking in their current glory.

'It could have gone so badly wrong, as of course we knew nothing about the helicopter. Just imagine how we'd all be feeling now if that pickup had gone according to plan. The press wouldn't be loving us, they'd be eating us for breakfast! I can see the headlines now: "Most wanted killer opts for James Bond escape under the noses of senior police officers!"'

There was general laughter and agreement.

'Knowing the size of the grounds of Woodcanton Hall, Alex and I were trying to figure out exactly what happened,' said Matt. 'If you were all inside the house, it would have been easy for a helicopter to land and take off before you even realised it was on site. The walls of that house aren't like your normal semi-detached – they're really thick – and then there's the distance from the house to the far end of the grounds. How did anyone get there in time?'

'I'm reluctant to say this but it's one we owe Charles Ferguson. He knew about the arrangements to get Ahmed out by helicopter and he was happy to go along with it. That was until I arrested him and he realised that he was going to have to face the music alone. He took us all by surprise when he sprinted off, either to stop Ahmed getting on board or to join him.'

'Which was it?' asked Matt.

'At the moment he's saying nothing about that. It's either "no comment" or someone else is to blame. His mother was his main target, and I let him hang himself before telling him that I had copies of her papers. To say he's a consummate liar is the understatement of the year. He denied having the originals and I listened to him lying through his teeth to save his own skin. If we hadn't photocopied them, he could have got away with many things – but his mother documented everything. We've got names, dates, and lots of evidence of money transfers and some of it makes very unpleasant reading for us.

'There are people, who were at quite senior levels in the South Wales force at the time of Dalmar's death, who received considerable rewards to look the other way. I'm sure you must have suspected something of that sort made the case falter, and then it was conveniently shelved. Do the names DI David Williams and Sergeant Mick Walker mean anything to you? There's also someone called Stella Powell, but she was just at PC level so I'm not sure what influence she would have had on things.'

Martin shook his head, but then he remembered the conversation he'd had with Ian Baker. 'Not to me personally, but they are names that have come to my attention since I've been investigating Dalmar's case. Apart from being corrupt it's likely, from what I've heard, that they were also responsible for ruining the careers of some promising young officers.'

Mortimer swore. He loudly suggested that everyone on both sides could do with some well-earned rest. As the team filed out, Matt offering to treat everyone to coffee, Mortimer asked to speak to Martin in confidence.

'What is it?' asked Martin.

'There's one name in what I'm inclined to call Catherine Ferguson's *memoirs* that is politically sensitive. Patrick Stone is one of the senior civil servants in the UK Border Force. According to Catherine he could be relied upon to do some creative accounting for her so-called charity. We've already got one political scalp – what do you think?'

Martin didn't hesitate. 'I think you've got enough to ask him to help with your enquiries. I'd go and see him at work, that often rattles people. We'll link up tomorrow morning, arrange how we're going to do interviews, and report to the CPS. I think Matt and I could spend the day in your neck of the woods – that would make it easier all round.'

'It's always a bit of an anti-climax, tying up loose ends and getting the paperwork sorted, but it's a brilliant feeling when it's done. It was well worth spending the day with DCI Mortimer and his team but I'm glad we're on our way home. There's heavy snow on the way, and I don't want to be stranded the wrong side of the Severn Bridge.'

Matt was speaking as he stretched out as best he could in the front of Martin's car and they compared notes. They'd both interviewed Ahmed Hassan, albeit in relation to two separate and very different murders.

'What did you think of him?' asked Martin.

Matt glanced up. 'What do you mean? He's a thug and a cold-blooded killer, so that just about says it all, doesn't it?'

'Maybe, and I thought that when I met Dalmar's killer I'd hate him on sight.'

'And didn't you?'

'Well, I didn't exactly fall for his brutish charms, but I didn't feel the same loathing as when I interviewed Charles Ferguson. There could never be any excuses for him, but there is an element of self-preservation involved. You could perhaps understand how he ended up that way. Ferguson, on the other hand, was born with a silver spoon in his mouth and had every opportunity to do something good with his life. For me he's the more evil of the two!'

Matt thought for a moment. 'It's his sister I feel sorry for. How the hell is she going to cope with everything? Both her parents are murdered, she finds a daughter she hasn't seen since she was a baby, and now her brother is in prison. And all in the space of a few days!'

'It's incredible, really, but I think she'll be OK. She was

upset by her father's death, but as far as her mother and brother are concerned they've been distant for a very long time. I only hope she gets herself a decent solicitor, and that they get her father's will properly actioned before her brother finishes whatever stretch he's given. There are a lot of charges being thrown at him but some will be difficult to prove. I'm hoping a good leftie judge will use him as an example, put him away for a long time, but I'm not holding my breath. We've seen it before, haven't we! People that the public should be able to look up to and respect are sentenced, and in no time at all they're back out to resume a life of leisure. I'd like to lock him up and throw away the key.'

Matt raised an eyebrow. 'I thought I disliked the man, but he's really got under your skin, hasn't he? What about the others mentioned by Catherine Ferguson?'

Martin handed over the toll for the Severn Bridge crossing and they headed for Goleudy. 'Every one of them will be followed up, even those currently out of the country, but I'm glad to say it's a long and tedious job for someone other than us.

'Talking about us, what's next, d'you think? Are you going to continue investigating specific unsolved cases, or has the chief super got other plans?'

'Nothing he's shared with me, but then we've both got a debriefing session with him later so perhaps he'll tell us then. I still can't believe we came up with the same killer in both cases – teamwork or kismet?'

Their expected debriefing with Chief Superintendent Atkinson was postponed, as he'd been called to an emergency meeting.

'It's late, so let's call it a day,' suggested Martin. 'Dalmar's funeral is tomorrow and I've got to sort out something other than a suit to wear. I've asked Shelley to see if she can find out exactly what Basra meant by that.'

'It usually means that the funeral isn't going to be sombre – more like a celebration of life. People who attend wear colourful clothing – no black allowed!'

'That's a new one on me. Have you been to one?'

'No, but Sarah has. I do remember seeing an amazing send-off when I was on holiday in San Francisco. There was a New Orleans-style brass band, and on top of the hearse was a smiling photograph of the deceased surrounded by flowers. It looked as if he was enjoying his last journey. That's the way I'd like to go!'

'Well, OK, mate. If I'm still around when you pop off I'll ensure you get your wishes!'

Matt laughed. 'Is it just you going tomorrow?'

'No, Basra has issued a general invitation to anyone who's ever shown an interest in her quest to find her brother's killer. I know for certain that Sergeant Evans is going and so are Alex and the Prof. You'd be welcome, I'm sure.'

Matt grinned. 'Funerals aren't really my thing – but in the interest of never passing up on a new experience, why not!

Cardiff had seen its share of stately and well-attended funerals but this one was unique. The small suburban chapel had never seen such activity. People had flocked from all over Cardiff and beyond to say goodbye to Dalmar. After a few days of high-profile reporting on the interlinked cases, Laura Cummings had turned the public's attention to the human interest story that had started it all off. She'd said that sort of reporting wasn't her bag but she was attracting a lot of interest.

Laura had captured the public imagination with the story of a brother and sister who'd been let down by people they should have been able to trust. She had been unable to reveal details of why the original police investigation failed, as that was under internal investigation, so the focus of her reports had been on what she called the circle of stones, and how Basra's yearly pilgrimage to Dalmar's shrine had been the key to finally bringing his killer to justice. There was a brief mention of Martin in her reports and it amused him to realise that it was probably back to business as usual between him and the press.

The public had taken on board the 'no black allowed' theme with relish. It was a freezing cold day, but even with the temperature at or just below freezing point there was no sign of the usual dark overcoats with upturned collars. Guests wore sweaters, bobble hats, scarves, and gloves of every imaginable colour, and in spite of having the appearance of a carnival there was complete respect and dignity.

The chapel was packed to capacity and the crowds filled the surrounding streets. Laura Cummings had been allowed inside the chapel for the service and the whole thing was broadcast live. The service was simple, but made memorable by the few words spoken by Basra.

'From the bottom of my heart I want to thank you all for giving my brother Dalmar the send-off he deserved. If someone you love has been wronged, never, never give up the fight to get justice for them.'

The songs that rang out in that normally quiet area of the city ranged from upbeat songs from *Mamma Mia* and *Hairspray* to soulful numbers made famous by Shirley Bassey and Tom Jones. Basra had taken absolutely to her new Welsh roots, but her devotion over the past eleven years showed that she'd never forgotten her past. With the guests in full voice, a small party moved through a door beside the altar and into the graveyard, where a corner plot had been prepared to receive Dalmar. No television cameras followed, as this was for Basra and her new family only.

As requested, Martin had sat near the family for the service but he'd not even considered being part of the graveside party.

When Basra turned back and requested that he join them he felt unable to refuse but stood back from the family group. Martin hadn't been formally introduced to them but he guessed that the elderly Somali woman who stood close to Basra was Elmi. The others he guessed were Elmi's husband and son, possibly the one who had been punished to ensure her silence some years ago. Craig's parents and what looked like his brother and sister made up the rest of the group.

The first things his eyes rested on in the graveyard were the smooth stones that were carefully laid out alongside the plot. They were no longer in a circle, no longer in the desolate spot where her brother's body had been callously dumped. He suspected that they would soon occupy a place of honour on top of Dalmar's grave, and that her future visits to the stones would not be the lonely ones she'd endured for eleven long years.

Basra showed the first signs of her pent-up grief as Dalmar's body was lowered into the ground, and her fiancé hugged her. It was such a private moment that Martin took a few more steps back, and at that moment he felt the vibrations of his phone. Most people knew that he was attending the funeral and so he wasn't expecting any calls. He walked to the edge of the path, checking to see if he recognised the caller's number. He did.

'Yes, sir?' he whispered.

'I'm sorry, Martin. Until I heard the tone of your voice I'd forgotten where you are. I take it you're in no position to speak, and I've no wish to be disrespectful, but I've got something that can't wait.'

It was obvious from Atkinson's voice that he was excited.

'I take it Matt Pryor is there with you. As soon as you can both politely leave I'll be waiting for you in my office. I've got something to say that's going to keep you both out of mischief for some considerable time!'

Author Inspiration

Some of my more cynical readers may think that I spend my time roaming the most beautiful areas of South Wales looking for somewhere to place my next body! Thankfully, my experience of crime is only on my pages, and in reality I always enjoy the fantastic Welsh coastline, the parks, the castles, and the stunning countryside – all close to my home.

One of my favourite places is Roath Park, and each time I visit I get the feeling of being transported from the hustle and bustle of Cardiff city centre back to a quieter period of our history. The park is surrounded by some splendid Victorian houses, and the layout of the park itself reflects that period. The people of Cardiff can thank the third Marquess of Bute and other landowners for bequeathing the land upon which the park was built. The whole area was originally marshland, and made an ideal foundation for the construction of a lake.

A major feature of the lake is a lighthouse, built in 1915 and dedicated to the memory of Captain Robert Falcon Scott. Scott sailed from Cardiff in 1910 on board the *Terra Nova*, but their mission to be the first group to sail to the South Pole was ill-fated. On January 17th 1912 they did reach the Pole, only to discover that Roald Amundsen's expedition had beaten them to it. Scott and his men all perished on the return journey, and the lighthouse, a well-loved feature of Roath Park, stands in fitting tribute to him and his comrades.

There are quiet areas where visitors are able to watch a diverse variety of wildlife. The lake with its small islands provides ideal conditions for over-wintering and breeding birds, and the wildflower garden is a haven for butterflies. In part of the famous rose garden visitors can see trial beds for the National Rose Society. There are plenty of open spaces for children to run about and play games, and a visit wouldn't be complete without some time being spent boating on the lake.

Wonny Lea
2014

Jack-Knifed

Jack-Knifed is the first novel featuring DCI Martin Phelps and his team, based in the world-famous and vibrant Cardiff Bay.

Mark Wilson, a decent, well-liked gay man, lives alone in Cardiff. One Saturday evening, his closest friends go to his house for an evening of drinks and catching-up Finding no answer, they break in – to a horrific murder scene. For Mark Wilson has been brutally, sadistically murdered in his own home.

As DCI Phelps investigates, Mark's traumatic early life is revealed. Was his killer someone from his past? Was his sexuality a motive? What about his violent, homophobic father– a man who has already killed more than once.

As the body count rises, Phelps and his sergeant, Matt Pryor, soon realise they might be on the trail of a serial killer …
…

The Coopers Field Murder

The Coopers Field Murder is the second in Wonny Lea's DCI Martin Phelps series, set in the thriving Welsh capital city of Cardiff.

Phelps and the team are faced with a body found in Coopers Field, a Cardiff beauty spot – a naked body that has lain there so long it is almost unidentifiable. Pathology reports establish that the body is that of a woman – but who is she, and how did she die?

Local nurse Sarah Thomas, a helpful passer-by when the body is found, soon finds that she has another unexpected death to deal with – at Parkland Nursing Home where she works. Colin James, one of her favourite residents at the home, dies suddenly – but the reactions of those closest to him are surprising. Was Colin's death due to natural causes – or is there something more sinister afoot at Parkland?

The Copper Field Murder

260

Killing by Colours, the third in the DCI Martin Phelps series, takes Martin in search of a serial killer who appears to have somewhat of a personal interest in the DCI himself.

When the body of the killer's first victim is discovered at a popular Cardiff leisure attraction, key elements of the murder link her death to a macabre colour-themed poem recently sent to DCI Phelps. As the body count rises, the killer teases the team by giving possible clues to the whereabouts of victims and the venues of potential murders, in the form of more poems. Are the killings random acts by a deranged individual, or is there something that links the victims to one another – and even to the DCI himself?

Meanwhile, Martin's sidekick, DS Matt Pryor, is worried about the safety of his boss. Are his fears warranted? Is Martin Phelps on the colour-coded list of potential victims – or is he just the sounding board for the killer's bizarre poetry?

Money Can Kill

The fourth volume in the DCI Martin Phelps series.

A school trip to the National History Museum of Wales at St Fagans ends early with the disappearance of a child. Is he just playing hide and seek – or is it the work of a criminal? Perhaps a kidnapper with designs on the boy's mother and her recently-acquired millions?

DCI Phelps and his team are back together just in time to take on the case – one that starts off as a possible kidnapping but soon descends into something even more sinister …

As the investigation exposes the complexities of family relationships, another long-standing mystery is solved – all while Martin and his colleagues anxiously await the results of a major police review that may result in them losing their jobs …

The DCI Martin Phelps Series

Wonny Lea

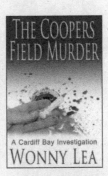

266

For more information about **Wonny Lea**

and other **Accent Press** titles

please visit

www.accentpress.co.uk